Demon's Delight

Demon's Delight

MaryJanice Davidson

Emma Holly

Vickie Taylor

Catherine Spangler

BERKLEY SENSATION, NEW YORK

THE BERKLEY PUBLISHING GROUP
Published by the Penguin Group
Penguin Group (USA) Inc.
375 Hudson Street, New York, New York 10014, USA
Penguin Group (Canada), 90 Eglinton Avenue East, Suite 700, Toronto, Ontario M4P 2Y3, Canada
(a division of Pearson Penguin Canada Inc.)
Penguin Books Ltd., 80 Strand, London WC2R 0RL, England
Penguin Group Ireland, 25 St. Stephen's Green, Dublin 2, Ireland (a division of Penguin Books Ltd.)
Penguin Group (Australia), 250 Camberwell Road, Camberwell, Victoria 3124, Australia
(a division of Pearson Australia Group Pty. Ltd.)
Penguin Books India Pvt. Ltd., 11 Community Centre, Panchsheel Park, New Delhi—110 017, India
Penguin Group (NZ), 67 Apollo Drive, Mairangi Bay, Auckland 1311, New Zealand
(a division of Pearson New Zealand Ltd.)
Penguin Books (South Africa) (Pty.) Ltd., 24 Sturdee Avenue, Rosebank, Johannesburg 2196,
South Africa

Penguin Books Ltd., Registered Offices: 80 Strand, London WC2R 0RL, England

This book is an original publication of The Berkley Publishing Group.

This is a work of fiction. Names, characters, places, and incidents either are the product of the authors' imaginations or are used fictitiously, and any resemblance to actual persons, living or dead, business establishments, events, or locals is entirely coincidental. The publisher does not have any control over and does not assume any responsibility for author or third-party websites or their content.

DEMON'S DELIGHT

First edition: March 2007

Berkley Sensation trade paperback ISBN: 978-0-425-21381-0

An application to register this book for cataloging has been submitted to the Library of Congress.

PRINTED IN THE UNITED STATES OF AMERICA

10 9 8 7 6 5 4 3 2 1

CONTENTS

Witch Way

MaryJanice Davidson

*To my husband, who is my opposite in every way:
politically, religiously, economically, and neurologically.
Do I believe in love at first sight? You bet! Do I believe
opposites attract? I have two children (both look like him)
who would testify to that fact.*

ACKNOWLEDGMENTS

Thanks again to Cindy Hwang at Berkley, who never clutches her head (at least in my presence) when I pitch a new idea. And thanks to the fabulous cover artists and the flap copy techs; I could never sum up a book (or four novellas) in two paragraphs, but those bums make it look easy.

AUTHOR'S NOTE

Not all witches were bad. Not all witches were even witches, particularly during the madness of the Salem witch trials.

But some were. And they got pissed. That's all I've got to say about that.

She turned me into a newt! It got better.
—Monty Python and the Holy Grail

My mother says I must not pass
Too near that glass.
She is afraid that I will see
A little witch that looks like me.
With a red mouth to whisper low
The very thing I should not know.
—*Sarah Morgan Bruamt Piatt*, The Witch in the Glass

There is no hate lost between us.
—The Witch, *Act iv, Sc. 3*

There is no love lost between us.
—*Cervantes*, Don Quixote, *Book iv*

Prologue

TUCKER Goodman did not take his hat off, a whipping offense if anyone else dared try it. He pointed a long, bony finger at the witch in the blocks and said, in a voice trembling with rage and age, "You are an unnatural thing, cast out by the devil to live among good people—"

"Good people," the witch said, craning (and failing) to look at him, "like the Swansons? You know perfectly well the last three littluns born on that farm weren't got on the missus, but instead, the eldest daughter. Not to mention—"

"Liar!" Farmer Swanson was on his feet, his face purpling, while Mrs. Swanson just huddled deeper into the bench and cried softy into her handkerchief. "That *thing* filled my girls' heads with lies!"

"Silence, Farmer Swanson!" Silence reigned, as the witch knew it would. There was no reasoning with a mob. Unless you were the leader of the mob.

"I think we can all agree—"

"That you're a creaky old man who likes having marital congress with fifteen-year-olds to keep the evil spirits away." The witch laughed.

"—that since you were sent here, there has been naught but wickedness afoot."

"Except for all the children I cured of the waxing disease," the witch pointed out helpfully.

No one said anything. The witch wasn't surprised. Say just the wrong thing at the wrong time, and things like guilt or innocence didn't matter. Defend a witch, and you'd be burned alive, too. Just a handy scapegoat to roast and dance about. That's all they really wanted.

"You will die in agony, yet cleansed by fire."

"Terrific," the witch muttered.

"And in penance for your evil deeds, your children and your children's children, down through the ages, will be persecuted and hunted until you share your powers with your greatest enemy."

"I see no logic in that order of things," the witch commented. "Why not just kill me and get it over with?"

"Because you keep coming back," Goodman said, clearly exasperated. "My great-great-grandfather told me all about you. You bring your mischief to the town and have your fun and then are burned and show up in another town a few years later."

"I like to keep busy."

"This time, if you don't give over your powers to your greatest enemy, you'll be doomed to walk the earth forever, alone and persecuted."

"And if I do give over my powers to my greatest enemy?"

Goodman smirked, revealing teeth blackening with age. "But you never will, unnatural thing. You don't have a heart to share, to open. And so I curse you, as this town curses you, doomed to walk the earth forever, alone."

"How very Christian and forgiving of you," the witch muttered.

Goodman, wrapped tightly in his cloak of smug judgment, ignored the witch's comment. Instead, he sprinkled a foul-smelling herb poultice in the witch's hair and clothes, ignoring the sneezes, then stood back as flaming chunks of wood were tossed, arcing through the air and landing on the pile of wood the witch was standing on.

The witch wriggled, but the town elders knew their business: The witch was trussed as firmly to the center pole as a turkey on a spit. An unpleasant comparison, given what was happening right now . . .

"Well, if I *do* come back," the witch shouted over the crackling flames, "you can bet I will never set foot in Massachusetts again!" Then, as his feet caught fire, Christopher de Mere muttered, "Fie on this. Fie all *over* this."

The villagers watched the man turn into a living candle, making the sign of the cross, as he hardly made a sound, except for the occasional yelp of pain or muttered taunt. And later, scraping through the ashes, they never found a single bone.

Things were quiet.

For a while.

Chapter 1

RHEA Goodman sat at the broad wooden table in her mother's farmhouse and waited expectantly. Her parents, Flower and Power (real names: Stephanie and Bob), were looking uneasy, and Rhea felt in her bones that It Was Time.

Time to explain why she'd been brought up a nomad, moving from commune to commune.

Time for Flower and Power to explain why they clung to the hippie thing, even though they were in their fifties and ought to have ulcers and IBM stock.

Time to explain her younger sister's insistence on playing "kill the witch! kill the witch!" with the kid as the hero and her as the witch.

Her theory? Flower and Power had robbed a bank. Or blown up a building. Because they were on the run, no question.

Only . . . from whom?

And her little sister was just weird.

"Rhea, baby, we wanted to sit you down and have a talk." Flower ran her long, bony fingers through her graying red hair, waist length and for once not pulled back in the perpetual braid.

"About your future," Power added, rubbing his bald, sun-burned pate. He was about three inches shorter than her mother, who, at five-five, wasn't exactly Giganto. She had passed both of them in height by the time she was fourteen. "And your past."

"Super-duper." She folded her hands and leaned forward. "And whatever you guys did, I'm sure you had to do. So I forgive you."

"It wasn't us," Flower said, sitting down, then changing her mind and standing. Then sitting again. The sun was slanting through the western windows, making the table look like it was on fire, and for the first time in memory, Rhea saw her mother wince away from the light. "It was destiny."

Yeah, you were destined to rob a bank. Or free test animals. And then have kids and spend the rest of your life on the run. Homeschooling, ugh!

"As the eldest—"

"Yeah, where *are* the other ankle biters, anyway?" Rhea had four brothers and sisters: Ramen, Kane, Chrysanthemum, and Violet, aged nineteen, fifteen, twelve, and eight, respectively.

"Away from here. This is business strictly for the eldest of the family. For centuries it has been this way."

Abruptly, Flower started to cry. Power got up and clumsily patted her. "We can't tell her," she sobbed into her work-roughened hands. "We just can't!"

"We must," Power soothed.

"Hey, whoa, it's all right!" She held her hands up in the universal "simmer down" motion. "Whatever you did, it's cool with me." *Good God, did they kill someone?* "I'm sure we can figure something out."

"It's not what we did, it's what you're going to do."

"Go back to college? Forget it. Like the man said, it's high school with ashtrays. Get a new job? Working on it. Try to get one of my poems published? Working on that, too."

"No," Flower said, lips trembling. "Nothing like that."

"Then what is it?"

"It's destiny."

"Yeah, great, what does that mean?"

"You're going to kill the greatest evil to walk the earth, and you'll die in the process," Power told her. "So it is, so it has been, so it shall be. Only if the hunter makes the ultimate sacrifice will the witch be vanquished." He sounded like he was quoting from a book. Then he continued, and his voice no longer sounded like a recitation. "I'm so sorry, Rhea. I'm just so, so sorry."

Her mother was beyond contributing to the conversation and simply cried harder.

Rhea felt her mouth pop open in surprise. "So, uh, you guys didn't rob a federal bank?" Then, "Don't tell me all those fairy stories you told me about witches and witch-hunters and demons are *true*. Because if they are—"

Flower and Power nodded.

"Jinkies," she muttered and rested her sharp little chin on her folded hands.

Chapter 2

CHRIS Mere tried. He really did. If his family history wasn't reason enough not to draw attention to himself, ever, the fact that he had parked in a rough neighborhood was.

But the girl was screaming. *Screaming.* And as he approached, he could hear the man ripping her clothes, talking to her in a hissing whisper, could see the moonlight bounce off the blade he held at her neck.

Chris cleared his throat. "Uh. Excuse me?"

Victim and would-be rapist both looked at him.

"Yeah, uh. Could you, uh, not do that?"

"Fuck off, white bread. Me and the bitch got bidness."

"I guess you didn't hear. Times have changed. *No* means *no,* and all that. And it looks to me like the lady is saying *no.* Emphatically. So why don't you let her go, before I turn you into a turnip?" *And what the hell rhymes with turnip, anyway?*

"You come any closer, I cut the bitch!"

"With what?"

"You blind? With this!"

"You who have a knife at her throat
Put it down or be turned into . . . shit!"

They were both staring at him. And the knife was still jammed against the underside of the woman's chin.

"What's this? Rhyming an' shit?"

"Help me, you idiot," the woman practically hissed, glaring at him.

"Wait, wait, I've got it." Chris closed his eyes and concentrated on the mental image he needed.

"If you keep robbing ladies,
You'll come down with rabies.
Not to mention scabies."

"Stop with the poetry and call. The. Police," the woman grated.

"Man, you are *nuts*. You—" He stopped suddenly and clutched his throat. "Oh, man . . . I am so hot. Are you guys hot?" He coughed and spat and spat again. "Where am I? Who the hell are you guys?" He dropped the knife. "I've got to get out of here!"

"That seems like a good plan," Chris agreed.

"I—I—garrggh!" The would-be rapist started foaming at the mouth and actually barked at him.

"What the hell?" the woman said, twisting away from her assailant. "Did you just give him *rabies*?"

"Uh, yeah."

"Will he die?" The woman warily watched Sir Foams-a-Lot, as he darted in and out of a nearby alley.

"No, it's only temporary. Of course, every time he tries to bother a lady, it'll come back. Either that," he added thoughtfully, "or scabies will get him. That's some kind of skin condition, isn't it?"

"He was right," the woman said, backing away from him. "You're nuts."

"Hey!" he yelled at her rapidly departing form. "Don't thank me or anything!"

She waved a hand over her shoulder, but never slowed down.

Chris sighed and kept walking, stepping over the knife like

most men would step over dog poop. He was not really thinking about what he was doing, he was just automatically avoiding something unpleasant. He thought about turning it into a banana, but for the life of him couldn't remember anything that rhymed with banana.

Why did he even bother? They never hung around. No matter what he did for them, what magic he could make, they always got scared and ran away. For two cents, he'd give them something to *really*—

He stopped walking and pressed his palms over his eyes. *Don't think like that. You're one of the good guys, remember?*

Yeah, sure. As if he could fight three centuries of ingrained behavior.

You'd better.

Or what?

You know what.

He snorted. His inner voice sounded weirdly like his late grandfather . . . who had been killed by a witch-hunter from the Goodman line. His father had died at the hands of a Goodman twenty years later.

Now it was his turn. Unless he could prove to Goodman that he wasn't a danger to society.

Because if *he* could fight three centuries of conditioning, *she* sure as hell could.

Hell, he was as much of a demon fighter as a witch . . . how many demons had he vanquished? How many lives had he saved?

Did you do it for them, or for you?

What difference did it make?

But sometimes, when sleep wouldn't come, he'd burn with the desire for revenge. The Goodmans had been killing his family for centuries. Wasn't it time the de Meres got back some of their own?

He'd shove the thought away, try to be a good enough guy, but it always came back. Freakin' *always*.

Mixed feelings or not, he'd spent the last five years tracking down just about all the Goodmans in the country. And he had satisfied himself that, in every past case, the surname was just a coincidence. And he'd had many pleasant conversations as a result . . . and even a few free meals. Not that, as a Mere, he needed free anything. But still, they had been nice. They gave him hope for what was to come.

Annoyingly, the last batch lived in—ugh—Massachusetts. Salem, to be exact.

Salem. Just reading the name on a map gave him chills, never mind driving there.

Salem, land of the disenchanted and intolerant. Salem, the killing grounds for twenty accused witches (only one of which, by the way, had been a witch). Salem, where hundreds were accused of witchcraft during the rising hysteria between June and September 1692.

Come to think of it, he probably should have started there and saved himself several years of looking, but he couldn't bring himself to take that step until it was absolutely necessary. As far as he knew, a Mere hadn't set foot in Massachusetts in more than two hundred years, maybe longer. And there was a good reason for that. The freakin' state motto was, "By the Sword We Seek Peace," for God's sake! No, he had been right to avoid the state, at least until it was absolutely necessary to his plan.

Unfortunately, now it was. It gave him the creeps to even be crossing the state line, never mind lurking in Boston's dark alleys, tracking down more friggin' Goodmans and vanquishing the occasional smelly demon.

Not that he expected the witch-hunter to be listed in the Yellow Pages under "Hunters, Witch." Fortunately, lots of things rhymed with Goodman, and his magic was helping him methodically track them all down. And—and maybe it was just a fable, after all. Maybe all his antecedents had died of natural causes.

Ha. Were being burned at the stake or hanged on the gallows natural causes anywhere but Salem?

Still, he'd go. Then he'd talk, try to make peace. If only Goodman wouldn't set him on fire before he could explain that he was one of the good guys . . .

Assuming he actually was. Sometimes he wasn't too sure.

Chapter 3

AGAIN, Rhea. Again!"

Panting, she lowered the crossbow and glared at her father. "I don't see you out here slinging arrows of misfortune. And for an ex-hippie, you know entirely too much about how to kill people."

"I watched my father train my older brother," Power replied, absently running his hand over his bald spot—a sure sign he was distressed. "We never did find his body."

"Oh, *great*." Disgusted, she aimed the crossbow, and the arrow thwacked the mannequin right in the groin.

"That's not a lethal wound," her father snapped.

"No, but I bet he wishes it was."

"Rhea, stop it! This is a serious business. You have to fulfill your destiny, to—"

"That's another thing. Why did you wait until now to tell me?"

"Think, Rhea. Why?"

She sighed and reloaded the crossbow. "Don't even tell me. Twenty-first birthday ritual?" Oh, *great*. She'd been legal-drinking-age for twelve whole hours and was doomed to kill a powerful magic user and get killed in the process. "So you let me have twenty-one years of blissful ignorance, is that the way it works?"

Power nodded.

"Great. Any idea when Hot Shit Magic Guy is going to show up?"

"You've got a couple more years to train. So we have to be ready. Again."

None of the weapons were new to her. She'd been training (for fun, she had thought) in the barn for more than ten years. But shooting a man-shaped mannequin or a scarecrow wasn't the same as pointing a gun or a crossbow or a knife at a real man and finding the will to drive home a lethal stroke.

She'd never killed anything in her life. Heck, she'd never even swatted a fly.

But her parents pooh-poohed her worries, telling her that killing was in her blood, that with proper training she would do her duty when the time came.

"For what?" she had asked.

Her mother had finally stopped crying. "What do you mean, Rhea?"

"What's the point? According to you guys, another witch and another Goodman—one of the ankle biters' kids, I'm betting—will be born in the next generation, and the whole stupid thing starts all over again."

"Your point?" her father had asked.

"Why do it at all? It's fruitless."

"We do it," her mother had said, sounding firm for once, "because it is our family duty. And we do it to rid the world of evil. I don't want to lose you, Rhea, but I'll see you dead by my own hand before I'll let you turn your back on the world, on your family."

"Great, Mother. Just wonderful."

Still trying to reconcile the fact that her parents were fine with seeing her dead—by a witch or by their hands—Rhea groped for her Beretta and obliterated the mannequin's face with eight rounds.

It didn't make her feel much better.

Chapter 4

CHRIS drove the rental car through the gate and up the winding driveway, admiring the trees lining the drive, their leaves in full summer glory. *It must be amazing in the fall*, he thought.

The house and barn loomed before him, the barn a traditional red, the two-story house cream-colored with black shutters. Horses grazed in the field beside the barn, their coats glossy in the July sun. It was too idyllic for a hotbed of born-and-bred killers, which cheered him. He braked, yanked on the parking break, shut off the engine, and got out.

Just in time to practically shit his pants when a voice behind him shrilled, "Kill the witch! Kill the witch!"

He whirled, frantically trying to think of a rhyme to save himself, only to see a girl around seven years old pointing a toy six-shooter at him.

"Yeesh," he said.

"Kill the witch! Pschow, pschow!" She aimed the toy gun between his eyes and fired twice. She was grinning hugely, showing the gap between her front teeth, the sun bouncing off the golden highlights in her light brown hair, dark eyes sparkling with fun. "You're dead, witch!"

"Uh, run along, kiddo."

"You're dead, witch!"

"Okay. Bye now."

With a final "pschow!" she darted past him and up the porch steps, disappearing around the corner.

Chris took long, steadying breaths. *Okay. I clearly have not prepared for this encounter. It's okay. Deep breath. The kid caught you off guard, and you're on edge anyway, because nobody's tried the "let's just talk" approach, ever. And you're breaking years of tradition by showing up before your official "coming of age" ceremony. Deep breaths.*

He attached little importance to the witch game; the kid had, after all, grown up in Salem. They probably soaked up "kill the witch" with their mother's milk. Instead, he shrugged off the encounter and mounted the front porch steps, then rapped politely at the front door.

It was opened almost immediately by a middle-aged woman, late forties or early fifties, a woman who would have looked very nice if her eyes weren't so red and swollen. *Allergies*, he thought. *Or she's been crying for a while.*

"Yes?" she asked in a watery voice.

"Uh, hello, I'm looking for your eldest."

"My—you mean Rhea?" She pulled a tissue out of her sleeve and blew her nose. "Who are you? Are you from her school?"

"My name's Chris Merees," he replied, not expecting much in the way of consequences. He'd done this thousands of times in the past five years.

So the woman's reaction was startling, to say the least. Her eyes widened, then narrowed, and she started to slam the door, on his foot, which he'd thrust forward.

Bingo!

"You get out of here, foul thing! You're two years too early!"

"I like to plan ahead. Uh, ma'am, you're crushing my foot."

"Pity it isn't your head," she snarled, shoving harder.

"Look, I just want to—ow—talk. I'm not here for a fight."

"Too bad," the woman replied, half a second before a walloping pain slammed into his left ass cheek.

He staggered and went down on one knee. "Ow, damn it!"

"You get away from her *right now*," a female voice said coldly, behind him and to his left.

Shot me in the back, he thought, astonished. He clutched his ass and fell on his side. His other side, luckily. *One of the friggin' Goodmans shot me in the back!* The pain of it was like nothing in the world; the thing felt like it was coming out his belly button.

He heard steps running up the porch and rolled his eye up to see her. Arrows? Flying? Flying arrows? No, arrows flying true. That was it, by God.

"Rhea, watch out! You're not ready yet!"

Rhea, he thought.

She pointed the crossbow at his forehead. Not ready, his bleeding butt! He assumed she was the eldest Goodman; she looked about the right age. And the good looks he'd hardly noticed in the child and hadn't seen in the mother were unmistakable in this one.

She stared down at him, and time seemed to slow down, giving him a chance to take in her excellent good looks. Shoulder-length brown hair with gold and red highlights. Fair skin, freckled nose. Big dark eyes, currently narrowed to thoughtful slits. About five-seven, one-thirty. A foxy little pointed chin. Curves in all the right places, though the muscle definition was clear, because she was wearing khaki shorts and a red tank top. Red, the color of blood.

Her finger tightened on the trigger. From his vantage point (writhing in pain on the front porch) the arrow looked very, very big and very, very sharp. He could actually see her finger whitening as she slowly squeezed. Summer sunlight bounced off the arrow's silver tip.

I'm going to be killed, he thought, *by the prettiest girl I've ever seen.*

Chapter 5

RHEA heard the car come up the drive, but paid little attention. Her parents were always having friends over, salesmen often called (her parents were notorious for having trouble saying "no, thanks"), old school chums dropped by, people occasionally got lost in the country and stopped for directions. So she kept practicing until her father decided to check the stock. Then she made her escape.

Fuck destiny, she thought. *It's too nice a day to think about killing. Or being killed.*

Weapons were so much a part of her upbringing that she actually forgot to put the crossbow and quiver away; the bow was like an extension of her hand, and she didn't even notice the weight of the quiver. By the time she realized it, she saw her mother try to slam the door on the tall stranger.

In all Rhea's twenty-one years, her mother had *never* slammed the door. Not even on the Jehovah's Witnesses.

So she shot him. Not to kill. To get him to remove his foot from the bottom of the doorway. And it worked splendidly. He went down like a ton of saltwater taffy. She was more than a little amazed; had she worried so much, just an hour ago, about her ability to wound or kill?

She darted up the steps in time to see the tall man curl on his side like a shrimp and frown up at her.

"Rhea, watch out!" her mother shrilled. "You're not ready yet!"

She stared down at him, bringing the crossbow up in slow motion. At least, that's what it felt like. Everything was happening so slowly, she had plenty of time to get a good look at the guy.

Unmistakable: a de Mere. Short, sandy blond hair. Eyes the color of wet leaves. Tall, very tall (his head had almost touched the top of the doorway, before she shot him). Thin, but his broad shoulders were in evidence through his black T-shirt. His long legs looked even longer in the tight, faded jeans.

He looked exactly like the pictures of the de Mere her great-great-great-great- (how many greats was that?) grandfather had burned at the stake (except for the modern clothing). She had seen the archives, the drawings. *Fairy stories*, she had thought. About witches and the warriors who protected the world from their evil. And the demons some of the witches would call forth.

At last, the crossbow was in place. Her finger tightened on the trigger. *This is it! I'm going to kill him on my own front porch, and I'll live to a ripe old age. Why the hell were my folks so scared of him?*

"*Arrows, arrows, flying true,*" he rasped.

"*Form instead a cloud of blue.*"

The arrow in his butt vanished in a puff of blue smoke. The arrow loaded in her crossbow vanished as well. And her quiver suddenly felt pretty light. Horribly light.

"That's better," he mumbled, climbing to his feet with difficulty. He staggered for a few seconds, clutched his butt, then muttered,

"*Arrow's wound paining me,*

Form instead a—shit!"

"Are those supposed to be poems?" Rhea asked, reaching for her Beretta, then remembering she'd locked it in the barn after practice. *Oh, great.*

"You shot me in the back," he snapped, still massaging his ass.

His hands were red to the wrist. "That's why I'm the good guy, and you're the bad guys."

"The hell!" she almost shouted, then realized her mother was still standing in the doorway, utterly shocked. Rhea darted forward, shoved her mom back, and slammed the door. Meanwhile, the witch was hobbling around the porch, dripping blood all over the place and mumbling "Ooh, ow, ouch, God help me, ow ow ow . . ."

"You're wrong," she snapped, freshly outraged. How dare he accuse her of villainy? He'd come to her home uninvited and terrorized her mother. For that last one, if nothing else, she'd see him dead.

Her blood was still humming; her heartbeat thundered in her ears. She itched for a weapon, or a stake, some rope, and a box of fireplace matches. Because she wanted to kill him. She needed to kill him. Everything that was in her, centuries of tradition, cried out for it.

It was like, until she saw him in the flesh, her life had been rudderless.

"The hell," he retorted, and she tried to remember what they had been talking about. "I've never shot anybody in the back in the twenty-eight years *I've* been running around on the planet. You can't say the same, Rhea. Hell, your little sister runs around yelling 'kill the witch' at complete strangers."

"Shut up." She wondered if she could kick him to death. Surely it was worth a try. "You're the foul evil magicks bringer and demon raiser, not me. *I'm* protecting the world from *you*. It's not the other way around."

"Magic," he sighed, straightening. "And I don't *raise* them. I just get rid of them. That's an old wives tale, that we raise demons. *Magicks*. Jesus!"

"What?"

"Not magicks. Magic. I can hear the *'ck,'* and you're wrong about that, too. What rhymes with wound?"

"Boon, dune, croon, cartoon, commune, swoon . . ." she

answered automatically. She'd been studying poetry since the seventh grade. Her other talent, you might say.

"Swoon!" he shouted. "That's it.
Unkind arrow, leaving a wound,
Fix me up before I swoon."

She gasped as the bleeding stopped, as the blood disappeared from his hands, as he straightened up with a sigh. "Oh, God, that's so much better. Christ, my aching ass."

Okayyyy. So, her parents were right to be scared shitless by this guy. It seemed her ancestors had the right idea: Wipe out the de Mere line, witch by witch. Funny, in all the archives and all the old records and during her training, no one had mentioned he could *bend the very fabric of reality to his will.*

"Nobody told me you could bend the very fabric of reality to your will."

"Gee, so sorry your intel isn't up to snuff. No pun intended."

"I thought you were supposed to curse cows and sour their milk, or be a bride of Satan, or something like that."

He stared at her, green eyes wide. "Do I look like I spend my days hanging around cows? And I'm not a bride of anything."

"Why didn't the archives mention your little poetry trick?" she mused aloud, not really expecting an answer.

"Nobody knows, except you Goodmans. My great-great-great-great grandfather couldn't."

"Not enough greats."

"Never mind. Anyway, Christopher de Mere couldn't do it, and none of his descendants could, for the longest time. And FYI, we dropped the 'de' about four generations ago."

"What do you mean, they couldn't do it? You can all do magic."

He nodded and even smiled. She couldn't believe they were having a civilized conversation.

She still wanted to kill him, though.

"Oh, they could do magic," he replied, "but it was a lot

harder—I mean, would real witches allow themselves to be burned at the stake if they could save themselves? Oh, and that's quite a family history of murder, mayhem, and close-mindedness you've got there."

"Shut *up*. It wasn't just my family," she added lamely. The insanity of the Salem witch trials, deemed so necessary three hundred years ago, were an embarrassment to the Goodmans these days. So many innocents. Not enough of the guilty. "Why are we having a conversation? You're a dead man walking."

"Takes one to know one, sunshine. Except for the 'man' part, of course. And to finish answering your rude and intrusive questions, the Mere family has been evolving each generation in order to better deal with *you* bums. Thus, I rhyme, things happen. I rhyme, your pretty shiny things go bye-bye."

"Oh, *great*."

"I thought so," he admitted.

She abruptly turned and marched down the porch steps, annoyed to hear him following her. "Hey! We're talking, here."

"We're done talking."

"Where are you going?"

"Shut up."

"Are you going into the barn?"

"Shut up."

"Rhea, Rhea, tell me true
What is in the barn for you?"

She felt an invisible hand seize her mouth and force it open. She stopped in her tracks, appalled, and fought with as much inner strength as she could muster, but still her traitorous mouth fell open, and she said, almost babbled, "Four nines, two crossbows, a twelve-gauge shotgun, a twenty-gauge shotgun, ammo for everything, four skinning knives, two filet knives, six switchblades, and a Magnum .357."

"But we were just talking!" he yelled after her, sounding panicked.

"There's no need to take out four nines! What the hell is a four nine?"

Since he hadn't done magic, she was not compelled to answer and did not bother to explain that she had four nine-millimeter Berettas in the locked chest under the floor of the barn.

"Don't you want to just talk?" The rhyming moron was still trotting after her. "We don't have to kill each other, you know."

What bullshit! She didn't trouble herself to come up with the scathing remarks he had coming. Instead, she made it to the barn without interference (magical or otherwise), and pulled on the trapdoor on the south side of the building. She leaned down, spun the combination on the safe, popped it open, reached inside, and pulled out two Berettas.

"Rhea, Rhea, with your guns,
Stop this madness before it . . . shit!"

He's not a god, she thought with not a little relief. *He can't rhyme for shit. And thank goodness. Because otherwise, we'd all be cooked.*

She cocked the guns (they were always loaded; no need to even check) and held them up, just in time to see him sprint in the other direction.

Yeah, you'd better run, de Mere.

She started to take the shot

(I've never shot anybody in the back.)

and hesitated. Was it true? Was it cowardly and sneaking and bad-guy-like to take a witch from behind? All her teachings cried out in the negative. But de Mere had the weight of a bunch of Westerns on his side.

Because the bad guys always snuck up and shot you in the back.

These outrageous new thoughts crowded her brain and she hesitated. Not for long, but it gave de Mere time to dive through the driver's side window. She put plenty of bullets through said window, but either he had perfected the art of driving while kneeling on the mat, or he had made a rhyme that made bullets bounce off, because the next thing she knew, the only thing left of Chris de Mere was a spume of dust in her driveway.

She lowered her now-empty guns and stared at the dust. She'd had the shot, and she bungled it. The Goodmans might be out of luck if they were counting on her to save them.

Chapter 6

A WEEK later, he returned. This time he had scribbled down several words on pink Post-Its, words that rhymed with arrow and Beretta and gun and Rhea. He had been careful to return the bullet-ridden rental and drive up in a different car (the Avis people had not been pleased, to say the least), hoping they wouldn't nuke him the moment he pulled into their driveway.

He convinced himself he was here because it was worth another try, that people could overcome centuries of conditioning, these were modern times, and witch-hunting was just silly.

But the reality was, he couldn't get the trigger-happy jerk out of his head. *That's* why he'd come back. Her "oh, *greats*" and "shut ups" were actually kind of funny. And that hot little figure she had wasn't bad, either. And he loved the pointy little chin. At six-four, he was taller, but he didn't tower over Rhea the way he did with most women.

Worst of all: He couldn't imagine killing her. He'd liked her right away (insanity!), even if she had shot him in the ass. Or maybe *because* she shot him in the ass. She had sure charged up the steps in defense of her mother without hesitation, and he liked that, too.

His parents were long dead. He tried not to blame the Good-

mans . . . the one who had done the deed was, after all, also dead.
For every Mere death, a Goodman had died, too. He tried to keep
it in mind at all times. It helped when he was tempted to abandon
the human race, let the demons swarm, and use his magic to win
the lottery. Repeatedly.

Anyway, he liked—what was the word? He liked her *moxie*.
And frankly, verbally sparring with a woman who could kill him
(who was *fated* to kill him) was an unbelievable rush.

He carefully drove up to the house, eyes peeled for Goodmans. But
the house and barn looked quiet, and he could see no cars in the drive.

He put the car in park, deliberately left the parking brake alone
(it had almost been the death of him last time; he'd wasted valuable
seconds releasing it before making his escape), and climbed out.

"Uh . . . hello? Anybody home? Goodmans? Rhea?"

He moved closer to the front porch, then heard a sound to his
left and turned in the direction of the barn. "Mr. and Mrs. Goodman? Rhea? Anybody up for a rematch?"

The attack came without warning; he hadn't heard a thing. But
a sturdy weight smacked him in the middle of the back, and he
went facedown onto the gravel driveway.

"Kill the witch!" a familiar voice shouted. "Pschow, pschow!"

"Kid," he said into the driveway, "get off me. Seriously."

"Die, evil fiend, die!"

"Kid."

"Pschow!"

"Kid. I'm serious." He tried to move, to gently shift her off his
back, but she clung like a lamprey. "I know it's not cool to smack
children, especially not your own, but if you don't get off me—"

"Kill the witch!"

"What are they *feeding* you guys? You're, what? Seven? And
you're already obsessed with witch-hunting? Jesus wept."

"I'm eight, not seven, stupidhead."

"Thank God. I can't for the life of me think of what rhymes
with seven.

"Great, great,
Hate, hate,
Off my back
Child of eight."

It was one of his worst rhymes ever (he felt like jumping rope to it), but it had the desired effect; he felt the weight disappear from his back and climbed to his feet. He dusted off his clothes and looked around for the kid.

She was scowling at him from on the other side of the rental car. "No fair. You cheater."

"You're one to talk—er, what's your name?"

"Violet Goodman."

"Of course. Anyway, who ambushed who? You Goodmans. Bloodthirsty savages."

"You wait 'til Rhea finds out what you—"

"DID YOU JUST USE MAGIC ON MY BABY SISTER?"

"Uh-oh," Violet said, looking, to her credit, worried for him. Then she added in a much lower voice, "I wasn't really going to tell. You're a good witch, I know."

"Thanks for that." He turned in time to see Rhea come storming down the front steps, headed for him like a flame toward kindling. "Listen, Rhea, Violet jumped me. All I did was pull into your driveway."

"You used *magic* on my *sister*."

"I didn't hurt her. And before you go running into the arsenal-slash-barn, I warn you that I'm armed with tons of gun-and-arrow rhymes." He patted his pockets, fairly bulging with Post-Its, for emphasis.

She wasn't heading for the barn. She was steaming straight for him, pale face flushed to the eyebrows with rage. He wasn't sure if he was aroused or scared. Or both.

"So don't do anything crazy," he added, standing his ground. "I come in peace, like a benevolent alien. I mean you no harm—ow!"

She'd dropped into a crouch at the last second and swept his legs out from under him with a lunge. Then she was on him, her small hands grasping his neck, squeezing.

"I don't know—if you know—but I can't breathe—when you do that," he gurgled.

"If you can talk," she said grimly, tightening her grip, "you can breathe. How dare you? How dare you come back to my home, threaten my baby sister?" She started to slam his head up and down. Gravel bounced and flew around his ears.

"He didn't threaten me," Violet quickly spoke up. "We were playing."

"Violet. Go in the house."

"But Mom and Dad said you had to play with me when you were watching me, and all you've done is work out in the—"

"Violet. House."

"I don't think you need to choke him," the girl retorted, then reluctantly left.

"I agree," he gasped. The only thing that was saving him was his upper body strength; he had two hands clamped around her wrists, barely holding her off. She might work out like a fiend, but her hands were small, and she couldn't get them all the way around his neck. And it wouldn't be long before she figured that out and starting beating the living shit out of him in earnest. "You should listen to Violet, a kindhearted but slightly disturbed third-grader."

"Don't talk about my sister," she said through gritted teeth, her face going even redder from her strangulation efforts.

Throttle? Bottle? Strangle? What rhymed with strangle? Maybe he could turn her hands into flippers. Flipper, slipper?

Oh, to hell with it. He tightened his grip on her wrists and abruptly rolled over. *Thank you, Mother Nature, for making me a guy.*

Now he was on top, still encircling her wrists with his fingers, and she glared up at him with such malevolence that he almost let go of her. Which would have been a disaster.

"Okay," he said, and coughed, politely turning his face away.

He hated to think how his throat would feel if she'd had bigger hands. "Okay. Listen. I just came here to—"

"Get the *hell* off me!"

"—talk and try to convince you that this is a dance we don't have to do—"

"I am going to kill you a *lot*."

"—because after all, this is the twenty-first century, and don't you think witch-hunting should have been left behind with slavery?"

"Not as long as any de Mere descendants are running around on the planet now *let go*!"

"Oh, shut up," he said, and bent down and kissed her.

She went rigid with astonishment, which was a relief, because he didn't care to be bitten at the moment. He'd just meant to give her a peck, but the taste of her soft, sweet mouth worked on him like a hormone shot, and he slid his tongue between her lips, tasting her, relishing her the way he relished a ripe piece of fruit in the summertime.

She didn't make a sound. Just laid there like a board. An amazed, totally shocked board. So he let go of her wrists and cupped her face and deepened the kiss, and he thought he felt her respond, and then—

—and then her face shot out of his line of sight, and he realized she'd slapped him so hard he'd flown off her.

"Ow," he groaned, once again face down in the dust.

"What did you think you were doing?" He rolled over in time to see her spring to her feet. "What the hell is wrong with you?"

"Well, at the moment, I've got dust all over me and a piece of gravel up my nose and maybe a nosebleed, too."

She stood over him, jabbing her finger in the air for emphasis. He tried not to flinch. "We are supposed to be killing each other, not kissing. So cool your gonads and get your head in the game."

"That's what I've been trying to tell you," he said patiently, staring up at her. "I'm not in the game. I'm not going to play. I think our families have been killing each other long enough, don't you?"

"As long as a de Mere is around, a Goodman has to kill him."

"Who says?"

Her mouth popped open, and she appeared to be struggling for words, then burst out with, "Everybody! My parents and tradition and—everybody. All the way back to the first Goodman and the first de Mere."

"Yawn," he said.

"It's my duty to kill you and be killed doing it. Just like it's your family duty to try to kill me and be killed doing it."

"Don't you think that's just about the dumbest fucking thing in the world?"

"Well. Yes," she admitted. "But who are we to break from tradition?"

"And that's the second dumbest thing. Oooof!" She had dropped to her knees—right on his chest. "Gkkk! Air!"

"You listen to me, de Mere. You—"

"Chris," he groaned. "Christopher Mere, do I have to carve it into my forehead?"

"Shut up. You go away and do whatever you have to do until your thirtieth birthday, and I'll do what I have to do, and then the next generation can worry about it."

"Forget it," he gurgled.

"And no more of this showing up at my house being all chatty and shit. Stay away from my family and stay away from me. For the next couple of years at least."

"Sorry. Can't do it."

"You'd *better* do it. And keep your Mere lips to yourself."

"What's wrong with my lips?" He put his hands around her small waist and tossed her off him. She hit the dirt (literally), planted her arms, and spun right back over him.

He shoved. She shoved. Soon they were rolling around in the driveway like a couple of kids having a playground spat.

"Go away!"

"No."

"Buzz off!"

"No."

"I hate you!"

"Well, I hate you, too, sunshine. But you taste pretty good, I must—ow!"

"And don't even *think* about using your rhymes on me. You're a lousy poet and an evil magic-doer."

"Yeah? Well, you come from a long line of cold-blooded murderers."

"I do not!"

"Do too."

"Not!"

"You totally, completely do."

"Shut up!"

"Make me, sunshine."

"I'll make you, all right." She had temporarily gained the upper hand and was again on top. "I'll make you wish you were never *born*."

"Don't you think we're a little too old for this kind of thing?" He brought his legs up, hooked them around her neck, and rode her all the way down. "Now will you stop trying to beat the hell out of me—ow—and listen? Ouch!" He wondered dizzily if that last punch had given him a concussion.

Beneath him, she wriggled and squirmed in the dirt like an outraged snake. That was actually a big, big problem, because the fight (and the kiss) had seriously turned him on. He prayed she couldn't feel his erection. She'd cut if off. He pressed down harder, careful not to hurt her, inwardly groaning as he tried to hide the biggest boner of his life.

A boner for the witch-hunter! Jesus wept.

"Will you stop wiggling and listen?"

Gasping from her efforts, Rhea wheezed, "There's nothing to listen to."

"Oh, that's the spirit."

"We don't talk, we fight. And kill. You'd better reread your archives."

"Rhea, I can see how it is with you, but you don't know how it is with me. I won't kill you."

She blinked up at him. Her eyes were watering from all the dust in the air. "You'd better," she said. "Because I'm going to do my damnedest to kill you."

"I won't fight back, Rhea. It'll be murder. Cold-blooded murder."

"It isn't murder."

"It really, really is."

"De Mere, you'd better fight!"

"No."

Before she could screech at him some more, he heard a car pull into the drive, then skid to a halt with the left front tire no more than six inches from the top of Rhea's face.

Car doors were flung open, and quite a few Goodmans piled out and swarmed (how many *were* there, anyway?) around him. He realized he was pinning their eldest into the dirt and the two of them were filthy and sweaty. And their clothes were ripped.

He craned his neck to look up at Rhea's father, who looked about ready to start breathing fire. "Hi, Goodmans. Uh. This isn't what it looks like."

Then somebody came up behind him and turned off all the lights inside his skull.

Chapter 7

RHEA'S lips were still burning from the kiss.

She thought of a line from *King of the Hill*: "That boy's not right." It perfectly explained Chris Mere, the big grabby rhyming kissing dolt.

And the bastard was strong. Well, he was big, so she should have expected it, but she'd had no idea how much physical power was lurking within those ropy muscles. She'd tried her very best to beat the hell out of him, and he'd come away from it with only scratches.

But he'd be sore tomorrow, by God.

Her parents had been utterly at a loss. It was inconceivable that a Mere showed up years early, that a Mere was talking peace. Neither of them knew what to do, and both of them thought it might be a trick or a trap of some kind. The de Meres had a centuries-old rep for treachery.

Interestingly, Violet spoke up for him. And Rhea had been forced to admit to Power and Flower that not only had he not hurt the little girl, he'd taken several blows to avoid hurting *her*. That made her folks reel all over again.

After some discussion, they decided it would be disrespectful (not to mention leaving them open to embarrassing questions if someone stopped by) to leave an unconscious Mere in their driveway, so they dragged him inside, all the way to the guest room.

Her mother had hesitantly brought a warm, wet washcloth, tiptoed to the bed, then handed the washcloth to Rhea and hurriedly left, clearly not interested in hanging around the unconscious witch.

Rhea considered gagging him with the washcloth, then gave it up and gently wiped the gravel and small trickles of dried blood off the left side of his face. Once she had that clean enough, she moved to the right side—

—and quick as thought, he was awake and grabbing her wrist, yanking it back from his face. That startled her even more than the kiss, the way he went from flat-out cold unconsciousness to being wide awake, if a little disoriented.

"Oh. It's you. Hey, sunshi—oh, God, my head. My aching, breaking head. How long have I been out?"

"An hour," she said, handing him the washcloth. He folded it into a small square and rested it on his forehead. "Give or take a few minutes."

"Who hit me from behind?" he asked groggily. "Fucking Goodmans; do you ever try a frontal assault?"

"Me," she replied, ignoring the very uncomfortable feeling his comment planted. "I brought my leg up and kicked you in the back of the skull."

"So that's why the room is spinning. I thought we were on a merry-go-round with a bed."

"Not hardly."

"I am totally astonished—yet grateful—to find myself not dead. I don't know how you were all able to restrain yourselves."

"Even we cold-blooded murderers wouldn't slit the vocal cords on an unconscious witch."

"Slit the—"

"Sure. That's how I'll have to kill you. You won't be able to rhyme—make magic—and you'll bleed out in about a minute and a half."

He touched various cuts and scrapes, wincing as he did so. "If anybody can do it, you can."

"Oh, stop."

"No, really."

"You're just saying that."

"No, I'm not. You could absolutely do it."

"Well, thanks. I appreciate that. But if you're feeling better—"

"I am not."

"—you'd better hit the road. My dad's pretty upset, and my mom's not too happy, either."

"Why am I in a bedroom?"

"Well. We couldn't just leave you in the driveway like a dead earthworm."

"How charitable."

"Damn straight, considering the fact that your father killed my dad's older brother."

"I'm pretty sure it was the other way around."

"Either way, time to go."

"But I have contusions," he moaned, as she pulled him into a sitting position. "And possibly a fractured skull. You can't just turn me out into the cold."

"It's eighty degrees outside. And make a rhyme to fix your hurts."

"What rhymes with pain?"

"What doesn't? Chain, brain, drain, mane, main, champagne, bloodstain, complain, disdain, explain, ingrain, migraine—"

"That's it!" he shouted, startling her.

"The man on the bed
With a migraine
Fix his head

And take away his pain."

Rhea covered her eyes. She probably should have covered her ears. "That's really horrible. You're an *awful* poet."

"Hey, it got the job done, didn't it, sunshine?"

"Quit calling me that."

"Why?"

"We're fated to kill each other, not give each other nicknames like Sunshine and Stupidhead."

He sprang out of the bed, fully healed, and examined his filthy, shredded clothes in the mirror. "I am absolutely billing you for the clothes I must now go buy at Neiman's."

"You will not. And did you hear what I said?"

"Sure. How come you can always come up with a bunch of words that rhyme?"

She studied the pattern of the quilt, rather than look directly at him. She'd been feeling weird, staring at his broad shoulders. Almost . . . tingly? "It was my minor in college. I still, you know, write them. Poems." She wouldn't say it. No, she wouldn't. Okay, maybe she would. "You should get yourself a rhyming dictionary." *Good work! You've just put a powerful weapon into the hands of your greatest enemy.*

"Yeah, well, I don't have a lot of leisure time to hang out in bookstores and—" He spun around so quickly she nearly jumped out the window. "What? You're a poet?"

"Apparently, I'm a warrior for the honor of the Goodman clan," she said dryly.

"Yeah, tell me about it. I got the whole song and dance by the time I was sixteen. How long have you known?"

"Since last Monday," she admitted.

"Oh, shit! Why did your folks wait so long?"

"Tradition."

He had turned back and now scowled at his reflection. "I'm really beginning to hate that word." Then, quick as thought, he spun back. "Wait just one minute. You were going to be a poet, weren't you? But then you had to do . . ." He gestured to his (broad) chest. "This."

"Well . . ." She looked away.

"And you've only known this since *last week*?" He marched to the door and yanked it open. "Where's your dad?"

"Uh . . . target practice, I think."

"Because I'm off to kick his ass."

"Better not," she said, hiding a grin. It wasn't a laughing matter, not really. "He taught me everything I know, not everything he knows."

"I can take him," Chris said confidently.

She snatched up the water glass from the bedside table and flung it toward him, missing his nose (on purpose) by half an inch. The glass exploded against the wall, and he ducked (about two seconds too late).

"What the *hell*?"

"I could have thrown that at your left eye. But I didn't. It's why we always vanquish you, Mere. You can't do magic fast enough to save yourself from our reflexes. All you can do is—"

"Yes?"

"Get your licks in."

"Very nice. I'm out of here. You think I've got nothing better to do than hang out with a girl who wants to ice me?"

"Woman," she corrected.

"Please. I've got almost a decade on you."

"Are you leaving, or do I have to talk to you some more?"

"I am leaving. Right now. I'm sure there's a demon to vanquish or a damsel in distress to rescue."

"Demon?"

"What do you think I do," he snapped, "when I'm not here trying to talk you out of murdering me?"

"Make evil happen?" she guessed.

He rolled his eyes and stomped out the door. She couldn't help it; she ran to the window and watched as he stormed out, kicking up tufts of dust, then climbed into his car and roared out of the driveway—backward.

"And don't come back!" she shouted after him, wondering why that sounded unconvincing.

Chapter 8

WHERE is he?" Power demanded.

"You let him get away?" Flower asked, aghast.

Rhea rubbed her eyes. She *had* let him go. What was wrong with her? Other than being attracted to the man she was supposed to kill. A man who had been very, very careful not to hurt her, despite almost constant provocation. A man she almost wanted to . . . help? Had she gone crazy in the past week? Or had she always been crazy?

Still and all, he sure didn't *seem* evil.

"Answer me," Power said.

"What, you wanted him to spend the night? Have a slumber party with cookies and warm milk? I thought you'd be glad he beat feet out of here, not bummed because you don't have a jammy buddy."

"Watch your mouth."

"The *hell*. You two are egging me on to kill this guy and get killed myself. Then he shows up and not only doesn't kill me, doesn't hurt any one of us. Then he came *back*. And didn't hurt us again."

"He isn't in his prime quite yet. When he has thirty years, he will be formidable. And you. You're already distracted."

"He said he wouldn't fight me."

"He's a liar."

"He said it'd be cold-blooded murder on my part."

"And he has no respect for tradition," her mother added.

"That's true," she had to admit.

"Rhea. You can't be fooled by his tricks and his charm." Flower paused, then took a deep breath and continued. "I admit he's attractive. And he seems harmless. But he's a Mere, descended from de Meres. He. Will. Kill. You."

"And then one of Violet's kids will kill his kid."

"Yes, or one of your other nieces or nephews, assuming he has already fathered a child, or will in the next couple of years."

For some reason, that caused her a stab of anxiety right in the gut. Chris Mere kissing some bimbo? Touching her, whispering to her, caressing her?

"—be distracted."

"What?"

"You cannot be distracted. This is a trick. On top of everything else, he's probably afraid to face you when you're in *your* prime. So he showed up early and tried the de Mere charm. But it didn't work. Right?"

She said nothing.

"Right?"

"Why do we always take people from behind?"

Her father blinked. "What?"

"I was taught to strike from the rear, every chance I could get. Even most of the practice mannequins are facing away from us. How come?"

"Because we need every advantage over a magicks user."

"Magic," she corrected.

"Yes."

"Well. Our family has a rep for cold-blooded murder—"

"Defending the family and the town is not murder!"

"—we always hit from behind—"

"Because we cannot do magic!"

"—and we've been killing his family for centuries. Some of them a lot more helpless than Chris Mere."

"That is our duty!" her father practically screamed, his bald spot turning purple with rage.

"You know what? I think we *are* the bad guys."

"Rhea!" her parents howled in unison.

"No, really. We are. He came in peace—twice—and all you two can do is talk about how it's some cruel trick. Because you'll never trust a Mere."

"True enough," her mother said.

"But I think *I* can."

"Oh, Rhea."

"You guys weren't here. I was beating the shit out of him, and he took it. Not only did he not use magic on me, he didn't use his upper body strength, either. Well, not too much."

"That was not how it appeared when we drove up," her father said sharply.

"You're right. That's not how it looked. Which proves my point: Appearances are deceiving. What if we've had the wrong idea for three centuries?"

"That's—that's—" Her father shook his head. "I would have to give the matter some thought."

"Also, I think I know how to break the curse."

Her mother slumped wearily into one of the kitchen chairs. "This *is* the curse. To kill and be killed, again and again and again. To bury your mothers and your aunts and your sisters and your nieces."

"No. There's a loophole, and you know it."

Her parents were silent. Finally, her father tentatively said, "If he shares his powers with you?"

"That and one other thing."

"What?" her mother asked.

"Never mind. I don't know if I can pull it off. The important thing is to find him."

"*Find* him?"

"Yeah. I have to find him before he turns thirty and I have no idea where he is. Too bad for him I memorized his rental car license plate. It'll be a start."

"Rhea, you cannot do this."

"I'm calling your bluff, Mom. Because I'm *not* going to kill him. If you think killing me will fix that, you've gone over to the dark side for sure. And we're already there, damn it."

"Rhea, you know I—you know I would never hurt you. I—I was angry and I didn't mean—"

"Don't do it, Rhea," Power said quietly, sounding for the first time in a week like the superb trainer and parent she adored, instead of the shrill, easily angered man he had become after Chris showed up. "It's a trick. He'll kill you. Please don't go after him. Stay here and train. Maybe—maybe you can break the curse if you break him."

"You guys. I have to do this my way, because the old way doesn't work. I'm telling you: *I can break the curse.* Isn't that worth the risk? Think about it, Dad. No more training, ever. Not having to flinch every time a stranger shows up in town. Saving Violet's baby! Or Ramen's, or Kane's. Not having to bury me."

Her father couldn't meet her gaze and turned to stare out the north window. Her mother, however, looked hopeful for the first time in a week. "Oh, Rhea, do you really think so?"

Actually, I have no idea if my plan will work, but don't give it another thought. "Absolutely," she lied.

Her father stood with his back to her, still staring out the window. "Then go," he said, "quickly. While there's still time to catch him. Do—do you want me to come with you?"

"I'll come, too," her mother added, though she wasn't a Goodman by blood, of course.

"My, my, look at you two. I'm shocked to my very core. Breaking tradition like that? No chance," she teased.

"Mmm. And Rhea . . ."

"Yeah?"

"If it goes badly—"

"I know, Dad."

"Because it may be an elaborate charade on his part."

"I know, Dad."

"To trick you into lowering your defenses."

"Gotcha."

"Why was he the one on top when we drove up?"

"Uh—gotta go, Dad."

Chapter 9

CALL girls—or "soiled doves" as Chris preferred to think of them—had been disappearing in Boston for more than two months. Chris drove yet another rental down to the harbor for a quick look. And a finder spell, of course. Because he had a good idea what was happening. A K'shir demon: The Taker of the Lost. Looks like a man, feeds like a devil, then looks like a man again. Only a magic user could spot it for what it was—a creature so unnatural to this world that it actually made his head hurt.

In fact, it hadn't hurt so badly since the day Rhea had smacked the shit out of him.

Don't think about Rhea.

He tried. He really tried. He'd spent the last two days holed up in his hotel room, determinedly not thinking about Rhea. Trying to become absorbed with the Call Girl Killer. And in all the not thinking about Rhea, he'd decided what to do: stay away. Don't go looking for her on his thirtieth.

And don't knock anybody up, for the love of God!

He swallowed at the thought. Did he have the courage to end his family line? Could he? *Should* he?

If it kept Rhea and the next Goodman safe, then yes. Absolutely.

Feeling a bit better about his decision, he'd decided to look into the missing soiled doves. All had been lured down to the harbor. Other than that, they had nothing in common, except for the way they died—in great terror and pain.

The police thought wild animals were on the loose, even though no one had reported a pack of wolves gone missing. And Chris couldn't blame them—he'd seen the crime scene photos. A quick show-me spell, a quick forget spell, and he had copies of everything. He had seen. Nothing human could do that to the poor girls. Frankly, he hadn't been able to eat a thing for quite a few hours after looking through the case files.

He had a strong hunch that the cops weren't going to be able to solve this case. Ever. So he would step in, again. In truth, he couldn't wait. All the pent-up anger and frustration at his situation—his and Rhea's, whom he wasn't thinking about—could be poured into his attack.

Go back, the rat in his brain whispered. *Do a spell. Make her come with you to the hotel. Make her take off her clothes and yours and—*

He shoved the thought away. It would reappear in another half hour or so, much to his disgust. After all the lectures Rhea had endured, it looked like he was the bad guy after all. How she would have liked to hear him say so!

But she would never hear him again. He would see to it. And he would end his line and break the curse. And she could live happily ever after, and so could her niece, the player-to-be-named-later.

He parked near Faneuil Hall and walked toward the harbor. His head hurt more and more with each step—excellent. The Taker of the Lost was planning on feeding tonight. Good. Chris was in a skull-cracking mood.

He stopped near a relatively deserted side street, read a Post-It, then stuffed the note back in his pocket and chanted,

"Taker of the Lost
Show your true face.

Then you'll be bossed
And I'll hit you with mace."

Okay, as far as poems went . . . not so great. Really kind of dreadful. But that was the trick. They didn't *have* to be good poems. They just had to rhyme, even clumsily. What had Rhea said? Get a rhyming dictionary? How had he never thought of that? The girl—woman—was a genius! But more important, why had she given the suggestion? It was kind of out of character for her—for any Goodman—to help a Mere. Frankly, it—

A startled roar from two blocks over smashed up his chain of thought; he started to sprint. The demon was likely to lash out at anybody near it; they hated—*hated*—being forced to drop their disguises. He heard a car pull up behind him and slam on the brakes, and was absently grateful not to be creamed by what sounded like a typical Boston driver.

He rounded a corner and ran another block, then checked himself before he could run blindly into the alley. He looked up. And there it was, hanging twelve feet up like a bloated bat—all dark leathery wings, two hearts, and bad smell.

"Don't you want to come down here and kick my ass?" he called up to it, hoping it understood English.

That was when the one behind him slammed into him, shoving him so hard into the wall that he almost lost consciousness.

Two of them? Oh, *great*, as Rhea would say. It certainly explained the number of missing girls . . . he'd assumed it was a ridiculously hungry demon, not that it had a mate. Demons of any kind were not known for teamwork. He should have remembered there was an exception to every rule.

Too bad for him.

He rolled away just as the demon's left foot came down where his head had been, cracking the cobblestones. He felt something warm drip into his eyes and realized he was bleeding from a scalp wound.

It's possible, he mused, that I jumped into this without planning it so well. Anything was better than wondering how things might have been between him and the girl

(woman)

he wasn't thinking about. Even facing an extra demon on a Wednesday night.

He watched with something close to disinterest as the male scuttled down the wall and the female edged closer.

He couldn't think of a thing that rhymed with demon, and he was too woozy to grope for a Post-It and try to read it in the darkness of the alley.

This is it. Heaven, here I come. I'll go to heaven, right?

There was a shhhhk-THUD and another shhhhhk-THUD, and the female, who had been once again getting ready to stomp him, screamed. Chris wiped more blood out of his eyes and saw two arrows sticking out of the female's back.

The demon popped her extra elbow joint loose and was able to reach far enough up her back to yank at them, and then screamed again—in anger as much as pain—when she moved them in her flesh but did not dislodge them.

Shhhhhk-THUD, shhhhhk-THUD, shhhhhk-THUD. More screaming. Now the male was roaring in a rage, but (typical of demons) did not come closer to help his mate, preferring to wait in the shadows to ambush—who?

"You dumb shit," Rhea observed, marching into the alley. She was dressed in super-cool badass black from neck to ankles, and—was that a Kevlar vest?

"It's nice to see you, too, sunshine. Dressed for the occasion, I see. And by the way, ow, my head."

"Taker of the Lost?" she asked, studying the wounded female, who had gone down on her knees and managed to claw out one of the arrows. "To think I thought all those stories my dad told me were fairy tales." Her hand snaked behind her back and she came out with a gun—a really big-ass gun—and emptied six chambers into the female's head. "And for the record, you stinking big bastard, the only one allowed to make him go 'ow' is *me*."

"Stinking big bitch," Chris said helpfully. "This is the female."

Despite their exotic mythology, demons could be killed with conventional weapons: Destroy enough of the brain and it was a fait accompli. So Chris was not surprised to see the female slowly topple forward and lie still.

He *was* surprised to see Rhea squat in front of him and hand him a Wet Nap, which he batted out of her hand. He'd stupidly assumed she had seen the male as well—which was a gross disservice to the girl. Woman. She'd only known about her "duty" for a little over a week, and damned sure didn't spend spare time casting spells on demons. She was a fucking poet!

Those thoughts whirled through his brain in half a second, and he brought his knees up and kicked her as hard as he could, square in the chest. She flew away from him like he'd shot her out of a cannon,

(God, God, don't let her be hurt, please God, I'll owe you one, okay?)

and then two black feet smashed into the spot where Rhea had been crouching.

"Ow," Rhea bitched from eight feet away. Then, "Two of them? In all the stories I heard—"

"Yeah, and all those old stories are always totally truthful."

"Good point," she admitted, climbing to her feet and popping the cylinder on her six, grabbing a speed loader and sliding it home, even as she edged toward the male, who, in a rage, was still stomping on the spot she'd recently occupied.

"Jesus, what are you waiting for? Shoot him! He's alone now, so he's being careful. Which is the only reason he hasn't eaten our heads. Shoot!"

"No. You might be killed in the crossfire."

"Who cares? Shoot the fucker!"

"I care. Freeman, gleeman, semen, seamen, Philemon, cacodemon. Lost, boss, floss, gloss, toss."

The male twisted toward her, hissing, but it had to climb over the body of its mate to get to Rhea, so he had maybe three seconds.

"Taker of the Lost
Begone to where lives a demon
Lest I give you a toss
Then drown you in semen."

"I think I'd rather have my face clawed off than listen to another one of those," Rhea commented as the advancing male suddenly vanished with a loud "pop!" . . . the sound of air rushing into the space it had so recently occupied.

"Shut up. It worked, didn't it?"

"You couldn't think of anything that rhymed with demon, could you?" she asked kindly.

"Shut up," he said, trying not to sulk. They stared at each other from opposite sides of the alley. Then he wondered why he was sulking. She had come! She had (somehow) tracked him down and found him and come armed and—

"Before I embrace you and cry like a little girl, you didn't bring all that stuff and wear all that stuff to kill me, did you?"

"Only if you misbehave." She grimaced, stood, and rubbed the small of her back. "Thank goodness for body armor. You kick *hard*, Mere."

"Chris. And thanks. My fault, by the way. I had no business assuming you knew there were two."

"And I had no business charging into an alley before I effectively deduced the threat level. So we both fucked up. That's why we can't kill each other."

"Really?" he asked, almost afraid to hope.

She bent, found the Wet Nap, skirted the dead female, and handed it back to him. "Really. If we try to kill each other, we'll just screw it up. Excuse me." She leaned against the wall and efficiently threw up.

He climbed to his feet, wiping more blood out of his eyes, then went to her and patted her shoulder while she vomited. "Sorry,

sorry," he said, as distressed as he'd ever been. "It's awful, I know. The smell and the—the general unnaturalness of them." He couldn't believe she'd walked into a dark alley to save his ass. "It hurts my brain to look at them."

She coughed, pulled an arm across her mouth, then said, "It hurts my stomach."

"Then why did you come?"

"Oh, I broke into your hotel room and found all the police reports. After I tracked your car rental. It wasn't hard to figure out where you went next—I was right behind you those last few minutes, but you ignored my honking."

"This is Boston," he said, as if that explained everything.

She laughed, a sound that caused his heart rate to double with pure joy. Then her eyes narrowed, and she cut off her laugh and said, "You didn't raise those two, right? You just get rid of them. Right?"

"Rhea. You really have to ask?"

"Sorry. Distrusting you is going to be a tough habit to break."

"Sunshine, you don't even know how tough. So now what? Since you're sure if we turn on each other we'll screw it up. What does that leave? Teaching each other to knit? Taking a judo class at the Y? What?"

She laughed again. "Now we go back to your hotel room and make a baby."

"*What?*"

Chapter 10

I CAN'T believe this is happening. I just can't believe it."

Rhea actually had to lead Chris through the lobby like a Seeing Eye dog. He was so shocked by her plan, he'd almost gone catatonic.

"I've been spending all this time not thinking about you, and now you want a Mere baby."

"A Goodman-Mere baby."

"I can't believe this is happening," he said again, following her robotically into the elevator.

"Are you all right? You're like kind of . . . out of it."

"I can't believe this is happening."

"It's a good way to break the curse, don't you think?"

"Curse?"

"The *curse*. The one that's been on our families for three hundred some years? *The* curse."

"Oh. That curse."

She pressed the button for his floor. "Are you sure you're okay?"

"Sure as sure can be," he replied absently. "It's just that I fell in love with you and was resigned to never seeing you again, and then you saved me in the alley, and now you want to have sex. I'm feeling a little like a Powerball winner. Also, I think we already broke the curse."

"When you shared your powers with your greatest enemy. And we teamed up and kicked some demonic butt."

"Right, right."

The elevator dinged, and they walked out. She used his key card to pop the door open, and inside they went. The hotel had already done turn-down service.

"Look!" Rhea said. "Chocolates!"

"Help yourself." He was just standing in the middle of the room, like he wasn't exactly sure what to do. Which was problematic.

She gobbled both chocolates, then started taking off her body armor, short-sleeved T-shirt, black leggings, black socks, black running shoes, and white panties.

"What are you doing?" he said, sounding almost—startled?

"Like I'm going to make a baby with body armor on. Don't just stand there. Strip."

"I can't believe this is happening."

"Yes, Chris, I *know*. Strip."

Still moving like his limbs were barely thawed, he started taking off his clothes. Belt, shirt, khakis, socks, shoes (in no particular order, she noted). Simpsons boxer shorts.

"I'll overlook the shorts, but afterward, we really have to talk."

"Did I make fun of your underwear?"

"You were thinking it," she said, taking his hand and leading him to the bed. She was trying not to stare, and failing—miserably. He was just—superb. Long lean limbs, broad shoulders, lightly furred chest, slightly dazed green eyes. And what looked to her like a rather sizeable erection, jutting stiffly upward toward his taut stomach.

"Chris?"

"Mmmm?"

"Do you *want* a baby with me?"

He blinked. "A Goodman-Mere baby? I could care less. *Our*

baby? Sure. Oh. You'll have to marry me once you're knocked up. Or maybe next week."

"Good," she whispered in his ear. "Because I want one, too. So get me pregnant. Right now."

Finally, he snapped out of the trance and nearly fell on her as he bore her to the bed, his lips frantic over hers, his tongue probing, his teeth gently nibbling her ear lobes, her neck, her cleavage. His hand spread her thighs apart and stroked the tender skin of her inner thighs, which made her shiver beneath him.

He moved lower so he could pull her nipples into his hot, wet mouth, sucking greedily, even gently biting her, and the sensation shot from her breasts to her toes in half a second. And now he was gently stroking the hot throbbing center between her thighs, making her strain against him, making her groan, making her plead.

He needed no such encouragement, just returned his attention to her mouth while spreading her legs a little wider. He broke the kiss to gaze into her eyes, as his hips thrust against hers, hard.

"Ow!"

"What, ow?" he panted.

"I just wasn't quite ready for you."

Sweat stood out on his forehead, and she could see him gritting his teeth as he forced his hips to be still. "Wasn't ready for me?"

"Well. This is kind of my first time."

He gaped at her. "Kind of?"

"Okay. It's my first time."

He started to roll off her, but she grabbed him by the elbows and managed to keep him in place. "A virgin?" he practically yelped. "You're a virgin, and you didn't say anything? And *why* are you a virgin?"

"Why wouldn't I be?" she snapped back. "I've spent my whole life training to kill you, or in school. When the hell would I have time to lose my virginity?"

"Okay, okay, don't get your guns. I was just—surprised. I've never done it with a virgin before." He squinted thoughtfully. "I'm pretty sure."

"Could you not reminisce about other sex partners when you're inside me?"

"Sorry, sorry. Does it still hurt?"

"It's a lot better." A whole lot better. Almost . . . delightful? Yes, delightful, the hot friction between her legs was no longer a burning pain but instead a thrilling amusement park ride, where she went up and up and up. He was thrusting against her with such care she almost wept. And he watched her face every moment.

Again, shuddering all over, he stopped. "Hurts?"

"No." She strained against him, trying to create her own friction. "Oh, no."

"You're . . ." He wiped his thumb on her cheek and showed her the tear. "Crying."

"I'm just so happy. Right this minute is the happiest moment of my whole life."

"What whole life?" he teased, continuing to stroke and surge into her. "Ah, God, Rhea, you really shouldn't say things like 'give me a baby' and 'I'm so happy.' It's hell on my self-control."

"You're doing all—oh!" She felt an all-over tightening and held her breath, and then her orgasm—her first *assisted* orgasm—blew through her like a hurricane, leaving her trembling in his arms.

"Oh, Christ!" Then he was groaning and shuddering against her, and she felt even more warmth between her legs than before.

"Uck. You made me sticky."

His head, which had been resting on her shoulder, jerked up. "Uck? *Uck?* You're hell on the self-esteem, too."

"Not uck for the sex. Uck for immediately after the sex. I mean—yeesh. I'd better clean up."

He clamped down on her arms and squeezed. "Don't you dare move," he growled. "No fair ruining the afterglow."

"Oh, was I wrecking pillow talk?" she teased.

"To put it mildly. You came, right? I was pretty sure you came."

"Oh, yes."

"That's great. Usually I have to go down on—"

"Stop."

"Sorry. Boy," he added cheerfully, grinning at her, "your dad is going to shit when we tell him what we were up to in Beantown."

"Now who's wrecking the afterglow? Why did you bring up my dad? Now I have to call them so they won't worry."

"Be sure to mention your recent deflowering."

"Thanks for the advice."

"And our upcoming wedding."

She shoved and punched and finally kicked him off her. She sat up in bed and didn't bother with the sheet, and could see the admiration in his eyes as he looked her over from head to foot. "I didn't hear a proposal, buster."

"Oh, stop it. You totally fell under my spell, and you know it."

"Ha!"

"What else do you call this?" he asked, gesturing to them both. "But magic?"

"You're a bag of sentimental mush."

"One of us should have a feminine side."

"Shut up," she retorted, then grabbed the phone and started dialing.

Epilogue

POWER and Flower made it to Mass General in record time, given rush hour traffic, and went at once to the maternity ward. Flower was carrying a teddy bear. Power had a gaily wrapped box with a big blue bow on the top.

"Excuse me," he said to the charge nurse. "My daughter, Rhea Goodman Mere? She's having a baby? Can you tell me what—"

A shout interrupted him. "And stay out!" Punctuated by the clatter of an emesis basin slamming into the wall.

"Never mind," Flower said. "We can find her."

They turned and walked down the hall in time to see their son-in-law practically sprint into the hallway. "All right, all *right*!" he yelled back. "Don't come crying to me when you forget how to do your breathing!"

"Chris, darling!" Flower called, hurrying up to him and giving him a hug. "We came as soon as you called."

"Happy birthday, by the way," Power added, handing Chris the gaily wrapped box. "A milestone. You're to be congratulated."

"I found *three* gray hairs on my head this morning, and your daughter—and my daughter—are directly responsible. I'm only thirty-two, and I'm going gray!"

"Well, nobody forced you two to get married and have babies," Flower said gently.

"Quite the opposite," Power muttered.

"And don't worry about Violet Number Two; she's at home with her aunties and uncles."

"Great. If she points a toy gun in my face and pretends to shoot me, I'm holding both of you responsible."

"We can't help it that 'kill the witch' is everyone's favorite childhood game."

"It's not everyone's—"

"What are you doing out there?" Rhea shouted. "Taking a poll? Get your ass in here!"

"Coming, coming!" He gave his in-laws a final, harassed glance before going back through the gates of hell.

"The baby will be your birthday present!" Flower called after him.

"Doubt it," Power said, glancing at his watch. "It's almost midnight."

"Second babies always come faster."

"She's only been in labor for four hours."

"Darling. It's *Rhea*."

"That's true," Power said, and sat down with his wife to wait for another Goodman-Mere baby.

———

"And . . . it's a boy!"

"Oh, *great*," Rhea groaned. "What was I thinking? I *knew* it hurt like a bastard, and I let you knock me up again anyway."

"Hold on a minute, Mom, we'll get him cleaned up, and then you can hold him." The nurse had to shout over the baby's wails to be heard.

"Listen to the lungs on that kid," Chris said happily. "A chip off the old maternal block."

"Shut up."

"And he's gorgeous."

She perked up, as much as she could in her exhausted state. "He looks okay? I figured he was okay from all the yelling. Violet Number Two did the same thing when she was born."

"Here he is, Mom!"

Rhea stared down in wonder at the tiny, perfect face. The baby was looking up at her with the blue eyes of a fair-skinned newborn, and she wondered if they would go dark like hers, or green like Chris's. She hoped they would be green, because . . .

"Welcome to the world, Christopher Goodman Mere," she said softly, and kissed her baby at the exact moment her husband kissed her on the top of her head.

Street Corners and Halos

Catherine Spangler

*To all those who have ever suffered loss of family or home,
or been affected by hatred and intolerance. May you find
inner peace and joy in living every day to the fullest.*

*Special thanks to Roberta for the title and the ending.
You're amazing.*

For, remember, man looks upon the things of the day
but God looks upon the heart.
(Edgar Cayce Reading 3253–2)

Chapter 1

THE high heels of her boots made a distinct click on the sidewalk, amplified by the exaggerated swing of her hips. She knew that the strut and the boots, along with the rest of her skimpy outfit, were terribly clichéd, but why should she care? After all, she was what she was. She saw no need to pretend otherwise.

Winter was creeping in early in Dallas. There was a distinct nip in the October night air. The cooler temperature seemed to lessen the stench of unwashed bodies and vomit and urine that drifted from behind the shabby buildings.

The unpleasant smell was further masked by the tantalizing scents of cooking food and burning wood. The food aromas came from the restaurants and clubs along the strip; the wood odor probably from a homeless person's fire—which would be extinguished if the police who occasionally patrolled the area saw it.

Both food and wood aromas stirred nostalgic memories. *Home and hearth, dinner cooking, family, warmth, love.* Vague, distant memories that refused to be completely vanquished.

Rachel Stryker shook those thoughts away. Hunger gnawed at her, and it was time to get down to business. She continued her strut down Harry Hines, letting the darkness wrap her in anonymity, although she could clearly see every detail of the debris-and-hypodermic-littered street.

Midway down the block, a man got out of an older, battered, maroon Toyota Camry. He looked around, attempting a nonchalance that told her he was after either drugs or sex—or both.

She walked faster, her long strides eating up the sidewalk between them. He saw her and stopped short, his gaze skimming down her. He was middle-aged, balding, nondescript—like hundreds of other marks. He straightened and tried to smooth his shabby jacket as she reached him.

"Hey there," she said, letting her allure drift around him. "You look like you could go for a little recreation."

He wet his lips, his gaze still roaming over her. "I don't think I can afford you."

"Oh, you can," she said, drawing the net tight. "Because I'm worth it. I'm the best you'll ever have." She eyed him, recognizing his type—he either was paid his wages in cash under the table or cashed his paycheck as soon as he got it. "Fifty dollars will get you whatever you want, baby."

"Sure," he muttered, staring into her eyes, firmly in thrall. He fumbled in his pocket, pulled out a money clip and peeled off a fifty-dollar bill. She found it odd that poorer people tended to carry more money on them, in larger denominations, as if it made them feel richer.

"Come on." She took his arm, guided him into a nearby alley. It was easy enough to maneuver him, since she matched him in height, and was far stronger than he'd ever comprehend.

He was dirty, his foul breath and body odor an unpleasant affront to her highly developed sense of smell, but again, what did it matter? She was just what he needed, and he . . . he was key to her existence.

She slipped the money into her fanny pack. "Well, let's get started then." She stepped close and placed her hand on his chest, savoring the rapid beating of his heart. *Is there anything more exhilarating,* she thought, as she always did, *than the blood—a life force essential to survival—thundering through a living, beating heart?*

"So," she breathed, lowering her face against his neck, "how do you want it?" She nipped the side of his neck, slipped into his mind. She wouldn't begrudge him his fantasies, as long as he gave her what she needed. Ah, he was easy to read . . .

She quickly unbuttoned his coat, then his shirt, jerking them open so that his bare chest was exposed to the cool air.

"Hey, you're movin' too fast," he protested. "I want my money's worth, lady."

"You'll get it. I promise." She undid his pants, slipping her hand inside and wrapping her fingers around his cock.

"God, that feels good," he groaned, fumbling for her breasts. She wasn't wearing a bra, so it was a simple matter to unzip her bodice with her free hand, allowing him to fondle her breasts. Since he was focused on getting inside her rather than her taking him into her mouth, she squeezed him, stroked his balls.

Still groaning, he jerked up the hem of her dress, exposing her slender thighs and pubic hair. He seemed excited about that, clumsily touching the thick thatch of hair. "You don't shave down there like most whores," he muttered, slipping a thick finger between her nether lips and probing inside her.

She opened her legs farther, let him finger her a moment, then grabbed the lapels of his coat and jerked him against her, turning so that her back was against the gritty cinderblock wall. She hitched one leg around him, fitting herself against him and urging him to slam home.

"That's it," she crooned, meeting his thrusts as she again pressed her lips against his neck. "That's it. Take what you want, what you're paying for."

She opened her mouth, sank deep. Life gushed into her, a hot surge more potent than pure adrenaline. Gulping the intoxicating liquid, she became omnipotent, flashed to the stars and back in a wild, heady rush. At the same time, a part of her managed to remain grounded and keep the mind lock on her mark. In return for her personal nirvana, she hurled him over the edge.

"Oh God, oh God!" he screamed, in the throes of the most powerful orgasm of his insignificant life. He emptied himself inside her, in long, drawn-out waves of sensation. He'd never felt such pleasure. He was dying, dying . . . God, God!

Then blackness closed in around him . . .

Rachel stared down at the prone man, noting the even rise and fall of his chest. Since he was completely dressed, and it wasn't that cold, he'd be fine until he came to in twenty minutes or so. He'd be weak and possibly have a headache, but he'd also have the memory of a hot sexual encounter that had left him completely satiated—even though it had all been in his mind. She smoothed her shawl and stepped out of the alley, another business transaction completed.

Strolling away, she ran her tongue over her fangs to catch the remaining film of blood. They were already retracting, the earlier heated flush receding. Fading way too quickly, like her john's simulated orgasm. Leaving her cold and bleak until the next fix.

———

The next john, obviously more affluent, was better dressed and better spoken, but he was a cold, unemotional man with gutter morals. He was able to pay a lot more for Rachel's services than her last customer. "Don't you have a place where we can go?" he asked, as she grabbed his expensive coat's lapels and maneuvered him behind a tattoo parlor.

She refused to do her transactions in the confines of a car. She never allowed johns to take her to a hotel, either—although there were numerous dives and flophouses in the general vicinity—not even for exorbitant amounts of cash. She didn't need that much money, nor did she have to worry about her personal safety—it was difficult to kill a being without a soul. But she needed the cover of night, and she needed the blood, and her profession was perfect for those needs.

"I want to go somewhere where there's a bed or a hot tub," he said imperviously, obviously used to his orders being obeyed. "Or I want my money back."

"No," she whispered, flowing into his mind. "That's not what you *really* want, is it? I know what you want, and I can give it to you."

She slid down him, going to her knees where he wanted her, subservient and willing to do what his wife wouldn't. Her fingers rubbed his thighs, circling upward, almost—but not quite—touching his straining erection.

He moaned, thrust his pelvis forward and said, "Get on with it!"

She unzipped his pants, eased his cock out, gave him what he demanded, teasing and tantalizing him with her mouth and tongue.

He was vaguely aware of her long fingers digging into his bare buttocks, and found that incredibly erotic. He grabbed her head, pressed her closer, and she took more of him. Jesus, she was good.

Then she took him really deep into her mouth, deeper than any woman had ever managed. He wanted to hold back, he tried to hold back, but her mouth was moist and her throat tight, creating an exquisite suction around his dick, and suddenly he was exploding. Oh man, oh man, he'd never experienced such pleasure. He didn't know if he could take it, if his heart could hold out.

His world went dark with stunning, ruthless suddenness.

———

Rachel left the back alley and its fully dressed occupant without a backward glance. She felt the warm glow of his blood in her veins, given in exchange for another illusion of a sexual act that had never really occurred. She considered it a fair trade.

This was her last "business transaction" of the evening. She knew, without the benefit of a watch, that the night was waning, with about two hours remaining until sunrise. She'd had enough blood, and she had more money to add to her hoard. It was time to call it a night, although there was certainly nothing awaiting her at her condo.

She slipped behind the buildings fronting Harry Hines and walked past stinking Dumpsters and litter scuttling along the ground until she found a bedraggled and pitiful group of people huddled around a fire in a trash can. The stench was overwhelming, the atmosphere of despair and mental confusion oppressive.

Most of those living in the streets were mentally ill, homeless through no fault of their own, shunned by the rest of society. Rachel had long ago accepted that justice was a jaded crapshoot. Drawing some bills from her pack, she approached the group.

"Hey Paul, Sam, Martha," she said, acknowledging the people she knew. "If I give each of you some money, will you promise to share with everyone here?"

They nodded enthusiastically, toothless smiles splitting filthy faces. "Thank ye, Rach," Sam said, snatching the bill she offered him. "God bless ye."

"Same to you." She couldn't bring herself to say "God." She didn't believe He existed—just a useless myth. "Don't spend it all on booze, okay?"

They all nodded their agreement, but she knew they'd make a run for the Centennial liquor store as soon as she was gone. Maybe some food would make it into their bellies—she could only hope.

She headed for her car. She lived in a modest condominium in Oak Lawn and could walk the miles to get there, but she preferred to travel by automobile, as a hedge against being caught out in sunlight. The years had taught her that anything could—and did—happen and that she must always be prepared. The instinct to survive was strong, even if she no longer remembered the reasons to persevere.

Her car was at Parkland Hospital, a few miles south on Harry

Hines. Rachel always used the visitor parking garage. She could afford it and didn't have to worry about her vehicle being vandalized. And if someone tried to question her appearance or her regular use of the garage, she could always glamour them into forgetting they'd ever seen her.

She'd gone one block when she saw him. He was standing beneath one of the streetlights that still worked, and its fluorescent glow gave him the unsettling illusion of being framed in a halo. His body language was different from the usual Harry Hines crowd.

He appeared to be expectant, almost waiting for something—or someone—although he didn't emit the threatening hostility of a criminal, the hardness of a drug dealer, the apathy of a drug addict, or the general despair and hopelessness that swirled in varying shades of darkness in the area.

He wore gray slacks and a navy sports coat over a dark gray sweater, and his swept-back dark blond hair gleamed in the light. Despite the strongly chiseled features of his face, the slightly over-large nose, and the surprisingly sensuous mouth, he had a wholesome look—a glaring indication that he was totally out of place here, in the bowels of Dallas. He might be an undercover cop, but she didn't sense it, and she was rarely wrong about cops.

Police, like soldiers, had a distinct aura surrounding them. Generally it was an air of power and arrogance, sometimes cruelty and finding sadistic pleasure in the fear of others; although some cops did radiate a genuine concern to help. But the compassionate ones were rarely seen here among the depravity and hopelessness. Not that it mattered; Rachel was well acquainted with the cruelty of corrupted power—and she was no longer helpless.

A chill swept through her. Mentally damning the stranger whose presence had raised unwelcome memories, she started past him, but he stepped into her path. Surprisingly, he met her gaze, another anomaly for the area. His eyes were dark, intent.

"Hello," he said.

She shifted around him, kept walking.

"Wait!" he called out. "Please."

Ordinarily she wouldn't have stopped, but the *please*—the rareness of hearing that word—startled her. She paused, looked back over her shoulder.

"I'd like a few minutes of your time." His well-modulated voice was pitched low, as if someone might actually care that he was negotiating a transaction, but no one around here cared about anything except their next fix, whether it be drugs, alcohol, or sex.

He definitely wasn't her type of mark, and she'd had enough blood tonight. "Sorry, not interested." She pivoted back around.

"I'm not asking for sex," he responded quickly. "I just want to talk."

They all did. They wanted to tell her about their rotten lives, cheating spouses, unemployment, and the crap the world dumped on them in general. Or they wanted to brag about their sexual prowess, or their domination over women, or how important they were—despite all evidence to the contrary. She'd heard it all, seen it all, when she slipped into the pathetic and weak minds she encountered virtually every night of her existence.

"No," she said firmly. "I'm done for the night." She started to walk away.

"I know what you are."

She rolled her eyes. Great. He was a missionary, intent on saving the soul of a lowly prostitute. Or a do-gooder, trying to meet his quotient of helping those "less fortunate."

She glanced over her shoulder again. "Hooray for you. News flash, mister—I don't want to be saved, and I don't want to be helped. But there are plenty of the *less fortunate* back that way. Just leave me alone."

She'd only made it two steps when he spoke again. "And I know who you are, Rachel Emma Stryker."

His words stopped her cold. She'd never given her full name to *anyone*. She had used a false identity for buying her condo and her car and establishing credit.

Tension lacing through her, she faced him. "You've mistaken me for someone else."

His gaze remained steady, his eyes an indeterminate color in the artificial light. "Your mother was Gertrude Marie Gutmann Stryker and your father was Abram David Stryker. Aaron was your younger brother."

Shock staggered her, but she managed to keep her outward composure. How could he possibly know that? Who or *what* was he? He certainly wasn't her kind. She would know if he was. "Who are you?"

"I'm Gabriel Anthony. But my friends call me Gabe." The light around him seemed to intensify, and she had to avert her eyes. He took a step closer. "I'm here to help you."

Fear and irritation comingled. She was certain now that he was a do-gooder, determined to "rehabilitate" her, that he had somehow managed to trace her to that other life so long ago. Although she had no idea how, and his accomplishment left her shaken and concerned.

She took the step that brought her in close proximity with him. Looked him in the eyes, despite the pain of the light. He radiated a surprising warmth that almost had her leaning into him. And he smelled great, reminiscent of fresh bread, coffee, cinnamon, and all the other enticing scents that had once permeated her mother's kitchen.

Damn it, she wasn't going there. "Let me make this very clear. You are mistaken about me. You have me confused with someone else. I repeat, I don't *need* and I don't *want* your help. Now leave me the hell alone."

She turned and strode off, determined this would be the end of it.

"I'll see you around." His words sounded like a promise—or a threat.

"I don't think so," she called back without breaking stride.

He didn't speak again or try to stop her. But she was very aware of his presence behind her as she walked away. She went another two blocks before she looked back. He was still there, watching her. And the light still surrounded him like a sacred nimbus.

She didn't like halos or anything associated with them.

She walked on, disappearing into the shadows.

Chapter 2

H ERE, kitty, kitty! Come here, kitty. I have something for you."
Rachel crouched at the Dumpster where Gertie usually lurked. She
rattled the paper bag, pulled out a pouch of Friskies Fine Cuts and
a paper plate.

A faint meow came from behind the Dumpster, and there was a
flash of white and gray as a small cat edged around and trotted
toward Rachel. It meowed again, then rubbed against her legs. She
petted the cat awkwardly, feeling rather foolish, as she did every
night. It butted its head against her hand.

"Are you hungry? I brought your favorite brand." Rachel opened
the pouch and dumped the contents on the paper plate. The cat
started gulping the food.

Rachel allowed herself one more stroke along the cat's soft fur
before she stood. She'd found the animal a month ago, just a kitten,
ragged and starving and feral. The kitten's skeletal state had resur-
rected terrible visuals of the starving humans in Dachau. Something
about its weary, distrustful eyes had touched Rachel. That, and the
fact that it would only come to her, despite efforts from Caitria and
some of the homeless men. Rachel could only guess that the animal
was attracted to her because of her allure.

She couldn't bring herself to take the cat home, but she couldn't leave her to starve, either. So she'd started bringing food for her every night, although she only allowed herself brief contact. She didn't want to become attached to the animal. She'd had enough loss in her life.

Rachel turned to go, starting when she careened into a man standing there. She moved back, her eyes narrowing when she saw who it was.

"*You.* What are you doing here?"

The do-gooder from last night, Gabriel something-or-other, squatted down, held out his hand. "I'm here to see you—and Gertie."

How did he know the cat's name? Rachel usually only called her "kitty," rather than use something as personal as a name. Squinting against the light that seemed to emanate from the man, she stared as Gertie left her food and went right to him, rubbing against his hand. The cat had never let anyone else near her. And she was purring loudly.

"You saved her life, you know," he said, scratching under Gertie's chin. She angled her head back to give him better access, and he smiled.

The light around him brightened, and Rachel had to look away. "I haven't saved anyone. It's enough just to take care of myself."

He stood and faced her. Tonight he was wearing a dark brown leather jacket over a tan sweater and jeans. "I think you've done a good job of surviving. But there's more to life than simply existing."

They were back to that. "I'm not interested in preaching or a helping hand. Leave me alone."

He stared at her a long moment, the light around him painful. Was it just her imagination, or were his eyes glowing? "I'm afraid I can't do that," he said softly.

This—*he*—was making her crazy. "You'd damn well better," she snapped. "Stay the hell away from me, or I'll go to the police and tell them you're stalking me."

She turned and stormed away. The man was unnerving, in more ways than one. One was the light around him—she guessed he must have an unusually powerful aura, although she knew very little about that stuff. Another was him knowing so much about her and her family, which should be impossible. They'd been dead for decades, perishing in the concentration camp at Dachau. The only reason she hadn't died with them was because an SS soldier, who happened to be a vampire, had turned her—after he and his comrades repeatedly raped her.

She realized she was shaking and tried to calm down. She couldn't change the past, couldn't change what she was. Her only two choices were to meet the sun and end it all—or to survive. Maybe she was a coward, but she wasn't ready to face eternity, and most likely the fires of hell, just yet. That meant she had to feed.

She drifted through the shadows of the underbelly of Dallas, walking past bars and strip clubs and adult bookstores. She didn't pass any other hookers. Very few prostitutes actually walked the streets anymore. Most cruised northern Harry Hines in their cars, talking to clients on their cell phones as they looked for other johns to flag down. Then they either conducted business in their cars or at an hourly rate hotel.

But Rachel preferred to troll for marks as she had always done—on foot, and at the quieter end of Harry Hines. She didn't have to worry about her personal safety, and if the police stopped to question her, she could glamour them into forgetting her. She also knew quite a few of the homeless people along this stretch, although they were scatted throughout the area.

She found her first mark for the night. He was a tall, beefy man in a work uniform, topped with an insulated vest. His complexion was ruddy, his hands rough and callused, with dirt crusted beneath his fingernails. But his money was green, and his blood red. Rachel tucked the crumpled bills into her fanny pack. She ran her hand up his chest and stroked his neck, her attention focused on his powerful jugular veins.

"So, big guy, tell me what you want," she murmured, slipping into his mind.

He was a tits and ass man, wanted to see the goods before he sampled them. "Take off your shirt," he ordered. He watched as she pulled her tight black sweater over her head, shaking her long, dark hair loose. She was braless, and her tits jiggled a little from her movements. His cock came to attention. She wasn't all that large in the boob department, but they were nice and round, with pink nipples that puckered when he pinched them.

He told her to turn around and raise her skirt, and her nice, firm ass made him rock hard. He liked doing it from behind, liked to fondle the woman's tits and rub her ass as he fucked her. And this woman was prime, nice and tight, bracing herself against the wall as he pounded into her, jerking her upward with each thrust. Yeah, tight like a fist, milking him in greedy gulps. He cried out as the best orgasm of his life crashed over him, wave after wave, riding him right into oblivion . . .

Rachel left him unconscious behind the *Chicas Sexual* club, wiping her mouth with the back of her hand as she reached the street. He was so big she'd been able to take a lot of blood without endangering him. She came around the corner of the building and almost shrieked in frustration when she saw Gabriel leaning against the front of the building. She glared at him, wondering what it would take to get rid of him.

He straightened. "Now that you're not so hungry, we can talk. Why don't you let me buy you some coffee?"

She was shocked. Had he seen her taking her mark's blood? She always used allure to blur her activities, so passersby wouldn't see what was happening. Yet this guy had apparently seen past her shields, which should be another impossibility. "What do you mean by that?"

He had the most intense gaze she'd ever seen. "I know what you were doing back there, Rachel. I already told you I know what you are. You just don't want to believe me. You're a little weak in the faith area, too. We'll have to work on that."

"What did I do behind this building?" she challenged. She had to know what he'd seen.

"What you have to do to survive. That's not a sin." He raised his hand, rested it against the side of her face. He was so warm, his gesture so tender, she felt herself softening inside. Not good.

She knocked his arm away. "So you were spying on me?"

He nodded. "I saw you take his blood. I would apologize for watching you, but it's necessary that I understand every aspect of your life to help you."

Incredulity and anger and consternation all rolled through her in one tsunami-level wave. "You had no right to do that. Fuck you!"

"Like you did for him?"

How could he have known about that? It was all fantasy mind sex. There was nothing to see, even if Gabriel had been watching. She had to put a stop to this immediately. Last night, he had so imbalanced her she hadn't thought to glamour him. But she intended to wipe his memory clean now.

She moved closer, let her hands slide up his arms, feeling some impressive muscles beneath the leather coat. She stared into his eyes, for the first time, seeing their true color, a deep blue, with golden sparks of light. For a moment, she felt their pull, as if they were mesmerizing *her*. She felt sluggish, disoriented. *Whoa!* She shook her head, broke eye contact. The odd sensation faded.

Still determined, she leaned within inches of his face, again gazing into his eyes. "You will forget everything about me," she said in a low voice, directing the full force of her allure toward him. "You won't remember my name, or what you just saw in that alley. If you see me again, you won't recognize me. I'm a stranger to you."

He blinked. Convinced she'd had him firmly in thrall, she turned to leave.

"I'm not going to forget you, Rachel. And I'm not judging you for what you have to do to stay alive."

Panic stirred. She spun around. "Maybe I can't make you forget me, but I can hurt you very badly."

He didn't seem at all perturbed. "But you won't. It's not in your nature."

He was wrong. Her nature—the freakish thing she'd become—contained inherent violence. "You don't really know as much as you think," she hissed.

"Oh, I know a lot more than you realize." He tilted his head, as if studying her.

He really did have a nice face, strong . . . noble—except for that sensuous, suggestive mouth. *What was wrong with her?* Was he enthralling her? Not possible.

She drew back, wrapped her shawl protectively around herself. She wasn't sure what to do about him, but he was wrong to trust her. Even so, she didn't want to inflict physical harm unless it was absolutely necessary. She'd seen way too much violence in her human existence, knew how its aftereffects reverberated through lifetimes. For now, she'd use words as a weapon.

She started to tell him what he could go do to himself, when his gaze shifted away from her. She turned to see what he was staring at, saw two punks threatening a homeless man, trying to get his bottle away from him.

"Sorry. We'll have to resume this discussion later." Gabriel headed toward the men.

She snapped her mouth shut, watched him reach the group and insert himself between the punks and the man they'd been hassling. She recognized one of the aggressors, knew he was a bully who could get violent if provoked. And here was this do-gooder, stepping into the middle of three guys who were either drunk or high, and most certainly crazy.

He raised his hands, and she could see he was talking, probably trying to calm them down. But the flash of a blade in one man's hand was a pretty good indication it wasn't working.

Damn, damn, damn! Gabriel was an idiot—and he was going to be one dead idiot very shortly. She should leave him to his fate, should let those punks take his money and whale out their hatred and anger on him. It would serve him right—and would certainly solve her problem of what to do about him and the information he possessed. But . . .

Her feet were moving before she'd made the conscious decision. *This was crazy*, she told herself. The man was obnoxious, and he was a threat to her existence. So why was she going to keep his handsome face from being bashed in? Good question.

She didn't have time to ponder it before she reached the group. She grabbed the knife-wielder by the back of his coat, easily lifting him off his feet. "Hey Bubba, that's enough fun for tonight." She threw him against the closest building; he hit the wall with a thud, slid to the ground, stunned.

She spun as the second punk rushed her, landed a kick in his solar plexus that sent him flying backward a good twelve feet. He crumpled into a moaning heap. The first punk struggled to his feet, brandishing the knife.

Rachel glared at him. "You want some more of this, you bastard? Then bring it on."

He took a staggering step toward her, grabbed his head with a groan. He glanced past her to the other man heaped on the sidewalk. "You're crazy, bitch," he growled. He looked at Gabriel. "And who the hell are you, man? Fuckin' stupid. I'm outta here." He limped off, leaving his companion behind.

The homeless man was long gone, having bolted at the first opportunity. To Rachel's utter amazement, Gabriel walked over to the remaining punk, helped him to his feet. "You all right?" he asked him.

"Get the hell away from me!" Still groaning, the guy headed the same direction as the first one.

Gabriel walked slowly back to Rachel. "You are insane," she said. "More than the people around here. But maybe you're smart enough to remember what I just did to those guys, because I'll do the same to you if you don't leave me alone. Got that?"

He just looked at her with those glowing blue eyes. "I'm not afraid of you, Rachel." He straightened his leather coat with a jerk. "You didn't have to interfere on my behalf. I could have handled those men."

She couldn't believe it. That was gratitude for you. "Fine, then, Gabriel whatever-your-last-name-is. I won't come to your aid again. And believe me, if you hang around here with that baby-faced innocent look, you will soon be facing those punks again, or others like them."

"Baby-faced?" He seemed genuinely affronted. "Is that how you see me?"

Not really, but she wasn't in the mood to stroke his ego. She folded her arms across her chest and nodded.

He looked heavenward. "She thinks I'm baby-faced." His gaze returned to her. "As I told you, I can handle anything that comes my way." He extended his arm, palm up. "Watch."

She didn't want to. What she wanted was to put as much distance between this man and herself as possible. Besides the fact that he made her very uncomfortable, there was the little problem of his knowledge about her and his being immune to her glamour. "Forget it. I'm leaving."

"Wait. Watch."

There was a powerful compulsion in his voice, and she simply didn't want to expend the energy to fight it. He wasn't a vampire, so what, exactly, was he?

A sudden shaft of light exploded from the palm of his hand, shooting upward. Rachel was so startled, a small scream erupted from her throat, and she stumbled backward. But she couldn't take her gaze off the beacon of light. It was both mesmerizing and terrible, a swirling mass of blue and gold flames within the brightly glowing beam, which went way up into the sky, disappearing into a starburst of more light. It crackled with energy she could feel, even as she backed away. The air around them was charged, sending tingling sensations through her body.

Gabriel was lit up like a freaking solar explosion, with bursts of light shooting out from all around him. And his hair was blowing around his face, even though there wasn't a hint of a breeze. All the while, that horrifying light kept streaming out of his palm. *Oh, my*— No. She was not saying *His* name. Add one more thing to her list of dislikes about this man: He scared the crap out of her. She was out of there.

Rachel whirled and ran. He called after her, but she only ran faster. Terror shot adrenaline through her body, making it hard to breathe, to think, to function. But the primal need to survive was strong and clear. It was no longer a question of *who* this man was, but *what* he was. She didn't want to know. In a world where vampires were a certainty, the possibility of numerous other monsters was too real. Not to mention the human monsters plaguing the world throughout history.

With her superhuman speed and the adrenaline jolt, she ran the miles to the hospital parking garage in record time. Heaving a sigh of relief, she dug her keys from her fanny pack as she jogged up the ramp to the third level. She looked toward her car, and utter shock jolted through her. The keys slipped from her fingers, clattered on the concrete.

"I didn't mean to frighten you." Gabriel pushed away from where he'd been leaning against her car and came toward her.

She backed away. "Don't come near me."

He stopped. "I won't hurt you, Rachel. If I had evil intentions, I could have fulfilled them at any time. Right?"

That made sense, except she was so freaked, her mind wasn't functioning very well at the moment. She took another step back.

"I'm here to help you," he said. "I swear on all that's holy it's the truth."

Holy didn't have a place in her life anymore. "I keep telling you I don't want any help. Go away."

He sighed. "I can't do that. Look, maybe I shouldn't have shown you that power flash, but I wanted to assure you that I can take of myself. And to give you a glimpse of who I am."

"I don't care who you are. I just want you to leave me the hell alone."

"I already told you I can't do that." He took a step closer, held out his hand as she turned to bolt. "Running is futile. I can track you wherever you go. Why don't you hear me out before you do anything rash? You know you want to."

There it was again—that hint of compulsion. She resisted it, as she debated what to do. She sensed sincerity behind his words. The fact he'd beaten her to her car—hell, that he even knew what she drove and where it was parked—showed he was very powerful. She probably couldn't defeat him. She hated feeling powerless. When she left Germany, she had sworn she'd never be helpless, or at anyone's mercy again.

"This isn't about control or domination," Gabriel said quietly.

Startled, she stared at him. Was he a mind reader as well? Here in the semilighted garage, he didn't look very threatening. He appeared to be just an attractive man with thick, dark-blond hair and unusual blue eyes. Even the brightness he emanated was less obvious here, probably because of the lighting.

"I know you've suffered a lot, Rachel."

She stiffened, realizing he was suddenly in front of her. How had he moved so quickly, without her seeing his movement?

He touched her, clasping her shoulders. Warmth tingled from his hands into her chilled body. She gasped, tried to step back, but he tightened his grip. "I'm here to show you how to move from a minimal existence to a full, meaningful life. The life you were denied in Germany. The life God wants you to have."

That word again. "I don't believe in Him. Let go of me."

He ran his hands lightly down her arms. The electricity followed. "That doesn't matter. She believes in you."

"*She?*" Rachel realized she was getting distracted, brought her attention back to the matter at hand. "Never mind. I don't want to know."

He grinned, and the light around him surged. Damn. She needed sunglasses. "We can accomplish a lot without talking about She whose name you will not say," he said.

How did he know about her aversion to God? And . . . *She?* "I still don't understand." Rachel tried to tug free of his grasp, failed. Tried again, using superhuman force this time. Failed again. "Damn it! Let me go." When he just looked at her, she considered, added, "Please."

He released her, and the chill returned. She rubbed her now-cold arms, her mind running through options. She was smart, had been very bright when she was human, the top of her class in school. But it really didn't take much intelligence to conclude she might as well listen to what he had to say. She couldn't glamour him, couldn't outrun him, and couldn't overpower him. He had the upper hand—for now.

"So talk," she said.

He stepped back, shoved his hands into his pockets. "You already know I'm here to help you. You suspect I'm some sort of monster. That's not exactly right. I am, however, a supernatural being. But I'm on the good side."

She couldn't stop the question that tumbled out. "What are you?"

His gaze locked with hers, and his eyes grew even more luminous, taking on an otherworldly glow. "I'm an angel."

Chapter 3

RACHEL stared at Gabe, her dark eyes huge in her porcelain-white face. She was fairly tall, probably around five feet, seven inches, but she was very slender, almost delicate. Her boots and suggestive clothing, along with her attitude, made her appear bigger and tougher, and her current incarnation as a vampire gave her superhuman strength. But he knew she was emotionally vulnerable.

"I don't believe you." She took a step backward. "Angels don't exist. Just like G— Just like He . . . Her—oh, hell, *whatever*, doesn't exist. You're just another weirdo. Go mess with someone else."

"We do exist. If I'm not an angel, how do you explain the burst of light from my palm earlier? Would you like a replay, just to be sure? Or some other display that might convince you?"

She shuddered. "No."

"Then I guess you're just going to have to accept my word in good faith."

"Faith," she scoffed. "Just what exactly should I have faith in?"

He hesitated, knowing she wouldn't be receptive to him suggesting she place her trust in a higher being, or in the basic goodness of most humans. "How about in yourself?"

"Oh, yeah, I'm the ideal role model for young girls everywhere."

She looked away, seemed to be considering. Looked back at him. "If you're an angel, where are your wings?"

"I don't happen to have any on me at the moment. I'm in a human body, just like you are." He felt a twinge of regret about the circumstances that had convinced him he needed to visit Earth in the flesh.

"But I'm not human."

"Yes, you are. You're just a . . . variation."

She gave a harsh laugh. "Yeah, right. That's a good one. Tell me something that's true."

"All right. Despite this body, I *am* an angel. You can't glamour me, beat me up, or outrun me. That should be proof of sorts."

She turned and walked slowly past several cars. Her shoulders were hunched slightly, as if she was protecting herself from the world. She stopped, stiffened. Even from here, he could feel the tension rolling off her, then the anger. She whirled, her gaze fierce. "If you're really an angel, where were you when we were being herded like animals into cattle cars and taken to Dachau? *Where, damn you?*"

She strode toward him. "Where the hell were you when my family was murdered?" She reached him, shoved him so hard, he stumbled backward. She followed, twisted her hand in his jacket, yanked him back him to her. "How about when those soldiers took me behind the barracks and—" Her voice broke, and her eyes glistened. But he could see the rage had not abated.

Could feel it, too, when she slammed him against a concrete support beam, knocking the breath from him, and probably crushing a few vertebrae. He offered no resistance. She was entitled to her pain and fury.

"And when that Nazi soldier decided to turn me, were you watching?" Her eyes bore into his, dark pools of eternity and suffering. "How about when I was in agony, begging for death, *praying* to be destroyed so I wouldn't become the monster he was? Why didn't *He—She—anyone* answer?"

He stared back, compassion and his own burden of failure beating at him. "Because of free will," he said quietly. "We can't stop events that are set in motion by free will and human actions."

"Then you're worthless, aren't you? Damn you to hell and back!" A new glow came to her eyes; her hand tightened on his mangled jacket. "Maybe I should make you a freak like me. Let you experience firsthand what it's like to be a monster that has to drink human blood just to exist in misery." She gave him a parody of a smile, let him see her gleaming fangs. "Yeah. That's what I should do."

With her free hand, she gripped his head, tilting it to the side and exposing his neck. She leaned so close, he felt her breath on his skin, felt the brush of sharp incisors. He wanted her to choose—oh, he wanted her to make the choice.

"Go ahead," he said. "Take what you need. I know you only had one client tonight. I can feel your hunger."

She hesitated, growled. Pressed her teeth closer.

"Yes, Rachel. Do it. Blood is life. You deserve to live."

He really thought she was going to. Steeled himself as her fangs scraped over his jugular vein. But then she jerked back, dropping him as if he were a white-hot brand.

"No! I wouldn't sink so low to drink from you," she hissed. "You're crazy, you know that? Why would you allow me to suck you dry, turn you into a monster, like me?"

"Would you really do that, Rachel?"

"Hell yes!"

He almost smiled at her belligerent tone. "But I wouldn't be *allowing* you to do it. You would be *choosing* to do it. Free will."

Her hands clenched by her side. "I don't remember my family choosing to go to Dachau. I certainly didn't choose to *dally* behind the barracks with those Nazi bastards, or become . . ." She gestured down her slender body. *"This."*

"I know." He straightened his clothing, tried not to groan as his abused spine cracked and popped. "The Holocaust was the direct result of many people's decisions and choices. Hitler's actions, those who chose to follow him; those who chose to live and have families in Europe. Celestial beings can't force decisions, choices, or actions on anyone. Nor can we interfere with the results of those actions. The Law is clear—humans have been given the gift of free will. All we can do is guide and encourage someone to take the higher path."

She tossed her dark, wavy hair over her shoulder. "I'm on a set path now. I can't change what I am. My only choices are to take blood and stay alive, or commit suicide. Do you think I should kill myself?"

"Certainly not!" he said, shocked.

"Then I have to drink blood, so there's nothing you can do for me, is there?"

"It's true there's nothing *I* can do for you, Rachel, except guide you. But there's a lot *you* can do. You can live the life you've been given. You can make choices that are fulfilling on physical, mental, and spiritual levels. Help others. Grow closer to Go—uh, do things that will purify your soul."

She rolled her eyes—a trait that was almost as endearing as it was exasperating. "I don't have a soul."

"That's a topic we'll be debating over the next week."

"*What?*"

"That's all I'm asking of you. A week of your time."

She stared at him, her eyes flared wide. "You want us to spend an entire week together?"

"It won't be that much. Just every night for a week."

"That's insane. I can't do that."

"Why not?"

"I have to . . . eat. And I need to earn money, too."

"That's fine. You can spend the first part of the evening with me, and then take the rest of it to attend to business. One week, Rachel. That's all I'm asking."

"But *why?*"

"If I could explain it all right now, we wouldn't need that week, now would we?"

She didn't want to do it. He could almost see the wheels turning in that quick mind of hers. Her full mouth took on a sulky slant. "You can't make me spend seven nights with you. Especially if I *choose* not to. *Free will.*"

"Yeah, yeah, I've heard it all before." He walked over and picked up her keys. "I can't make you do it, Rachel. But you can't make me stop hanging around every night, either. Can't keep me from observing as you 'do business.' "

She glared at him as he handed her the keys. "You're a real bastard."

"You need to expand your vocabulary. You're starting to get repetitive."

If looks could kill, his mortal body would be dead right now. She gripped the keys so tightly, her knuckles were white.

"It's just one week," he said persuasively, using a touch of compulsion. "Then I'll be gone from your life—for good, if that's what you want." He hoped that wouldn't be the case.

"So I really don't have a choice."

He shrugged. "You always have a choice. But then you have to live with the consequences."

She shook her head, rolling her eyes again and looking none too happy. "Fine!" she snapped. "I'll do it, if you give me your word that you'll leave me *completely* alone after that. Seven nights— that's all!"

He felt as if a ten-ton load had been lifted from his shoulders. "You have my word on it. I'll meet you at the corner of Harry Hines and Shea tomorrow night, at seven. It should be dark enough then. And don't think of reneging—I can find you."

Without another word, she whirled and strode to her black Honda. To her credit, she didn't slam the door when she got in. But she was driving overly fast as she screeched down the ramps.

He hadn't realized he'd been holding his breath, until it flowed out of him in a sigh of relief. He'd made the first hurdle. But Rachel was very strong minded, as well as resistant to mild compulsion, which *was* allowed. Not only that, she'd had more than sixty-five years of pain and misery to harden her. He'd known she would be one of his tougher cases, which was why he'd made the decision to enter a physical incarnation in order to help her.

His odds of success with her weren't any higher than those of his charges who had refused to be helped, despite his best efforts. He remembered each and every one of them, every detail of their hopeless faces, every sensation of their fear and despair. They, along with the weight of his failures, would be with him through eternity.

Gabe ran his hand through his hair. This free-will rule was a bitch.

Rachel strutted back and forth, waiting for Gabriel. It was quiet, way too early for much action, so she was alone with her churning emotions. She *hated* being manipulated, hated being forced to do anything against her will. Years ago—lifetimes ago—she'd sworn she would never be at anyone's mercy, or subject to their whims. *Never again.*

But here she was, stuck with an angel—an *angel*—for the next seven nights. She didn't see where she'd had a choice, though; it didn't appear she could shake Gabriel. Plus she'd given her word, a rare happening for her; but vampire or not, she did have some integrity. She hissed in frustration.

A car horn interrupted her fuming, and she looked over to see a white Acura turning onto Shea and stopping. Caitria rolled down her passenger window and leaned over. "Hey, lil' bitchhomie, how you doing? Haven't seen you in a few weeks."

Caitria was a black woman who'd been hooking a long time.

She was in her late twenties, but drug use and too many backhands from her long-term boyhomie, as she referred to him, had left her looking used up. She was a tall, hefty woman who liked her food. "Girl, you need to be eatin' more—do some of that carb loading," she often told Rachel. "Men don't like scrawny women. They like some meat on them bones, somethin' they can sink into, you know?"

They'd met when Caitria had been driving by, just as a street person went nuclear and attacked Rachel. Caitria had parked her car in the middle of the road and come out swinging a purse that had to weigh more than a bowling ball. Of course Rachel could easily have handled the man, but Caitria had no way of knowing that. She'd chased him halfway down the block and then strutted back in four-inch platform shoes, her ample hips swaying. "I showed his ass. You okay, girl?"

That had been the start of an unusual relationship—with them speaking when they saw each other, which led to occasionally having coffee, with Caitria venting about her abusive man. She'd been with him for years, had two children with him, and wasn't willing to leave him. Caitria apparently considered Rachel a friend, a baffling and uncertain experience for her. She'd avoided all relationships since she'd left Germany, but this woman had somehow barged past her barriers.

She walked to the car. "Hey, Caitria. I'm all right. How about you?"

"Business been a little slow." Caitria self-consciously raised a hand with inch-long, bloodred nails and numerous sparkling rings to a swollen cheek. "Them damned police makin' it harder and harder for a ho to earn a livin'."

Which meant her man Danyon was whaling on her because she wasn't supporting him in the manner he wanted. Rachel would love to meet him in an alley someday, give him some of his own medicine. But he never made the Harry Hines scene, so she hadn't met him at all.

"I know what you mean." She looked around the quiet area. "It will heat up later. You'll get more action in a few hours."

"So you want to have coffee or somethin'?" Caitria looked like she really wanted to talk.

"I wish I could, but I'm meeting someone." Rachel stood as she saw Gabriel. "Here he is now."

He wore a black blazer over a black turtleneck sweater, with khaki pants and sleek black loafers. His thick, wavy hair brushed his wide shoulders, and he looked fit and solid as he approached them. "Hello, Rachel." He smiled at her, strong white teeth flashing. Then he leaned down, unleashed that killer smile on Caitria. "Good evening, ma'am."

She swept him with appraising glance. "Ooooh, sexy. You are mighty fine prime. Rach, you been holding out on me? I thought you didn't do regulars, although with pretty boy here, I'd sure make an exception if I was you."

Rachel didn't know what to say, but Gabriel laughed. "We're just friends—for now. Going out for the evening."

"Sure, lova boy, whatever you say." Caitria looked past him at Rachel. "Looks like you're moving up in the world, lil' bitch. Have fun, now. Catch you later." She waited until Gabriel stepped back, then gunned the car and screeched away.

Rachel stared after the car, unwelcome concern gnawing at her. "Her man's been hitting her."

Gabriel's hand lightly touched her lower back. "I know."

She turned to face him. "He's been doing it for years, but she stays with him. Why?"

Compassion filled his dark blue eyes. "People do things for a lot of reasons. It's her choice, her decision. Only she can change her situation."

Rachel grimaced. "It's that free-will crap again, isn't it?"

A grin tugged at his sensuous lips. "Afraid so. Come on." He took her arm, started up the street.

"Where are we going?"

"First we're going shopping."

"Shopping? For what?"

"New clothes for you."

She stopped and looked at him. "I have clothes. I don't need anything."

"All you own is 'work' clothing." His gaze skimmed her. "And while it looks very . . . good on you, you need some play clothes."

"I don't play, Gabriel."

"Oh, but you're going to this week. You need something fun and relaxed to wear. And please call me Gabe."

Fun? Relaxed? As crazy as it was, she felt like she was dodging bullets here. In a single day, he'd managed to throw her well-ordered life into upheaval. *Seven nights*, she told herself. Then she could tell him to fuck off.

She stumbled along as he towed her up the sidewalk. "And who's going to pay for these new clothes?"

"You are. Use your credit card. You can afford it."

He was right that she had a fairly sizeable nest egg squirreled away. Her needs were simple, and she lived in a modest condominium and drove an older car. She doled out some of her excess funds to the homeless and put the rest into investments. Now that she had a computer, she'd become pretty savvy in that area. But her stockpiled money was her security against the unforeseeable future. She didn't like to spend it.

Gabe stopped at a sleek, silver Nissan roadster parked in front of an adult bookstore and opened the passenger door for her. She slid onto a buttery-soft leather seat, eyed the instrument-laden dashboard. She wasn't sure what she had expected him to be driving, but somehow had envisioned something more old-fashioned and sedate. "Nice car."

He glowed with male pride. "Sweet, isn't she? Six speed, V-6 engine, and handles like an angel." He grinned at her. "A little celestial humor there." He started the car, and rock music blared from the radio—another surprise. He pulled out and proceeded to drive like a seasoned race-car driver, flipping through the gears like they were light switches.

They went to NorthPark in north Dallas, and miraculously made it without an accident or speeding ticket. The mall was crowded, a lot of people in a confined place. She hated crowds. A familiar, frightening memory rose swiftly. *So many bodies crammed together in the cattle cars, so hard to breathe. . . .*

"Rachel! Snap out of it!" Strong hands gripped her arms.

Dazed, she stared up at Gabe. "Too many people."

"You're not *there* anymore. You're here, in Dallas, where there's always going to be a *lot* of people. That's just the way it is," he told her. "Take a deep breath and calm yourself."

Somehow, his touch and his voice helped settle her, and the tension eased. He took her hand and held it firmly as he headed for Dillard's—better than Neiman Marcus, which she couldn't begin to afford.

At Dillard's, Gabe was a man on a mission. He led her to casual wear, where he picked out jeans and sweaters, then to dresses, where he added a chic, black long-sleeved sheath to the pile. She was just along for the ride, she thought dourly, as he escorted her to dressing rooms and handed her the clothes to try on. Everything fit, and she stared at the strange woman in the mirror. First jeans and sweater, which made her look impossibly young and innocent; then the sleek black dress, which made her look sexy, but in a classy way.

She had to admit Gabe had good taste; unfortunately, it was also very *expensive* taste. She cringed as the merchandise was totaled, and the sales clerk had to pry the credit card from her clenched fingers. "It will take months to pay that off," she muttered as he picked up the bag and took her hand again.

"And you have lots of time, don't you? You work hard for your money, Rachel. You need to learn to enjoy it."

Then he took her to the lingerie department, where she dug in her heels. "I don't need undergarments." She never wore a bra—she wasn't that large, and it was easier to attract johns.

He looked pointedly at the outline of bare breasts beneath her spandex top. "Do you want every red-blooded male above the age of twelve staring at your chest wherever we go this week?"

"I don't care. In case you've forgotten, I'm a whore."

Gabe glanced at a nearby sales clerk, who was avidly listening to every word. Frowning, he took Rachel by the elbow, pulling her farther into the seemingly endless sea of brassiere displays.

"First off, I don't know of any whores who make a living without actually performing sexual acts. Secondly, do you truly view yourself that way? When you look inside yourself, Rachel, is that what you *really* see?"

She didn't want to delve that deeply, to even consider her self-image. Gabe was making this way too difficult. She fisted her hands on her hips and glared at him, her frustration rising. He stared back, calm, implacable, reminiscent of a cement wall. She had the feeling he could stand there all night until she gave in, and decided it wasn't worth it.

"Fine!" she snapped. "I'll wear some damned undergarments."

"Good decision." He scanned the displays, chose one and sifted through the bras, plucking out a lacy black one with a sexy décolletage. "Here. This should be your size." He held it toward her, as he continued looking, extracting a pair of matching panties. "And here. These should work under your new jeans. They're no-line."

She took them, surprised that he knew about such things as no-line panties. Since he'd been totally accurate on her size so far, she didn't try them on. She dug out the plastic again, ignoring the salesperson's piercing stare as she rang the sale.

Two more stops netted a pair of low-heeled ankle boots, high-heel pumps, a purse—and another sizeable charge. Rachel sulked about the expense all the way to her condominium, barely registering any surprise that Gabe knew where she lived. He dropped her off so she could unload her purchases and change while he waited.

He didn't ask to come in, and she didn't offer. She didn't allow visitors to her private lair.

She had to admit her new jeans, sweater, and low boots were very comfortable. And the bra . . . well, it wasn't too bad. It was all lacy and frilly and made her breasts look fuller; gave them a nice line beneath the rose-toned sweater. She put a few things in her new purse and went outside to where Gabe waited.

From there, they went to the Angelika—she didn't miss the fact it had "angel" in the name—a movie house known for showing offbeat films. It just so happened they were having a John Travolta movie fest, and were showing—of all things—*Michael*, which was about an angel.

"Why am I not surprised?" Rachel muttered as she settled into a seat next to Gabe.

"Great movie," he said, munching from the giant-sized bucket of popcorn he'd purchased. "Although it has some flaws."

She hadn't been to a movie since . . . since before the war. The film quality and the color were amazing. She quickly got caught up in the story; found herself laughing in places—she rarely laughed—even felt a twinge of sadness in others. She didn't miss the obvious point of the movie—an angel coming to Earth to help some poor, misguided humans. She scoffed at the comparison. She wasn't poor or misguided, she was . . . What?

Outside of a vampire and a prostitute, what was she? *No. She wasn't going there.* As she'd been doing for years, Rachel blocked off the should-have-beens and could-have-beens. She did find Gabe's muttered comments about the movie's inaccuracies amusing. By the time they left the theater, she didn't feel so melancholy.

Gabe said very little as they drove to Harry Hines. They had decided she could work in her new outfit rather than go back to her condo to change. He pulled onto Shea and parked.

"So that's it for tonight?" Rachel asked, perplexed. There'd been no deep conversation, no earth-shattering revelations. "Just shopping and the movie?"

"Sorry, but I don't do more than that on the first date." Gabe's eyes glowed with warmth and humor. "Simply having fun is a valid pastime. It's good for the soul."

Anger burst through her. "Are you telling me you're going to drive me around, make me spend my money, and then watch stupid angel movies for seven days? That's a bunch of crap!"

"Rachel, Rachel." He shook his head as if she were a child.

That steamed her even more. She balled her fist, ready to knock him into Tarrant County. The long, steady look he gave her made her think twice. She didn't normally resort to violence. Plus she probably couldn't hurt him, so what was the use?

"Emotion is good," he said. "Rage, hatred, love, joy—it's all good. It means you're alive." He shocked her by leaning over and kissing her on the cheek. "Have a nice evening, Rachel. Wear your new dress tomorrow. Same time, same place?"

She watched him drive away. Well. That had been . . . She touched her cheek, which tingled where his lips had touched. She didn't know what that had been. Shrugging, she hitched her new purse over her shoulder and started her strut.

She found her first mark a few minutes later, a soldier on leave from Iraq. Since he was laying his life on the line for his country, she cut her price in half. "Aren't you a little young to be doing this?" he asked, eyeing her jeans and demure sweater.

"I'm old enough to know what I'm doing." She cupped him, felt him harden against her hand. "And good enough you won't forget me." She led him behind the closest building, slipped into his mind.

He was the young one, barely out of school, but had already seen more atrocities than most people saw in a lifetime. She could identify.

He thought she was sexy as hell and was torn between asking her to go down on him, or fucking her until the memories of war were obliterated—if only for a short while.

She solved his dilemma, taking him in her mouth for some stop-

and-go action that heightened his anticipation. When he was about to explode, she stood and pulled him against her and inside her, wrapping her leg around him as he pounded into her.

Then she took his blood, giving both of them the things they so desperately needed—oblivion and survival.

Chapter 4

GABE pulled in front of the same adult bookstore where he'd parked last night. Rachel was standing across the street, nervously tugging at the black dress. It looked great on her, snug enough to emphasize her curves, and with a square-cut neckline that offered a hint of cleavage. The high-heeled pumps completed her outfit. She really did have nice legs.

He noticed her breasts looked higher and rounder, so she must have been wearing the new bra. Smiling to himself, he thought about the expression on her face when he'd insisted she buy one.

A group of guys in a passing car let out some lewd whistles, and she flipped them off. That was his Rachel. She was definitely going to be one of his most intriguing and engaging challenges. Gabe got out and walked over. "You look beautiful tonight." He took her hand and couldn't resist the urge to raise it to his lips. She nearly stumbled, her astonishment palpable. He hid a smile as he lowered her hand. "That dress looks wonderful on you."

"T-thank you." She eyed the dark gray sports coat he was wearing over a burgundy turtleneck and navy slacks; cleared her throat, obviously uncomfortable with small talk. "Uh—you look nice, too."

"Glad you think so." When he came into this physical incarnation, Gabe had been chagrined to find he had a penchant for nice things, like designer clothing and fine cars. But he was philosophical about it, accepting the fact he was in a material body, with material urges. There was nothing in the Celestial Laws that prevented an angel in a human body from acting like a human. When in Rome, and all that.

"Where are we going tonight?" she asked as they walked toward his car.

He heard the sullen tone in her voice, knew she was still chafing at having to bend to his will—not to mention parting with some of her hoard. He didn't like strong-arming charges, but he wasn't losing another one. "More playing," he said.

"Then why am I wearing this?" She gave an exasperated wave down her body. "The jeans worked fine last night. I didn't have to spend the extra money on a dress."

"This is adult playtime."

Her dark eyes narrowed, "Isn't *that* what I do every night? My johns sure think of it as recreation."

He opened her car door. "What you do every night is simply survive, Rachel. Nothing more, nothing less."

Her jaw tensed, and rebellion flared in her eyes. "Well, it's enough for me. It's what I want. Doesn't that count for anything?"

He started to respond, noticed her looking across the street. "What's wrong?"

She turned back. "It's probably nothing."

"*What's* probably nothing?"

Concern filled her eyes. "It's the cat. She didn't want her food tonight. And she seemed really tired. I'm sure she's fine, but . . . she's just never refused food before."

"*Gertie*. The cat's name is Gertie. It's all right to say her name. Are you telling me Gertie is sick?"

"No!" Rachel said vehemently. "She probably just played hard all night. Maybe someone else fed her. I'm sure that's it."

"Maybe." He closed the door and locked the car. "Why don't we go have a look?"

She followed him silently. They found the cat lying on her side by the Dumpster. She gave a feeble meow when Gabe squatted beside her. "Hey, Gertie," he said softly, his hand a gentle caress along her fur. "What's the matter, girl?"

She stared at him through dull eyes, a small twitch of her tail her only response. Gabe rested his hand on her side. "She's hot." He looked up at Rachel. "She *is* sick."

"She can't be sick." Distress emanated from her. "She was fine last night. She's still just a kitten. She's got a long time to live and—"

"*Rachel.* She's sick."

Pain swept across her face before she whirled away. "So she's going to die. Is that what you're telling me?"

Scenes of death flashed from her mind into his—the lifeless bodies piled up. Her family, all dead. He stood and placed his hand on her shoulder, squeezed gently, felt her stiffen. "I only know that Gertie is sick. I can't tell you what's going to happen to her. We need to take her to a veterinarian."

She turned to face him, a small ray of hope in her expressive eyes. "Do you think that might help?"

"Maybe. We can give it a try."

She nodded. "I guess so."

"Get her and let's go." He pulled his keys from his pocket.

"*Me?* I can't do that. I don't want—I might hurt her."

Gabe considered Rachel thoughtfully, noting the alarm on her face. *Ah.* He suddenly recognized this situation as an opportunity, for which he was vastly grateful. He knew what he wanted to accomplish with Rachel—for her to realize her full potential as a woman, as a human, and as a child of God—but he wasn't exactly sure how to go about it.

Contrary to popular belief, angels did *not* have all the answers. Not for the first time in his somewhat-tarnished career, he'd wished there was a celestial *How to Help Your Charges* guide for angels. But no assignments came with an instruction manual. He was on his own. Yet here was a chance for Rachel to cement a tie with a living creature—something she'd resisted since the loss of her family.

"She's your cat, so you have to carry her," he said. "I can't hold her while I'm driving, anyway."

"She's *not* my cat," she hastened to explain. "She lives behind the Dumpster, and I just . . . feed her sometimes."

"All right then. We don't have to do this. We'll just leave her here. No reason to get involved with a stray. Let's go."

"But . . . we can't do that. She's sick."

"What's it going to be, Rachel? It's your call. *You* found her, *you* rescued her, and *you* feed her *every* night. In my book, that makes her *your* cat, whether or not you're willing to admit it. If we're going to do this, get her, and let's go." He strode away without a backward glance, leaving it up to her.

He waited by the car, watched Rachel walk slowly toward him, awkwardly holding Gertie and looking utterly terrified. Keeping a straight face, he got them in the car. He used his cell phone to find an emergency vet, and drove there fast.

The animal clinic was busy, with at least ten cats and dogs in various states of illness or injury—and every one of them was wildly attracted to Rachel. She sat on a hard plastic chair with Gertie carefully cradled in her arms, as baffled pet owners tried to reign in their straining animals.

She looked completely out of place in her chic black dress—now covered with cat hair—and sleek pumps, like a real pearl amidst fake jewels. Gabe signed them in, completed paperwork, and came to stand beside her, as all the seats were taken. "Busy night," he commented, watching one particularly determined basset hound named Percy lunge to the end of his leash.

They finally saw a veterinarian, a compassionate young woman with wire-rimmed glasses and a golden braid down her back. Gertie cried pitifully when blood was drawn from her tiny leg, while Rachel stared intently at the tube, her eyes glazing over. "Stop looking at that," Gabe murmured, turning her away. "You'll get to eat later."

After another long wait, they received the diagnosis: Gertie had an infection that was readily treatable with an antibiotic. One problem—the medicine had to be given three times a day. "We can handle it," Gabe assured Dr. Conner, taking the bottle she held out.

Rachel missed the exchange, because she was too shocked by the bill, and by the fact that Gabe insisted she pay it. She watched morosely as the receptionist ran her credit card through. "Highway robbery," she hissed to him as they walked out.

"The price of being responsible for someone—or some animal— you love." He raised his eyes heavenward in silent thanks.

"What? I don't lov—"

"You know you're going to have to take Gertie home with you," he interrupted. "There's no other way you can be sure she gets her medicine three times a day."

Rachel stared at him, flabbergasted. "I couldn't possibly take her home."

He opened the car door. "She's your cat."

"No, she's not!"

"We've already been through this. If you don't take care of her, who will?"

"You?"

"She's not my responsibility. But if you don't want to do it, we'll just take her back to the Dumpster."

Rachel looked like she had a noose closing around her neck. "I don't know anything about cats."

"You'll learn. Come on." Gabe ushered her into the car. "We'll go buy everything the well-supplied cat owner needs."

They found a Wal-Mart that was open twenty-four hours a day; and in the pet department, a staggering array of cat products. Fortunately, Gabe knew a little bit about cat care, and piled litter pan, cat litter, food, dishes, toys, and fleece bed—a pink one—into the cart. Rachel practically snarled when he made her dig out her credit card again.

"I'll be bankrupt by the end of seven nights," she snapped at him. He couldn't help it—he laughed. Good thing her glare couldn't disintegrate him.

They went to Rachel's condo, and she reluctantly allowed him in, because she didn't have a clue about litter boxes and cat stuff in general. Like the rest of her life, her place was stark, bare, with only a few pieces of furniture and no adornments. Interestingly, she did have a CD player and a receiver, along with a large collection of classical CDs. So she liked music, a fact Gabe stored away.

A while later, they left Gertie there, on her new fleece bed, with bowls of food and water and litter box nearby. Rachel had changed back into her customary street attire, handing over the black dress to Gabe, as he'd offered to have it dry-cleaned.

He dropped her off at Harry Hines so she could conduct her necessary business. She looked unusually vulnerable as he drove away, standing in the shadow of the tattoo parlor and staring after him. He offered a prayer of thanks to a Higher Being for assistance, for the blessing of one small gray-and-white cat.

Rachel didn't know it yet, but between him and Gertie, her well-ordered life was about to be totally disrupted.

―――――

Rachel awoke to soft snoring. Her first, groggy thought was *Aaron*. Her younger brother had always been a mouth breather when he slept, and the whole family teased him about his snoring. *Aaron, you are loud enough to summon Elijah. Surely Hashem can hear you up in heaven.*

Could it be . . . ? No, Aaron was dead. The grief cut through her before she could head it off. She jolted upright and blinked as she stared at . . . the cat, curled on her pillow, right against the outline where Rachel's head had been.

With a high-pitched meow, the cat uncurled and did an amazing stretch before daintily treading across the pillow and butting her head against Rachel. Tentatively, she stroked the soft fur.

Obviously, the cat was much better tonight—livelier, its eyes bright and alert. The medicine must be working. It was time for another dose—and to feed the cat. Rachel wrinkled her nose as her highly developed sense of smell picked up a rank odor. And to scoop the litter box like Gabe had shown her.

She'd known no good would come of this. Better not to be responsible for anyone but herself. Better . . . and safer.

She told Gabe as much when he asked about the cat. "She followed me everywhere tonight," she said, still baffled over the cat's odd devotion. "And she kept batting at my robe, then climbed up the drapes, all the way to the top!"

Gabe smiled. "She's just being a cat. She follows you around because you're her surrogate mother."

His words made a funny feeling curl through her stomach. She shook her head in denial. "Cats don't think of people as parents."

"Sure they do. And you have adopted Gertie—or maybe it's the other way around." Gabe chuckled. "If you could see your face. Having someone or something to care about isn't a bad thing. No way around it, you and Gertie are stuck with each other."

She told herself he was wrong, but didn't waste her breath arguing. "Where are we going tonight?"

He accelerated the car down Harry Hines, shifted gears. "First, do you mind if I ask you a question?"

"I guess not."

"How old where you when the war started?"

Tension shot through her body. This was a topic she'd always avoided. "I don't want to talk about that."

"But—"

She whirled, her fangs bared. *"I don't want to talk about it, damn you!"*

"Sorry." He raised a placating hand. "It's just that the more I know about you, the better I can help you."

"I don't want your help! I keep telling you that, but you're too stupid to get it. I just want to be left alone."

He was quiet a long moment. "If that's what you want when the seven days are up, then that's what you'll get."

"Thank Go—uh, good." She sank against the seat, dismayed to find she was shaking.

"Do you mind telling me when you were born?"

He was relentless. Why couldn't she have gotten a wimpy angel who she could glamour or beat to a pulp? She knotted her hands in her lap, hissed out her breath. "May 17, 1921." She'd supposedly "died" in the concentration camp in 1940. She hadn't even made it to her twentieth birthday.

"Have any boyfriends when you were growing up?" he asked.

What did that have to do with anything? "No. My parents would never have permitted that until I was older."

"So you never went on a date?"

She turned and glared at him. "*No.* I was seventeen when they—" *When the soldiers came and took them away in the middle of the night.* She pushed away the pain, struggled to explain. "Back then, girls from conservative Jewish families didn't date like they do now. And when they did, it was a man their father picked. Now, can we change the subject? I might not be able to hurt you, but I can kick the shit out of your car."

He shot her a shocked look. "You wouldn't!"

"I would." She leaned back, quite pleased with this new power over him.

Gabe shook his head, a pained expression on his face. "Fine. No more questions for now. But I'm not telling you where we're going, either. It will be a surprise."

"*Fine,*" she mimicked back. "By the way, I *hate* surprises."

A smile flirted at his lips. "Better get used to them." He shifted gears again, and the car blasted down the road. "Man, this baby can hum," he said reverently.

———

The State Fair of Texas. Art deco buildings with their odd domes, countless exhibits and aromatic food stands, a cacophony of music blaring from various stages mingled with hundreds of voices, and a terrifying press of bodies. Rachel was overwhelmed as Gabe commandeered her hand and led her into the heart of the melee. Not even his hold on her could stop her panic tonight. She tried to break free, to run, to get the hell out of there.

"Rachel! Come here." He stepped between two food stands and pulled her against him, wrapping his arms around her. Under normal circumstances, she would have decked any man who did that to her, but right now, Gabe was her lifeline.

"Breathe," he commanded, his breath warm against her ear. "Just breathe, be calm." Gentle compulsion whispered through her, and she welcomed it over the dread suffocating her.

Miraculously, the magic of his voice and touch soothed her, gave her the strength to shove unwelcome memories and her compulsive reaction to them back into the secret corners of her psyche. Her chest heaving, she leaned against him. He had his own special scent, warm, musky, and—as much as she hated to admit it—heavenly.

"Why the hell do you always have to take me somewhere that has so many freaking people?" she muttered.

"It's not about the people. It's about experiencing life," he told her. "You never had a chance to enjoy life the way you should have. You were forced to grow up way too fast, without experiencing the fun years of college and dating and falling in love. The state fair is a great slice of life."

He turned her toward the crowds. "Look out there, Rachel.

Look at all those people, laughing and talking and having fun. Smell the food. Hear the music. Feel the joy and the excitement of being *alive*. Feel it sing through your body."

She found herself *wanting* to do as he suggested, wanting to experience, if only for the moment, what *real*, *normal* people did at events like the fair. Calmer now, she took another deep breath and inhaled the scents of fried food and sugary concoctions, cigarette smoke and beer, livestock dung. She saw the bright lights and rides, heard people laughing and talking, over the rhythmic beat of country, rock, and even Cajun music.

Resigned to the fact she was stuck there, she walked around with Gabe. He sampled different foods, sharing them with her. In general, most foods were too rich for her system and gave her indigestion, but she could eat small amounts. She had her first taste of cotton candy, was amazed at how it compressed from spun pink strands into hard lumps of sweetness. She wrinkled her nose at Gabe's beer, but took a sip.

He dragged her inside the auto exhibit before she knew what he was about. They spent thirty minutes there, him salivating over the newest sports cars, and her salivating over the sound of beating hearts and the scent of blood rushing through veins.

From there, they went to the midway, Gabe's hold on her hand somehow keeping her grounded, and watched the various games and the astounding amount of money changing hands. He talked her into playing some games, and for a few moments, she felt like a young girl again, the girl she'd been before war and hatred had permanently darkened her horizons.

He won a huge purple bear and stunned her when he presented it to her. "I can't take this," she said. "You won it. It's yours."

"That's what the guy is supposed to do, Rach. Win his girl a prize." Gabe tucked the unwieldy plush bear under one arm and playfully wrapped his other arm around her neck. "And you're supposed to kiss me for doing it, but I'll collect later."

They staggered along, his arm still around her neck, stopping near the Texas Star, a huge Ferris wheel. Gabe checked it out with a whistle of appreciation. "That looks like fun."

"Oh, no!" Rachel pulled free and backed away. "I'm not going on that thing. I don't like heights."

"What?" He followed, his voice low. "You're immortal. What have you got to be afraid of?"

"No. I'm *not* getting on that thing. Absolutely not!"

What the hell am I doing in a small cage, hanging more than two hundred feet up in the air?

"Contrary to popular belief, vampires are *not* bats. We don't like being airborne." Frozen with fear, she stared at the ground, which seemed dangerously, impossibly, far away.

"You're not going to fall." Gabe pried her fingers from the seat edge and took her hands. "Feel the night, Rachel. Feel the rush of the wind, the flutter in your stomach as we circle down and back up. Look at those glorious stars, at that full moon."

"Why don't you go howl at it? Then stick it up your—" She screeched as they started down again and clutched his hands.

He laughed and drew her against him. "Then think about something else." His voice dropped into a deep, seductive tone. "Imagine you're still in high school. Your boyfriend—who's angelically good looking, by the way—has brought you here. He wants to show you a good time, to let you know how much he likes you. And now that he's got you right where he wants you, high above the ground—"

He took Rachel's chin in one hand, tilted her face toward him. "He's going to do this."

He kissed her, just a brush of his lips, and she thought that was it. But then he was back, his lips a warm, sensual pressure. She felt his thumb push on her chin, forcing her mouth open, and then his tongue was dancing with hers in a full-fledged kiss.

If she hadn't been so shocked, she'd never have allowed this. . . . She'd *never* been kissed before. She put her hands against his shoulders, started to push him away . . . *wow*.

He wasn't trying to cram his tongue down her mouth like some johns visualized doing; instead his tongue stroked hers suggestively, created startling sensations. A tantalizing heat wound through her body, along with a little hum of pleasure. That jarred her back to reality, and she shoved Gabe away.

His eyes were glowing, and she could swear she saw stars sparkling against their deep blue. "Of course your boyfriend, being a red-blooded teenager, would want more than a kiss," he said huskily. "So he'd try to cop a feel, too." She jerked back with a hiss, and the idiot grinned at her. "But I want to get out of this gondola in one piece, so we'll skip that for now."

———

Later that night, as Rachel took a mark behind a building, she couldn't stop thinking about Gabe's kiss. How it had freaked her, yet at the same time made her body come alive with sensations she'd never experienced before. She was so distracted she almost lost her mind lock on her john.

"Hey!" he protested, as she paused in the middle of pulling off her sweater. "Whadda you doin'? I told you I want to see you buck naked. Get it on!"

She removed her sweater, kicked off her boots, and seductively shimmied out of her jeans. She wore a lacy thong, which excited the john, although he motioned for her to take it off. She turned for a moment as she did, giving him a nice view of her fine ass. Then she pressed her back against the wall, sliding partway down and spreading her legs wide so he could look at her like he wanted. As he freed himself from his pants and moved forward to bang her, she found her mind wandering to a different fantasy—one that involved a mind-blowing kiss that wasn't lewd or tainted by shadows.

And while the john experienced an explosive orgasm and she sank her fangs deep, it was Gabe's face she saw as she flashed to the stars and back.

The big purple bear was leaned against her front door when she got home two hours before sunrise. A spark of joy shot though her when she saw it, and she couldn't help smiling. She noticed a folded piece of paper tucked between its legs and pulled it out. Scrawled in a bold, masculine handwriting were the words: *Rachel, Another creature for you to care for. Stuffed toy bears need love, too. G.* Little angel wings had been drawn on each side of the *G*.

What an odd thing to say. Gabe was totally whacked out. Had a death wish, too, which might come to pass if he didn't stop messing with her. Still, she couldn't resist running her hand over the plush material. A memory flashed through her mind—that of a Steiff teddy bear she'd had years ago, a little golden bear named Ludwig. That was long gone, but for once, she didn't feel the rush of loss and pain that usually accompanied memories of her previous life.

She lugged the purple bear inside. The cat streaked toward her, meowing loudly. Rachel didn't even have the door closed before the cat twined around her legs, still crying. Almost tripping, Rachel set down the bear and her purse. "What?" she demanded. "What is it, cat? Are you hungry?" That must be it. She fed Gertie and gave her a dropper of medicine, then scooped the cat litter. Ugh. How could such a little creature make so much shit?

None of those things seemed to satisfy Gertie, and she kept dogging Rachel's steps with intermittent meows. She attacked Rachel's toes while Rachel was brushing her teeth, chased her own shadow on the wall, and then tried to catch her tail. Rachel found herself smiling at the cat's antics. When she finally sat down to relax and brush her hair, the cat leaped into her lap, turned twice, then settled down and began purring. Hesitantly, Rachel stroked the animal, and it pressed its paws into her thighs, purring even louder.

Rachel couldn't understand why this cat would want to be around *her*. With their exceptional senses, surely most animals recognized *what* she was—a monster, a depraved creature of the night. Yet Gertie didn't seem to care.

Rachel continued stroking the cat, found its purring was oddly soothing. Later, as she was sinking into the fathomless void of her kind, she was vaguely aware of the cat settling on the pillow beside her head.

She felt a sense of comfort she hadn't experienced for decades.

Chapter 5

THIS surprise business was fun, Gabe thought, watching Rachel's utter amazement as she took in the Meyerson. He'd gotten tickets for the Dallas Symphony, center floor—probably had been some heavenly intervention involved in that one. He'd also had the foresight to purchase rhinestone earrings, an evening purse, and wrap for Rachel.

Those had taken her aback, especially when he didn't ask her to pay for them. Then she'd been excited, although she'd tried hard not to show it. He had to help her put the clip earrings on her dainty, unpierced earlobes. He suspected she'd never worn earrings, just as he was pretty certain she'd never been kissed before last night.

That kiss had been pretty special. Heavens, it had practically blown his wings off, not to mention the wicked things it had done to his human libido. But more important, Rachel hadn't been immune to it. He'd heard her breath hitch, felt her heart speed up, been blasted by pheromones—from *her*.

Rachel had been turned on, although she might not understand exactly what had happened. But it was real progress, because part of living on Earth meant experiencing the sensations of the flesh—and not just through mind sex.

Gabe's flesh was having plenty of sensations of its own, but he would have to control them. Not that there was anything wrong with, or any celestial laws prohibiting, sex between angels and humans, as long as the angel was in a physical incarnation. But it wasn't the right thing for Rachel, at least not yet.

Beside him, Rachel turned full circle, gaping at the elegant Meyerson with its incredible expanses of glossy white granite, banks of exterior glass panels, and the two imposing radial stairways going to the upper level. It was crowded, but she didn't seem to be panicking tonight, although he kept a firm grip on her hand, just in case. It seemed like they were making progress in that regard, as well.

She looked fabulous in her black dress, which had been dry-cleaned. She'd put her dark hair up in an elegant twist, and it shone in the light. The earrings swung and sparkled from her ears. She could give every one of the elegantly attired patrons a run for their money. Gabe glanced down at his impeccable dark gray suit, crisp white shirt, and burgundy-and-gray striped tie. He wasn't too shabby, either.

They had arrived forty minutes before performance time, so they sat at a table in the west lobby and sipped wine—red, of course. Rachel kept looking around. "How did you know I like classical music?"

"That's the only kind of music you had next to your stereo."

"You still didn't have to get symphony tickets."

"Rachel, don't you get it yet? I'm here for *you*. To show you how to have fun and enjoy life. To do whatever it takes to bring you back to the living, to fulfill your potential."

She got the rebellious expression that usually indicated she was about to deliberately provoke him. "I do a damn good job as a whore. I don't need any improvement, or to develop my *potential* there." She turned and glared at the shocked faces staring at her from the next table, daring them to say anything. The elderly couple hastily looked away, and she lowered her voice. "And what exactly is the potential for a vampire? Drinking blood from higher-class humans?"

"That's not a bad idea. You can drink my blood any time."

She jerked upright, her eyes narrowing. "Wouldn't that be lowering myself?"

But he had her number, understood her need to erect defenses. "Rachel, you don't have to insult me every time I make you feel uncomfortable or mad."

She took a gulp of wine. "Is that what you think I'm doing? What the hell do you know?"

"I know you're running from yourself. From your pain and your fears."

She looked away, her jaw clenched. He could almost hear her fangs grinding. Taking pity on her, he rose and held out his hand. "Come on. Let's just enjoy the evening and the music."

Their seats were excellent, which they should be, considering they'd cost a small fortune. The orchestra was onstage, doing its disharmonious tuning and warm-up. The concertmaster came out, and the audience applauded. Gabe watched Rachel flip open the program, felt immense gratification at the expression of delight that filled her face.

"Beethoven." She said the name reverently, like a prayer. "One of my favorite composers. Symphony No. 3." She scanned further. "Rachmaninoff, Piano Concerto No. 2 in C Minor. Not one of my countrymen, but another favorite."

The lights dimmed, and the conductor entered to thunderous applause. Then the music swelled. Gabe watched Rachel more than he watched the orchestra. She was rapt, riveted, her body practically vibrating with the music. During particularly evocative passages, she closed her eyes, swaying slightly.

When intermission came, she looked at Gabe, her eyes shining. "Thank you." She leaned forward impulsively, brushed his cheek with her lips. She sat back, her face flushed.

He felt his own temperature rise a few degrees, along with a great satisfaction that he'd found something that gave her such pleasure. "You're welcome."

The second half of the program was also excellent, the piano notes soaring to mingle with those of the orchestra. During the slow, plaintive second movement of the concerto, a few tears slid down Rachel's face. Gabe rejoiced silently. Where there were tears, there was emotion.

"This was my mother's favorite concerto," she said, swiping at her face, her eyes still damp.

He took her hand. "Try to think of the joy it gave her. And the joy *you* gave her."

"It's so hard," she said sadly.

He squeezed her hand. "I know."

She turned her attention back to the orchestra. Gabe blew out his breath. *Progress.*

They went out for coffee afterward, then he took her home to change before he drove her to Harry Hines. He parked the car and came around as she got out.

Her demeanor, which had been relaxed and receptive, changed subtly as he rounded the car. She stiffened, watched him warily. "What is it?" he asked, perplexed.

"You'd better not be thinking about doing what you talked about last night."

He searched his memory. "What was it I said?"

Her chin went up. "That a boyfriend would cop a feel."

He almost choked, then struggled not to laugh. "Oh. Well. That was *last* night. Tonight, we're imagining that you've graduated from high school. Now you're more grown up and dating a more mature man." He stepped closer, ran his hands along her upper arms. "And while he, like every male who can get it up, would definitely like to jump your bones, he would never treat you with such disrespect—at least not the first few dates."

He leaned in, ignoring her flare of panic, and kissed her lightly. He stepped back, dropped his hands. "Of course, relationships do have a way of progressing, so I am going to take a rain check on that."

He grinned at the look on her face—relief warring with

disappointment and apprehension. She was so expressive, so easy to read. "Good night, Rachel. Jeans tomorrow night."

―――――

The next night, which was the fifth night—not that Rachel was counting, or anything—Gabe had another surprise. But this one wasn't fun. She stood inside one of the playrooms at Children's Medical Center, appalled by the illness and misery she saw. This hospital was for very sick children, and many of them were just babies, although there were older kids as well.

Apparently the mobile patients were encouraged to move around the hospital. Those who could walk rolled their IV stands along with them. Those who were too small or weak to walk were pulled around in little red wagons by parents or volunteers. Many of the patients were bald from treatments, or had various tubes coming out of them, or heavy bandages.

The vast majority had the sunken eyes and washed-out complexions of the very ill. It was a look that Rachel remembered all too well, and it raised horrific memories. She glanced over to where Gabe, who had brought two large bags of new toys and books, was reading to a small crowd of children. His wonderful voice rose and fell, changing to match whatever character he was portraying. The children were entranced.

Rachel walked in that direction. Several kids she passed smiled shyly at her, and she found herself responding, although she couldn't imagine what they had to smile about. She and Gabe spent two hours in the room, and she ended up playing with a few of the children, helping them to build Lego structures and do puzzles.

They were sweet and innocent, but she could hardly look at some of them, with their wounds and tubes, and the aura of impending death that lingered around them.

She was glad when Gabe was ready to leave. As soon as they got in the car, she said, "That place was awful! Why the hell did you take me there?"

He turned in his seat to face her. "It's not awful. There are a lot of miracles that happen at Children's Medical Center."

"There's disease and death there. Did you see those faces, those sunken eyes?"

"Of course I did. There are some very sick children there. When you looked at those faces and those sunken eyes, what exactly did you see, Rachel?"

She felt a cold fist creeping around her heart. "You know what I saw."

"Tell me."

She shook her head.

"Tell me, Rachel." This time the compulsion was there. She didn't want to, but she knew he wouldn't let it go.

"I saw death. I saw bodies, stacked like wood." She drew a deep, shuddering breath. "I saw despair and pain and no way out. No safe place, nowhere to run."

He placed his warm hands over her cold ones. "You saw those things because of your life experiences. Let me tell you what *I* saw."

One of his hands went to her chin, forced her to look at him. She stared into his deep blue eyes, mesmerized by the golden star-bursts in them. "I saw the resilient human spirit," Gabe said softly. "I saw the fierce will to live, despite failing physical bodies. I saw hope, determination, fortitude, amazing inner strength. I saw love, happiness, joy, even in the midst of pain and illness and uncertainty. *And* I saw *Her* there.

"These bodies—" He gestured from him to her. "These are just shells, temporary homes for our souls, which are eternal. No matter what happens to you physically, Rachel, your soul will always live on."

"You keep forgetting I *don't* have a soul. I'm a vampire."

"You *do* have a soul," he said firmly. "And you've been given your body and a life on Earth. Your own religion teaches it's a sin not to live that life fully, a sin to pass up opportunities for joy and happiness."

"Sometimes those opportunities are taken from us." She hated the quaver in her voice.

Compassion and wisdom glowed in his eyes. "Sometimes they are. Sometimes you have no choice over what happens to you or your loved ones. But you do have control over how you react to these things, and whether or not you choose to keep going. Those children in there live every moment to its fullest. They don't complain, they play hard, and they *fight to live*. That's what I want you to do, Rachel. *Fight, and live*."

He started the car. "Lecture's over. Let's do something fun."

Rachel was silent as they left the hospital, but her thoughts were whirling. Gabe was forcing her to think about things she'd never considered. To her amazement, one of those considerations was the possibility he might actually be right.

———

She'd never been bowling before. The thunderous noise of rolling balls and toppling pins was very disconcerting at first, especially since it reminded her of the sounds of war. But Gabe helped her breathe through it. When she was settled, he got her some bowling shoes. He was very patient as he showed her how to bowl, but she was sadly lacking in natural ability.

"Uh, Rach?"

Dismayed, she stared down the lane. "Yeah?"

"Try to *roll* the ball, not *throw* it. Especially since you have superhuman strength."

That *was* a pretty big hole in the bulkhead above the pins. She nodded. "Gotcha."

Later that night, as she was strutting down Harry Hines, she remembered the look on Gabe's face when her ball had crashed through the wall, and found herself grinning like a fool. Then she started laughing—*really* laughing.

Something she hadn't done for more than sixty-five years.

———

The next evening, she was relieved when Gabe didn't take them somewhere sad or depressing. Instead they went to the Pocket Sandwich Theatre and watched a live production like nothing Rachel had ever experienced. It was a spoof of *Phantom of the Opera*, and the actors responded to comments from the audience, even incorporating those comments into the play. The audience also participated by throwing popcorn at the actors.

It didn't take Rachel long to get into the spirit of things, especially since Gabe paid for the popcorn. She munched a few pieces and gleefully threw the rest, some at the actors, and some at him. He laughed at her antics. She laughed with him, which seemed to surprise and please him.

But it was the warmth in his gaze, the acceptance and approval in his incredible eyes that crept inside her, made her feel special, like maybe she wasn't really a freak. She felt more relaxed than she had in a very long time.

Later that evening, when he left her on Harry Hines with just a light brush of his lips on hers, she found herself disappointed that it hadn't been a deeper kiss.

Or that he hadn't tried to cop a feel.

———

The next evening, Rachel tried not to think about the fact that this was her last night with Gabe. After tonight, she'd have fulfilled her end of the bargain, and if he kept to his word—which she had no doubt he would—he'd be gone, out of her life. She'd be alone again.

She ignored the misery biting at her. It was her destiny to be alone, she told herself. It was better, safer, and less painful. Gabe was an angel. Sooner or later, he'd have to go off and do other angel things. She didn't even know if he'd remain in a body. If she let herself get attached to him, she'd only be setting herself up for more pain. She'd had enough of that to last a hundred lifetimes.

The sight of a white Acura pulling in front of the tattoo parlor drew her from her dark thoughts. She walked over to the passenger side of the car as the tinted window lowered. "Hey, Caitria."

Caitria looked tired, and she sported a black eye. But she managed a smile when she saw Rachel. "Ooooh, look at you, lil' bitch. Who'd you knock off to get that dress and those killer earrings?"

Rachel fingered the dangling earrings, smoothed her hand over the satiny evening wrap. This would be the last night she wore the black dress and the accessories Gabe had bought her. "Just meeting someone."

"Ooooh, girl. Is it that hot man with the great threads?"

"It's the guy you met a few nights ago."

"Oh, yeah, that's what I'm talkin' about. I bet he knows how to fuck a bitch right."

Rachel couldn't answer. The only sex she'd experienced had been more than sixty-five years ago—and it hadn't been consensual. But something about Gabe told her he'd know what to do in bed.

"Lil' bitch, you got a few to hang with me?"

"Sure." She got in the car, concerned about Caitria. It was obvious Danyon had been whaling on her. "You don't look too good."

Caitria lit a cigarette, her hand shaking. "It's been a tough few. Motherfuckin' cops caught me in the act, blowing a john. Arrested both our asses. I spent two days at Sterrit afore my momma got me out. Said she was tired of keeping the kids."

And Danyon had let her know he didn't appreciate the lack of funds, or the inconvenience—with his fists. "Why don't you leave him?" Rachel asked suddenly. She'd never brought it up before, had kept her distance from Caitria's personal affairs, but she was really worried.

Caitria shook her head with a sad smile. "Girl, I can't do that. Been with him too long."

"You could go away, get a fresh start somewhere. Find another job."

"There ain't nothing I can do but whorin'."

Rachel felt a rush of desperation for Caitria. "You *can* do something else. And there's got to be a decent man out there . . . somewhere. One who will treat you right."

"I don't got that kinda choice. Where would I go? How would I support my kids?"

"There's always a choice." Rachel sat back, stunned she'd just said that. Damn. Gabe was really getting to her. Speak of the devil. He was approaching the car, wearing the same suit he'd worn to The Meyerson.

"Ooooh, he do know how to dress." Caitria rolled down the passenger window as he walked up. "Sup, sexy man?"

Gabe leaned down. "Good evening, Caitria. How are you?"

"Things lookin' up, with your fine ass here."

"Not sure Rachel would agree with you." His tone was light as he opened the car door. "You ready to go?"

"That depends." She thought about the visit to Children's Medical.

Gabe flashed his killer smile. "Just a good time tonight."

"Sounds like fun." Caitria gave Rachel a thumbs-up. "Go for it, lil' bitch. Check you later." She started the car and roared off.

"Gabe, did you see her?" Rachel couldn't ignore her distress. "That bastard boyfriend is killing her."

He put his arm around her. "I know."

"You need to do something!" She whirled on him, suddenly furious, and knocked his arm away. "How can you stand by and let that happen?"

He sighed. "We've been over this."

"Fuck free will!"

"You may not believe this Rachel, but there are forces at work to help Caitria."

"What the hell does that mean?"

He took her arm, gave her a little tug toward his car. "Has it occurred to you that maybe you and Caitria are friends for a reason? That you might be able to influence her to make some positive life changes?"

"Me?" she scoffed. "I'm not in a position to help anyone."

"You underestimate yourself. Caitria likes you, and the two of you share a bond. She might listen to you."

"I already said something, and she blew me off."

"She might listen eventually, if you keep talking to her about it." Gabe stopped by the car. "Although sometimes all you can do is be there, be a good friend."

"Maybe you could help her," Rachel said hopefully. Gabe was pretty good at getting his way, as she well knew. She thought about the Ferris wheel and grimaced.

"I'm not part of her destiny. You are my sole challenge right now." His warm gaze swept over her. "And may I say you look beautiful."

His intense stare flustered her. "Thank you."

He stepped closer, his scent and heat drifting around her. His hands settled on her shoulders, sent tingling sensations down her arms.

"Tonight, imagine you're completely grown up. You've graduated from college, and are now a professional businesswoman." Humor tinged his husky voice as he leaned closer. "You have a date with an experienced, sophisticated man who knows how to treat a woman right."

His breath whispered over her hair, along her cheek, and she shivered, but not from cold. "Tonight," he whispered. "Anything could happen."

Chapter 6

GABE took Rachel to the West End, an area of downtown Dallas that had been restored and sported both trendy and funky stores and restaurants. Per their agreement, it was their last night, although he hoped that wasn't the case. He was a little anxious about the evening, because he was still feeling his way big-time, even though he was thrilled with Rachel's progress.

She'd adopted Gertie, not that she would admit it. She'd cried, she'd laughed, she'd expressed a wide range of emotions that had been bottled inside her for decades. She'd begun overcoming her terror in crowds, ridden a Ferris wheel, played games with sick children, and thrown popcorn during a theater production.

She had let him kiss her, with a sweet, hot response that had singed his wings. Still, he wasn't sure of the outcome—or if he should push her toward the next step; that of acknowledging her value as a woman, her innate sensuality, realizing she deserved to be loved. They hadn't dealt with the issue of her being raped, either. So much left to do. Gabe sent up a prayer for guidance, as he and Rachel parked and started walking.

They went to the West End Marketplace and browsed the shops. True to form, she didn't buy anything, but she did enjoy watching fudge being made at The Fudgery. She tasted a sample, and he had to laugh at her enthralled expression; she definitely liked chocolate. He bought her some chocolate pecan fudge to take home, loving her smile of delight.

They left the Marketplace and just strolled, taking in the sights and sounds. Rachel seemed more comfortable outside, with the fresh air and nighttime swirling around them. He hailed a horse-drawn carriage, and she eyed it warily as it pulled up beside them. "We're getting in *that*?"

"It will be fun." He helped her up, got in and slid his arm around her as the carriage jolted off. "While all males are basically cavemen, your more mature and experienced man will pick a romantic setting like this to make his next move."

"Next move?"

He answered her by leaning over and kissing her. She tensed, but she didn't resist him. When his tongue gently prodded her lips, she even opened her mouth for him. He sensed she'd been expecting him to kiss her, maybe even hoped he would, but she still wasn't sure about it.

Despite her occupation, she was innately innocent. He explored the softness of her mouth, savoring the taste and texture of her. When her tongue tentatively pressed back against his, a jolt of pure testosterone shot through him. He eased away before he did something crazy, like feel her up in public.

She stared at him, her eyes huge and her lips damp. "Did you like that?" he asked, brushing her hair from her face.

She touched her lips. "I don't know."

Gabe smiled wryly. "Good thing my ego's not too fragile." He sat back in the seat, but held her hand the rest of the ride.

After that, they went to a classy jazz club on the edge of downtown. The club was plush, with muted lighting provided by wall sconces and table candles. A soulful saxophone was conversing with a trio consisting of a piano, a double bass, and drums. A small dance floor was already catching some action. They got a cozy corner booth, and Gabe ordered wine.

Twisting her hands together on the table, Rachel stared at the couples on the dance floor. "Ever been dancing?" Gabe asked.

"No." She accepted her wine from the waiter, took a gulp.

"You're supposed to sip that."

A rebellious expression crossed her face, and she took another healthy swallow. Thoughtfully, he glanced from her to the dance floor. "What's got you so on edge?"

"Nothing."

He leaned forward, placed his hand over hers. "You know, I've been totally honest with you during our time together. In return, I'm asking the same from you. If you have any respect for me, then don't lie to me."

She drew back, pulling her hand free. "Why should it matter? This is our last night together. Isn't it?"

"I don't know. You tell me."

She was silent a long moment. "Yes," she said finally. "This is it, Gabe. Nothing has changed. I'm still a vampire—a *monster*. I have no future, and I basically have no past."

He felt like he'd been gut-punched, even as another part of him knew she'd come much farther than she realized. But she didn't yet recognize her progress, couldn't yet accept the truths he'd presented. That was *her* choice. He wasn't allowed to interfere further, once she'd exercised her free will.

"All right, then." He picked up his wine, took a gulp of his own. He drew a breath, shelved his deep disappointment. "But I have you until the stroke of midnight, à la Cinderella. So what makes you nervous about this place?"

She gestured around. "These people are normal. They're human." She looked at the couples so intimately entwined on the dance floor. For the first time, he saw longing in her eyes. "They have loved ones, families, lives."

"You could have that." *You could, Rachel. You could.*

"No." She shook her head vehemently. "Never again."

"Why?"

"You know why. I can't change what I am. I'll never have my family back."

"No, you'll never have your family back," he agreed quietly. "But you can change your life. You can forge new relationships. The only thing standing in your way is you." *Choose life, Rachel.*

She looked away, and he felt her grief.

"Dance with me," he said.

Her gaze swung back to him. "I don't know how to dance."

He held out his hand, used compulsion. "Come on."

"I know what you're doing. It doesn't work on me." But she put her hand in his and let him lead her to the dance floor.

Her body was stiff and unyielding as he pulled her into his arms. "Relax, Rach. Just relax and move with me." He pressed her flush against him, using his body to guide her. She was graceful and light on her feet. She quickly adapted to his moves, and some of her tension eased.

The music drifted around them, a low, seductive wail. Rachel felt soft and perfect in Gabe's arms. He rubbed his cheek against her silky hair, inhaled the natural, earthy scent of woman. His blood stirred, and desire rose, hot and hard.

His physical body reacted accordingly. His erection pulsed and strained against his pants, and her belly. Rachel might be innocent, but she was too experienced in the ways of lusting men to misread his reaction.

She shoved away and looked at the telltale bulge in his pants. Then she got the expression he'd never expected to be aimed at him—the disinterested, jaded look of a prostitute who's seen and heard everything. "So," she sneered, a bitter note in her voice. "Are angels allowed to solicit whores?"

Anger flashed through him like a lightning strike. Taking her arm, he guided her firmly off the floor and to the club entrance. "Be right back," he told the startled host as he dragged Rachel outside.

He took her around the corner of the building before he released her. He stared at her a long moment, willing his anger—and his body—to cool. She stared back defiantly. This was her way, he reminded himself—to build barriers whenever she felt threatened. He might only have her a little longer, but he could damn sure tear down some of those barriers before the proverbial clock struck midnight.

"Rachel, why do you always do that? Why do you always panic at normal emotions and reactions, and try to demean them? They're a part of being human."

She crossed her arms and looked away, her expression sullen. She wasn't even going to argue with him about her humanity.

His frustration spiked. "No, angels don't solicit whores." He grabbed her arms and pulled her forward. "But *this* angel is attracted to a beautiful, compassionate woman who has so much to offer the world. A woman who should be cherished by a man, not viewed solely as a sexual object. You deserve that, Rachel."

He crushed his mouth down on hers, willing a response. He kissed her hard, willing her to know she was every bit a woman; to know how much he wanted her. He felt her vibrating with hurt and anger and outrage and . . . passion. Her tongue engaged in a sensuous duel with his, and he sensed a new kind of tension in her. His own body hardened with need and desire.

"I think I'll take that rain check on copping a feel now," he murmured, sliding his hand upward to cup her breast. She gasped against his mouth, and he felt her nipple harden through the layers of fabric. He lowered his other hand and molded it over the firm curve of her rear. Her low moan was like music.

He raised his head, teased his fingers along her breast. "Come home with me, Rachel. Let me show you what it should be like between a man and a woman."

———

Rachel watched Gabe unlock the door to his apartment, panic edging out desire. What was she doing here? She'd been turned on like crazy when he'd kissed her outside the club and stroked her breast.

Sensations and unfamiliar physical demands had stormed through her, leaving her stunned and aching. In that heated moment of insanity, she'd agreed to go with him.

He'd kept her in a sensual fog by kissing and caressing her at every red light on the short drive to his apartment, in a gated community on north Maple. But now that they were here, sanity was emerging.

I can't do this, she thought, the panic growing stronger. Yet . . . the allure of *normalcy* hung in her mind, a tantalizing hope. She hated being a freak. Maybe, for one night, she could simply be a woman.

Gabe took her wrap and purse and tossed them, along with his suit coat, onto a nearby chair. Then he removed his tie and tossed it, too. Rachel tried to calm her jittery nerves. "Are you sure you can do this . . . that you're allowed to . . . ? I mean, if you're an angel, isn't this a sin or something?"

He smiled, and her heart stuttered. Taking her hand, he pressed it against the bulge in his pants. "Oh, I promise you, I can do *this*." She couldn't help herself—her fingers curled against his erection. Desire resurged in a staggering rush.

He groaned and pulled her hand away. "I'm not an angel tonight, Rachel. I'm a man, and I want you." He watched her intently. "You understand you don't have to have sex with me. This is *your* choice. Are you sure this is what *you* want?"

She felt no compulsion, only his need, warring with the innate honor that insisted he ensure she was willing. Her body certainly wanted to—every cell was screaming for more. She hadn't felt this vital and alive since before the war.

Oh, she wanted to be willing. Gabe had awakened a yearning in her, not only the fierce physical need she felt right now, but the longing to be human, to taste love and passion, to experience the things a cruel fate had denied her. "Yes," she whispered, before she could lose her nerve.

His face took on a fierce, triumphant expression. She felt a frisson of alarm, but then his expression gentled. "Thank God," he murmured, framing her face in his hands and kissing her senseless. Oh, yeah, she liked this.

She groaned a protest when he left her lips to trail kisses down her neck and over the slope of her breast, and he chuckled. "Soon," he promised in a low, sexy voice. "We'll get to the entrée, I promise."

He knelt and slipped her shoes off, running his hands along her bare legs, then farther up, beneath her dress. His fingers stroked dangerously close to where she was wet and aching, then retreated. She found it difficult to breathe, wanted to protest again when he stood.

He moved behind her, and she heard the sound of a zipper, felt the cool air on her back, followed by his warm hands. He slipped the dress from her shoulders and arms, letting it pool below her breasts. He reached around to cup her breasts as his lips seduced her neck. Helplessly, she dropped her head back against his shoulder.

"Nice bra," he whispered, his fingers teasing along the edge of the lace and then slipping inside.

She should have been lost in the pleasure, but something shifted inside her, a darkness welling from the depths of her soul. Fear came crashing out, colliding head-on with desire. Pain and grief and guilt—that she was still alive, while her family was dead. The knowledge that she was completely, utterly alone. The cruel faces of the three Nazi soldiers as they took turns with her, brutally destroying her innocence . . . *No.*

No! She *couldn't* do this, couldn't bear the intimacy, or the pain when Gabe left. How could she have even considered it? She felt herself withdrawing emotionally, even as his fingers stroked her nipple and his other hand slid down her belly.

Renewed panic pounded through her. Frantic, she reached out mentally to Gabe. She hit his mind barrier, remembered the futility of trying to glamour him. But then, she felt the barrier lower. He was letting her into his mind, inviting her to meld both mentally and physically with him. She was stunned by the depth of his gesture. He was giving her everything.

She swept inside his mind, grateful, relieved, now ready to offer her body.

Turning in his arms, she jerked his shirt out of his pants, anxious to feel his skin. He pulled back so that she could unbutton his shirt with shaking fingers. Then she slid her hands over swells of muscle and firm skin. Leaned in to press her mouth against his chest and lick a masculine nipple.

He groaned. "We've got to get you out of this dress," he said raggedly, slipping it over her hips. It fell in a silky pool around her feet. She stepped out of it, wearing nothing but the sexy black lace bra and panties that he'd insisted she buy.

Gabe stared at her, his expression reverent. "God, you're beautiful." He ran a hand down her trembling body, over her stomach, and between her legs, stroking her through the damp panties. His other hand drew her close, as he lowered his mouth to hers—

"Rachel!"

She jolted from the fantasy to find Gabriel glaring at her. Anger didn't begin to describe the expression on his face. He was *furious,* his features harsh and terrifying with the force of that rage. Fire sparked around him, forming a painfully bright halo. His hair and clothing blew wildly, although she couldn't feel any wind. *Avenging angel,* she thought, backing away.

"Damn it, Rachel!" His voice was pure, cold fury. "How could you try to force mind sex on me?"

"I don't—I just—" She couldn't begin to explain the demons that had driven her to protect herself from intimacy with him—not even to herself.

"I'm not one of your johns." He took a threatening step toward her. "I asked you for honesty, but apparently that was too much to expect. If you didn't want to have sex, all you had to do was say *no* or *stop.* That's all. But you couldn't even respect me enough to do that."

His disdain speared through her like a German bayonet. "I'm sorry," she whispered.

"You should be." There was no compassion or understanding in his voice.

The pain exploded inside her. She reached for her automatic defenses. "I don't owe you anything." She pulled the dress up and slipped her arms into the sleeves. "So I don't want to have sex with you. Big fucking deal. I gave you your seven nights. It's over and done."

Grabbing her purse and wrap from the chair, scooping her shoes from the floor, she told herself Gabe was being a bastard, and it was just as well they were through. But she felt shattered inside. She couldn't look at him as she went to the door and opened it.

"Wait." It was a steely command, and she froze.

She sensed him behind her, felt him zip up the dress. "As you said, our time is through. And maybe it meant nothing to you." His voice was emotionless. "What happens next—if anything—is totally up to you."

She closed her eyes against another wave of pain from those words and started through the door.

"Rachel." His voice stopped her. "I will be here a little while longer. If you want anything from me, you'll have to seek me of your own volition. But if you can't be totally honest with me, don't bother."

Then she was outside, and his door closed behind her with a terrible finality. She was alone again. This time forever.

———

Somehow Rachel got through the next days, although there were times when she felt like she was crumbling inside—which was ridiculous. Her life was exactly the same as it had been for more than sixty-five years. She was safe, she had a roof over her head, transportation, and ready access to blood and funds.

She was free of entanglements that could only bring more loss and pain into her life . . . well, except for Gertie. Now that the antibiotics were finished, she really should return the cat to the Dumpster, should get on with her life. But she just couldn't bring herself to do that.

The flash of gray and white following her around every night, chasing anything that moved; the warm body settling against her whenever she sat down or went to bed, offered the only relief from the bleak rote of existing.

This evening, Rachel walked along Harry Hines between Regal Row and Empire Central, feeling listless, trying to force the thoughts of Gabe from her mind. She hadn't seen him since that disastrous night, six days ago. Every time a silver sports car passed, she found herself looking to see if it was him, but it never was. How stupid of her. He was gone. She tried to tell herself it was for the best, but it was hard to be convinced when she felt so empty inside.

Even worse than the emptiness was the emotional pain, as if she'd lost a loved one. Not debilitating, like when her family had died, but it still hurt—like she was grieving. Damn it! She'd had enough grief during the war. Plus she'd been just fine before Gabe upset her life and messed everything up. She wasn't ever going through this again.

It was for the best, she told herself. As she turned and headed north on Harry Hines, she saw a white Acura driving south, slowly and erratically. Cars behind it were honking. It finally turned into a parking lot and jolted to a stop. She was pretty sure it was Caitria's car.

Perplexed, Rachel waited until it was clear, then crossed the street. When she saw the figure slumped over the wheel of the Acura, she ran to the driver's side and wrenched open the door. "Caitria, what's wrong?"

"Hey li'l bitch..." Caitria gasped weakly. "Not feeling... too ... good."

She was battered and bruised, her entire face swollen. Danyon had really done a number on her. Rachel felt rage bubbling inside her, but then Caitria groaned. "What can I do?" Rachel asked help-lessly.

"I'm thinking I might should go . . . to the doc. . . . Not sure I can get there."

Panic flared. Surely Caitria wasn't dying. She couldn't be. "I'll take you," Rachel said. But Caitria was too weak to get out of the driver's seat, and Rachel ended up lifting the large woman out and sliding her into the backseat. Caitria's cries of pain intensified her alarm. She drove to Parkland Hospital, pulled into the ER drop-off, laying on the horn.

The next hours were a blur. Caitria was rushed off to surgery, and Rachel used her allure to convince hospital personnel she was a relative. She sat helplessly in a surgical waiting area, unsure what to do.

A part of her didn't want to leave Caitria here, possibly *dying*, alone with strangers. Another part of her wanted to run, to put distance between herself and this place of death. Still another part of her yearned for Gabe, for his warm, calming presence. For him to assure her Caitria would be all right. On another level, she cursed Gabe for making her *feel* all these things. So, confused and battling myriad emotions, she simply sat and waited.

Finally a young female doctor in rumpled scrubs came through the doors and called, "Family of Caitria Washington."

Rachel hadn't even known Caitria's last name before tonight. She stood and walked slowly to the tired-looking doctor, who appeared surprised to see a white woman. "You with Ms. Washington?" she asked.

Rachel nodded, and the doctor, who didn't look a day over twenty, said, "Okay. Well, Ms. Washington suffered various blunt-force traumas, including a heart contusion and a broken rib, which punctured a lung. She's in pretty bad shape. But she's through surgery and in recovery. Later, she'll be put in Intensive Care, if she sur—" she caught herself. "We'll just have to see how she does."

Rachel hadn't understood much of what the doctor said, but she got the implication. "She's going to die, isn't she?"

"We don't know." But the sad compassion in the young woman's gray eyes spoke volumes. "Ms. Washington is heavily sedated right now," she added. "You can't see her until she's moved to ICU, and that will be in the morning. I recommend that you go home, get some rest."

Relieved to get out of there, Rachel headed for her condo. She stopped long enough to take blood from a panhandler who was too mentally ill to have sexual fantasies, so she paid him cash instead.

She returned to Parkland the following night, drawn there despite the almost-overwhelming urge to stay away, to avoid the pain of losing someone else. The news wasn't good. "I'm afraid Ms. Washington's internal injuries were pretty severe," Dr. Martin, the same young woman from the night before, told Rachel, outside Caitria's ICU room. "The cardiac contusion caused a severe arrhythmia, and we think there's still some internal bleeding. She might have to go back to surgery. It's still touch and go. I wish I had better news."

Very reluctantly, Rachel entered Caitria's room. She stared at her unconscious friend—although she had no idea how that *friendship* thing had happened. Caitria was lying there, completely still, with tubes running in her, and monitors humming and beeping. She looked awful.

There was death here, its black aura snaking through the room. It closed in on Rachel, and she couldn't stay there any longer. Couldn't watch Caitria die. She stumbled out, went down to the main lobby, intending to leave. But she couldn't do that either. She just couldn't totally desert Caitria. Freaked, she leaned against a wall, hugging her arms around herself.

Out of the blue, a memory rolled through her—that of family members taking turns to sit with her terminally ill Aunt Sophie. Jewish law and tradition demanded that someone always be at the bedside of a dying person. Yet no one had been with Rachel's family as they lay dying in Dachau.

No one had been able to sit shiva for them, either—the traditional seven days of mourning after a loved one was buried. In so many ways, Rachel felt she had let her family down, although she'd been in the throes of her own death, and rebirth as a monster.

Now she was letting Caitria down, because she couldn't bear to go back to that room, to watch another life fade away. But what could she do . . . ? *Gabe.* They needed Gabe—assuming he was still around. He might have some angel magic that could help Caitria. Rachel fumbled in her purse for his cell phone number. She found a pay phone and dialed with trembling fingers.

While a part of her anticipated hearing his voice, another part of her cringed at the thought of talking to him, after the way they'd parted. She got voice mail and almost disconnected. Hearing just a recording of his voice shook her more than she'd thought it would.

She marshaled her senses and said, "Gabe, this is Rachel. Caitria was beat up so badly by Danyon that she might . . ." She paused, drew a deep breath. "She's in ICU at Parkland. If there's anything you can do for her, please, *please* come. I— I guess that's it." She hung up, feeling totally lost.

Still unable to return to Caitria, but not able to leave, she roamed the hospital aimlessly, pausing when she saw a small chapel. She stared at the rose-glass panes in the door, feeling the tug of a long-forgotten lure, a call to worship: *Sh'ma Yisrael . . . Hear O Israel . . .* The ancient Jewish prayer echoed in her head.

Somehow, she found herself opening the door to the chapel. She took a small step inside, hesitated, wondering if she'd be disintegrated or struck by lightning. But nothing happened. She took another cautious step forward. The chapel was empty and quiet, with an air of holiness she hadn't felt in decades.

She walked tentatively to a bench. Well, she was still intact. She sank down, and the calm washed over her. More of the ancient prayer came to her: *And these words that I command you today shall be in your heart.*

She guessed she still had a heart, because of the pain beating inside her. She pulled her feet to the bench, resting her head against her knees. Then she did something she hadn't done since Dachau—she prayed. *Dear Go—Dear You. Please heal Caitria. Then help her leave that son of a bitch—oh, sorry for the profanity.*

She was quiet for a moment, before giving in to the urge to add, *And please, take away this pain inside me. I'm so tired of hurting . . . Amen.* She thought about what Gabe had said, and added, *Or maybe that's Awoman.* Who knew anymore?

A sense of utter peace flowed through her, and she stayed there a long time, resting both body and spirit. She might have even dozed. A stirring of the air pulled her from her drifting state. The bench shifting jolted her fully alert. She looked over, and there he was.

"I got your message," Gabe said.

Chapter 7

SHE drank in the sight of him, familiar and handsome in his brown leather jacket and khakis. She shouldn't have been so glad to see him, but she was.

"How's Caitria?" he asked. His voice was cool and impersonal, as if they were very casual acquaintances.

Rachel pushed away the regret and sense of loss. "Bad. She might not make it."

"And you're here instead of with her." His eyes were as cool as his voice.

Guilt speared her. "ICU visiting hours are over. And she's not even conscious."

"Do you care for her, Rachel?"

She nodded, too tired to fight it anymore. She finally admitted the truth to herself—she considered Caitria a friend.

"Then it's time to stop thinking only of yourself. Caitria needs you." Gabe rose from the bench. "Come on." He didn't offer his hand or take her arm, nor did he slow his steps for her.

They rode the elevator up in distant silence. Then Gabe strode to the ICU doors, supposedly locked at this hour, but they swung open at his approach. The hospital personnel didn't spare them a glance as he led the way to Caitria's room, without any direction from Rachel.

Caitria looked the same, unconscious, battered, and death-shrouded. Gabe moved to the bedside. He looked down at her, and his eyes lost their coolness, transforming to a deep, glowing blue. He placed his hand on her forehead. Light flared around him, so bright, Rachel had to squint against it.

"Caitria Shanice Washington," he said softly. "Someone is here to speak with you." He shifted his hand over her heart, and the light grew brighter. "Listen. *Listen*, Caitria Shanice."

Was it Rachel's imagination, or did her friend stir slightly? Gabe stepped back, his gaze pinning Rachel. "All right. Talk to her."

Shock barreled through Rachel. "*Me?* What can I say to her?"

"Tell her you're here. That you care. That she has more to live for than a life of prostitution and an abusive man." Gabe's gaze softened. "Speak from your heart."

Oh, man. Said heart was pounding so loudly, Rachel could hardly think. Wiping her damp palms on her jeans, she moved slowly to the side of the bed. Cleared her throat. "Caitria." She stopped, overwhelmed by the responsibility Gabe had just thrust on her. She understood instinctively that he had done as much as he could—or would—and the rest was up to her.

She drew a deep breath, focused on Caitria. "Hey, bitch. What the hell are you doing in that bed?" She stared at her friend's slack, bruised face. "You need to stop lying around on your fat black ass. There are people who need you. Your kids, your momma—" She cleared her throat again. "And me. I'm going to be really pissed if you don't get well and get out of this bed."

She paused, feeling her throat tighten. "You have a lot to live for, Caitria. You don't need that man, and you don't need to keep whoring. You're a smart lady. There are a lot of things you can do. You have all kinds of choices."

She felt a curious shifting inside, a flash of insight telling her she wasn't just talking about Caitria anymore, but also herself. "You can have a good life. But you have to choose to live." She realized there were tears on her face. She sensed Gabe moving behind her, felt the strength of his presence.

She swiped furiously at the tears. "Come on, Caitria, *damn it*, fight! Fight for your kids and for a better life. And if you— If you die on me, I'm going to kick your fat ass from here to Oklahoma. You got that?"

There was the slightest sigh, and then Caitria groaned. Her eyes opened slightly. "That you, li'l . . . bitch?"

Rachel felt her heart soar. "Damn right it's me."

"Where . . . am . . . I?"

"You're at Parkland." Rachel wiped away more tears. "You're a little punked out right now. But something tells me you'll be giving the doctors hell in a day or two."

"Sure . . ." Caitria's eyes drifted shut. "So long as they good lookin' and have big bangers."

———

Gabe and Rachel rode the elevator to the main level in silence. She hated the chasm between them, but she didn't know what to do about it. They stepped off the elevator, and he faced her. "Caitria's going to be all right. You said the right things, and she responded to you." His voice was cool, distant.

She felt a huge rush of relief that Caitria would pull through. "Thank you for coming and helping her."

"I merely raised her consciousness level so she could hear you. You're the one who persuaded her to remain Earthbound."

"I guess." But Rachel wasn't convinced. She stared at Gabe, wishing things could be different between them.

"Well." He took a step back. "Good-bye, Rachel. Have a good life." He turned and walked away. That was it.

She felt her heart twist, felt the familiar wrench of pain. Only, this wasn't the old pain. This was here-and-now pain of foolishly allowing herself to care for someone again. Of losing them. "Wait!" she called out. "Gabriel, wait."

He stopped and turned. She walked to him, stood there, uncertain what to say. "Are you still mad at me?"

He sighed. "I'm not mad at you, Rachel. Maybe a little frustrated—make that a whole lot frustrated. I care for you, more than you can know. But I can't help you any further, not until you choose to move forward. And the first step is being honest with yourself, and with others."

She accepted the truth of his words. Willed herself to take the first step. "I don't want you to go."

His gaze pierced through her. "What do you want?"

The second step was a little easier. "I want to go back to spending time with you."

"That's not possible." Her heart sank, but then he added, "Without total truth between us."

Relief slid through her. She knew honesty would be painful on many levels. It would involve intimacy and caring for someone, and those things still terrified her. But she also knew nothing came without a price. She didn't want to return to the darkness. So, taking a deep breath, she reached for the light.

"I'm ready to move forward. I want to be with you." Another deep breath, and then she let it tumble out. "I want you to show me what it should be like between a man and a woman."

She heard his sharp intake of breath, sensed his blood pulsing faster. But his voice was steady as he said, "Be very sure, Rachel. This is not a game. If you commit to this, there will be no turning back."

"I'm sure." She looked up at him, trying to ignore the fact her heart wanted to burst through her chest. "Very sure."

The warmth returned to his eyes, along with a dazzling display of tiny stars that took her breath away. "Good," he said, stepping forward. "That's *very* good." He kissed her, right there in the middle of Parkland Hospital.

They were at Gabe's apartment, in his bedroom, although Rachel barely remembered the blurred trip there. All she could think right now was that the man—or angel—certainly knew how to kiss. She thrilled at the way he cradled her head, his fingers tunneling through her hair, as he explored her mouth with slow, tantalizing strokes of his tongue.

He released her and stepped back. "No second thoughts?"

She was still afraid—terrified, actually—but not of him. Plus the thought of the alternative—the empty barren existence she'd known before he'd come into her life—was unbearable. He'd given her the desire to reach for something more.

"No." She took his hand and placed it on her breast, tried to ignore her racing heart, which hadn't slowed since Parkland. "I want to experience life."

"Thank heaven for that." He ran a finger down the slope of her breast, teasing the nipple through the sweater. "Undress for me," he said in a black-magic voice.

She sensed he was pushing her, testing the strength of her resolve. He wasn't going to allow her to be a passive participant. With shaking hands, she pulled her sweater over her head and tossed it to the floor.

His heated gaze swept her upper torso, and he gestured to her jeans. "Those next." His husky voice sent shivers through her. She unzipped the jeans, letting them slip down her legs, and stepped out of them.

"So beautiful," he said. Moving against her, he reached behind her and unhooked her bra. His hands slid underneath it, covered her breasts. The breath hissed from her lungs. "Like that, do you?" he murmured, his thumbs rubbing her nipples.

"Oh, yes." She closed her eyes and reached for him, finding his sweater instead of the skin she wanted. She tugged at the cashmere. "Your turn. Take this off."

He obliged, stripping down to black silk boxers, and her breath caught. He was stunning, golden skinned and beautifully muscled, like paintings of Adonis she'd seen years ago at the Alte Pinakotheka, in Munich.

He pulled her down on the bed, and into a sensual realm of thorough kisses and tactile exploration. The rest of their clothing managed to disappear, and flesh branded flesh.

It wasn't just the slide of his skillful hands over her body that melted her. It was the way he looked at her, the tenderness and caring in his eyes, and the way he touched her, as if she were a priceless treasure. She felt cherished, loved, maybe even deserving of those things.

In turn, she savored the feel of his body beneath her hands, the artistry of his physique. It was difficult for her to express her feelings, so she tried to show him instead. Coherent thought fled when he kissed his way down her breast and took her nipple in his mouth. She moaned, arching against him.

But she tensed when his hand swept down her abdomen and teased the dark curls there. He raised his head and looked at her. "What is it?"

She didn't want to remember the brutality of the Nazi soldiers, or for the ugliness to come between her and Gabe. Yet there was the issue of honesty. "I'm not right down there. I tore when they . . ." She closed her eyes against the memory. "I'd probably have bled to death if I hadn't been turned. I never healed properly."

"You're beautiful just the way you are," he said softly, "but we're going to ensure you can have a normal life."

His hand moved between her legs and stroked the tender flesh. She'd barely registered that incredible sensation, when he slipped a finger inside her. A heated tingling vibrated through her entire abdomen. "Gabe," she gasped.

"Shhhh. Just go with it, Rach." He slid down her body, as his finger continued stroking in and out. Then he lowered his head and licked her, and she almost came off the bed. "Gabe!" He splayed his free hand across her abdomen and held her still as he continued the sensual torment.

Her lower body was on fire, but pleasure overrode the pain, sweeping her along in a fast-moving current that shot her into an explosion of light and sensation. "Oh, oh . . . Gabe!" she screamed, flashing to the stars and back—only it was far more potent than when she drank blood. And it seemed to go on and on.

When she finally settled, and coherent thought started staggering back, Gabe moved up and took her in his arms. "You're perfect down there now," he whispered, his lips against hers.

"But, how—"

"What do you think?" He arched his brows at her. "I *am* an angel in my other incarnation." He rolled to his back, pulling her on top of him. "Now it's my turn to be all better."

He probed upward between her legs, lowering her slowly until he was deep inside her. Then he stilled, raised his hand to cup her face. "Are you okay with this?"

Taking a deep breath, she stared into his eyes, into an infinite universe of warmth and light and stars. *This was Gabe—not a Nazi soldier.* "I'm . . . good," she said, surprised to find it was the truth. She felt safe, and an incredible sense of freedom. She couldn't resist pressing her knees to the mattress and sliding upward, and found the friction sinfully pleasurable.

"Sweetheart, you are way beyond good." He groaned as she slid back down him. "Do that again."

She discovered how wonderful it felt to have him inside her as she moved, made headier by being in control, and by the power to render him at her mercy. She kept moving, caught up in his hoarse words of encouragement, urged on by his hands roaming over her. Then she was seized by a need so fierce, so intense, her body instinctively took over the rhythm, moving on its own accord, knowing exactly what to do.

"Yes, that's it," Gabe groaned. "Oh, yes. God . . . *yes!*"

And they both flashed to the stars and back.

Rachel lay in Gabe's arms, drowsy and pleasantly sore. Her body still hummed from the incredible sensations of two orgasms. She'd have gone for more, but he'd been firm in his insistence that she needed time to recover. "You're new at this," he said. "Your body has to get used to it."

"Oh, please. I've been a prostitute for over sixty-five years."

He smacked her bare butt. "Don't give me that crap."

"Ouch!" Rubbing her abused posterior, she glared at him. "I thought angels weren't supposed to mistreat their charges."

"Oh, well, then, let me kiss it and make it better." Laughing, he did just that, and then drew her into his arms with an angelic smile. "Now be good."

"That's your job." She sighed and snuggled against him. But soon, her acute awareness of his heartbeat and the blood rushing through his veins stirred a voracious hunger. She hadn't fed tonight; needed to take care of that before she lost control.

She rolled over and sat up. "I've got to go."

"Why?" He stroked her bare back.

"I have to feed. I haven't had any blood since last night."

"You can take my blood."

She glanced back and saw he was completely serious. "That's not a good idea." She got up and started gathering her clothes.

"Why not?"

"I don't feed from people I know."

"But why not?"

She gestured helplessly, struggling to put it into words. "I want to keep that part of my life separate."

Gabe stood and took her arm, halting her attempt to put on her jeans. "What are you keeping it separate from?"

She thought of the dark depravity of having to drink blood—which was forbidden in the Torah. Somehow, the only way she could do it was if she took it from strangers, and gave them something in return. "It's bad enough I'm a monster," she said. "Why would I want to expose anyone I know to it?"

"Because maybe it's part of who you are?"

There he went, getting philosophical again. She pulled away. "I have to go."

"No, you don't. I said you could take my blood."

"And I said I don't want to do that."

"There's nothing wrong with you drinking my blood, Rachel."

Her hunger was beating at her, fraying her nerves. She whirled on him. "Damn it, Gabe! I don't want your blood. I don't want you tainted by what I am."

His eyes narrowed. "First off, you're not tainted, and you're not a monster. Secondly, it would be nice if you would trust me for once."

"I do trust you," she said, frustrated.

"No, you don't. You've resisted me at every turn. Every victory with you has only been after a major battle."

"*Damn it!* What do you want from me?"

His eyes glowed, and the light around him brightened. "I want you to believe in me. And in so doing, accept that She loves you and wants you to live."

Back to *Her* again. It was becoming harder and harder to think clearly, with the hunger growling. Rachel sank on the edge of the bed. "Why does everything have to be so hard with you?" she asked wearily.

Gabe sat next to her, beautifully naked. "It's not me, it's the nature of free will. Each of us has to make our own choices. The most important decisions are rarely easy."

"Tell me about it." She thought about his request, and it made her stomach clench. "I don't want to do this."

"Do you love me?"

"What?"

"You heard me. Do you love me?"

"No! I can't love you." Utter panic exploded inside her. The beloved faces of family members flashed through her mind—Mother, Father, Aaron, grandparents, aunts, uncles, cousins—all murdered at the hands of the Nazis. "I can't."

"You either do or you don't, Rachel. Just because you're afraid of something doesn't make it go away."

She dropped her face in her hands, frustrated, confused, and trying to sort out the emotions swirling through her.

"I know you care," he said. "It's all right to feel love for someone. Love is divine, and it's the pattern in which we're supposed to live our lives."

"Love hurts." Sudden tears filled her eyes, tracked down her cheeks. "I can't love you, Gabe. That will only cause more pain when you go away. I don't want to take your blood. I don't want you to remember me as a monster."

"Blood is life, Rachel. Needing it does not make you a monster." He leaned closer, his voice seductive. "Use my blood for your hunger. Give yourself to me. Give me your heart, your soul, your trust. Choose life, Rachel."

He wasn't using any compulsion, but the bloodlust careened out of control, smashing her resistance. Her fangs elongated, and the darkness stripped away the tatters of her humanity. She lunged at Gabe, knocking him onto the bed. A strangled protest escaped her throat, even as she found his jugular.

"It's okay, Rachel. It's okay," he murmured, stroking her hair. "Take life."

She sank her fangs deep and greedily gulped his blood. It was fuller, richer, far better than anything she'd ever tasted. She felt the energy rush through her body, but this was very different from the other times.

Light and heat burst through her, and then she was flying through space, passing stars at a dizzying speed. But she wasn't flashing back to Earth. Instead, she hurtled faster and faster toward a dazzling starburst up ahead—a welcoming haven of brilliant light. And, oh, she wanted to go there, more than anything she'd ever wanted. She'd never felt such warmth, such acceptance, such love. She was home. At last.

———

The light teased her eyelids, disturbing the tranquil darkness in which she drifted. She tried to ignore it, but it kept intruding, until she finally roused herself and cracked open her eyes. The light hurt. She blinked, squinting against the brightness. It was warm, as if she were lying in the sun, which wasn't possible.

"Open your eyes, Rachel."

She knew *that* voice. But she couldn't quite remember . . .

"Rachel Emma Stryker, stop ignoring me and open your eyes," the voice said, but it was tinged with humor.

"Hurts too much," she muttered.

"That's normal. It's been over sixty-five years since you've been in sunlight."

Sunlight? That brought her fully awake, and her eyes flew open. Oh, no! She was lying in the center of a large sunbeam. Why wasn't she being incinerated? She tried to scramble up, found herself pressed back against a warm masculine body.

"No worry, Rachel. You're fine."

"Gabe? Is that you?" She was alarmed and disoriented.

"Yes, it's me. Be calm." His breath warmed her hair, and she realized his arms were wrapped around her.

"I've got to get out of the sun." She struggled, but he held her still.

"No, you don't."

She must be dreaming. "What's going on? Where am I?"

"You're in my apartment. On my bed."

"Your bed?" She squinted at the uncovered window, the sunlight streaming in. "I don't understand."

"What's the last thing you remember?"

"Flying through space." She closed her eyes. "Going to the light. Talking to . . . *Her.*" She shot up. "I'm dead, aren't I?" She twisted in Gabe's arms, faced him. "Am I an angel like you?"

His eyes glowed with warmth. "Look at yourself. Do you look like an angel?"

"I'm—" She looked down. "Naked. And . . . so are you."

A smiled teased his lips. "Well, we were both sans clothing when you drank my blood."

Her memory started returning, but nothing made any sense. "I took your blood," she said slowly, stricken with guilt. "I didn't want to do that. Did I hurt you?"

He leaned forward, kissed her gently. "No, silly. You made the right choice. Nothing could have pleased me more."

"I still don't understand. Did drinking your blood make it possible for me to be in the sun?"

"Yes."

"What the hell is going on?"

He threw back his head and laughed, then hugged her against him. "Haven't figured it out yet, have you?"

She balled her hand into a fist and pounded him on the back. "Stop playing games with me!"

"Ouch! No hitting. You're still pretty strong, even for a regular human."

She growled in frustration, tired of his games. "For a *regular human*? What are you—" She froze, as the implication sank in. "What do you mean?"

He leaned away, grinning like the idiot he was. "You're now a pure, normal, garden-variety human. On second thought, after last night, maybe not so pure."

She stared at him. "You're crazy. Or maybe I've gone crazy. Or maybe I'm dead."

"Rachel, you're *not* dead. When you drank my blood, you chose life. My blood transformed you."

She still couldn't accept it. "I don't believe you."

He shrugged. "Fine. You'll find out soon enough. Let's start with the fact that you're sitting in broad daylight at high noon."

She looked at the brilliant light streaming in the window and onto her bare, unburned skin. Couldn't argue with that. Hope began to bloom, and she got up and went into the bathroom. Stared in the mirror and opened her mouth wide. Her fangs were gone! She stumbled backward, almost falling, but Gabe caught her. She whirled to face him. "I'm really human?"

He nodded. "You're really human. I'll fix bacon and eggs in a little while, and you'll be able to eat as much as you want."

"I don't eat pork," she said automatically, then it sank in, and she screamed with joy. "I'm human! I'm really, really, human!" She grabbed Gabe and kissed him, then dashed to the bedroom. "I want to go outside. Right now."

She threw on her jeans and sweater and ran for the front door. Gabe followed, dressed only in his jeans. The day was cool and crisp and clear, and the sun shone brilliantly. Reverently, Rachel lifted her face to the light, not caring that the glare hurt her eyes.

"Oh. My." She couldn't think of anything else to say. She turned to Gabe. "But, *how? Why?*"

He took her hand, tugged her down on the steps. He settled next to her, and she took a moment to admire the sleek male body and how the sun reflected off his beautiful skin.

"Angels are pretty powerful beings," he said. "We have a lot of leeway in directing events, as long as a free-will choice is made. When we come into a physical incarnation, our bodies are very strong, and our blood very potent." He smiled at her, and his aura glowed. "When you chose to drink my blood, I was able to give you the gift of being human again."

"Wow." She shook her head, still stunned. "Thank you." Her voice shook, and she felt tears threatening. "Damn," she said with a shaky laugh. "I didn't cry for sixty-five years, and then you came along, and I've been crying ever since."

"I'll take that as a compliment . . . I think."

She wiped her eyes. "So, what happens now?"

He linked his hand with hers. "You'll live a normal, hopefully healthy and lengthy, human life."

"I still can't believe it." But despite the overwhelming joy, she felt a pang that he would probably be moving on to other angelic duties. "What will you do?"

"I'm allowed to live out this physical incarnation, if I so choose. By angel standards, a human lifetime is just a blip in the universe." Watching her, he raised her hand to his lips, pressed a kiss against it. "I've discovered that I have strong feelings for a very beautiful and headstrong young woman—and a nice Jewish girl at that."

It took a moment for his words to sink in, then she jerked back in surprise. "You have strong feelings for *me*?"

He considered. "Perhaps I didn't put that right. I think saying I'm in love with you would be more accurate."

Love? She almost fell off the steps. "You can't mean that."

"There are those who claim angels can't get it up, either. I don't generally listen to them." His eyes gleaming mischievously, he tugged her into his arms. "How about it, Rach? Want to hang out with me and do good deeds here on Earth?"

She couldn't think—everything was happening way too fast. "Well, I don't—"

"Good answer." He kissed her, his tongue doing a sensual sweep of her mouth. Her blood warmed, and she leaned into him. Of its own accord, her hand slid down, discovering he was as turned on as she was. He broke off the kiss. "If you're going to be *that* way about it, then there's only one thing to do."

He swept her up in his arms and carried her inside and to the bedroom. "This calls for a celebration." He tumbled her onto the rumpled, sun-streaked sheets.

Laughing joyously, she wrapped her arms around him and pulled him down on top of her. She was human again! And Gabe wanted her. *He loved her.* She intended to show him just how much she loved him in return.

They celebrated for a very long time.

Epilogue

HOW was I supposed to know Gertie was an escape artist?" Rachel fastened her seat belt, turned her face to the light, as Gabe opened the sunroof. She hadn't gotten tired of basking in the sunshine, even after six months. "I didn't even know she was in heat. She only got out that one time."

"Once is all it takes." Gabe listened to the small, pitiful meows and scratching sounds coming from the pet crate in the backseat, as he put the car in gear. "The kittens will be well loved at the women and children's shelter. And we'll have them all fixed, as soon as they're old enough."

"They won't dare fool around with Caitria in charge there. She doesn't allow anyone to turn tricks on her watch."

Rachel grinned as she said that. Gabe knew how proud she was that Caitria and her children had not only thrived at the shelter, but that Caitria's strength of character had helped her rise to the position of assistant director of the shelter.

He reached over to stroke her hair. "Speaking of fooling around, we've done our share."

"You think?" she asked sarcastically.

He laughed. "I definitely think." He slid his hand down over her flat belly. "I also think we have a bun in the oven."

"What does that mean?"

He loved the way her brow furrowed when she was confused. "It's an expression. It means, my love, that you're pregnant."

"*What?*" She stared at him, her eyes huge. "You can't possibly know that . . . can you? How could you?"

He gave her the arched brow *I'm-an-angel-that's-how* look.

"This can't be right. I can't be pregnant!" She shook her head. "*No.* Absolutely not."

He could see the panic setting in, and he took her hand. "It's okay, Rach. It's a good thing. You'll see."

She didn't look convinced. They still needed a little work on the faith issue. "When did this happen?"

"The day we went up on the roof and made love in the rain."

"Oh, *that* day." Despite her tension, a small smile teased her lips. "Hmmm. I think I might remember that."

"*Might* remember?" he asked in outraged male indignation. "Maybe you need a refresher course."

She ignored him. "A baby? What are we going to do with a baby?" Her panic level was rising again.

"We're going to love her and teach her about free will and how important it is to make good choices."

"*Her?*" Rachel looked terrified and utterly adorable. "It's a girl?"

"Yes, it's a girl." He felt a burst of joy and excitement. "Don't worry, we'll do fine, and so will she."

Gabe could already sense the strength and purpose of the soul choosing them for parents. You never knew which way a strong soul could go. Their daughter would either raise hell or lower heaven.

Regardless, he was looking forward to it. He figured he was up to the challenge. He had firsthand experience in dealing with—and loving—a strong-willed woman.

The Demon's Angel

Emma Holly

Chapter 1

THIS evening was either going to be the best of Dr. Khira Forette's existence, or it was going to be the worst. A single stroke of Fate would determine whether years of research would be rewarded with career advancement or consigned to the dustbin.

Seeing no other possibilities, Khira smoothed the form-fitting, sky-blue silk of her business tunic and strode across the echoing gray granite hall. Because she had been summoned here after hours, the ministry lobby was empty. The sense of being dwarfed by the shadows had the effect of winding up her nerves even more.

The entry hall alone was the size of a small palace.

In the silence, the perfectly trimmed ends of her ink-black hair swished against her trousered hips. Her silver brocaded shoes had never been worn before, and the matching briefcase was the pinnacle of style this week. She was as sleek as thirty very expensive minutes with a beauty consultant could make a less-than-fashion-conscious scientist.

If only those thirty minutes could have cured her anxiety.

This was Khira's first invitation to speak to the Ministry of Genetic Science. The forest of towering columns overawed her, gold and jewels spiraling up their height in an imitation of a DNA helix. Rumor had it that the first emperor's chromosomes had been their model. If that were true, Khira would be interested to examine, and crack, the gemstones' code. The origins of her people were somewhat lost in the mist. She'd heard things about the early royals that left her curious as to how much tinkering had been done with their genes. Too much, was what graduate students whispered—but only among themselves.

Knowing she was probably being watched from a dozen spyholes, Khira thrust her curiosity and her nervousness from her mind. She couldn't afford to let either emotion stain her aura. Her fellow Yama would have no trouble reading her energy sheath, and such displays of weakness might mean the difference between approval or rejection of her project. She'd come too far and had too much at stake to let anything stop her now.

Finally, she reached the silver arch the summons had instructed her to approach.

You are more than your eccentric parents' daughter, she told herself as the small of her back threatened to break into a sweat. *You are the product of a good Yamish education and your own strong Yamish will.*

The aide who guarded the door beneath the arch offered a small but respectful bow. "Please go in, Dr. Forette. The minister awaits."

Khira swallowed. *The* minister? She'd expected an audience with an under-minister at best, or perhaps some subcommittee.

"Thank you," she said faintly, and proceeded through the door the aide held open.

An elegant conference room lay beyond, its square, gilded windows overlooking the Forbidden City's grand plaza. Outside, large sandstone buildings blushed in the setting sun, a last few streamlined aircars zipping around them toward home. Inside, twelve tiny cameras sat in place of people at a long mahogany table. Every one of the lenses was aimed toward her.

With a jolt, Khira recognized the one Yama who was there in person. Seated at the table's head, he had the appearance of a typical inner circle aristocrat: dark-haired, narrow, and very tall. His robes were crimson, with polished sapphires set into their wide green trim. These were the colors of the emperor's house. This wasn't simply the minister of genetics; this was the emperor's minister of all the sciences, the emperor's favorite brother-in-law.

Apparently, her little project had elicited more interest than she expected.

"Your highness," she gasped, since all the emperor's in-laws had royal blood. Her own family was barely *daimyo*—strictly lower upper class. Shaken, her knee hit the granite hard as she dropped into an obeisance.

"'Minister' will do for tonight," he said with perfect supercilious dryness. He waved her into the seat opposite his.

She took it as steadily as she could, glad for the length of shining wood between them. "Do you wish to hear a precis of my project, sir?"

"A brief one." He nodded at the cameras. "For our guests."

She cleared her throat and pushed her new briefcase aside. She needed nothing in it, but it created a good impression. Style mattered in business almost as much keeping one's composure. Detachment was, after all, her people's highest ideal.

"As you know," she began, willing her nerves to settle, "only about eight percent of our species' genetic material directs the production of proteins and other body processes. In the past, genetic manipulation was aimed at that active portion, to correct inborn defects and enhance desirable traits. The remaining 92 percent of our genome was, up until the last century, regarded as 'nonsense' DNA and ignored."

"But it isn't nonsense," said the minister.

"Not remotely, your . . . minister. Other researchers besides myself have established that the totality of our DNA forms an organic superconductor that facilitates both the storage and communication of complex biochemical information, on a far higher order than formerly imagined. Now that the special vibrational language that the helix speaks is beginning to be deciphered, we realize that the supposedly nonsensical material may be more powerful than all the rest.

"I believe it contains, in potentia, the codes for every shape life has taken or ever could. Moreover, once you know its operating language, DNA can be given instructions to recode itself—without the deleterious side effects associated with previous cut-and-paste splicing technology. Gene-splicing defies nature. Gene-modulation simply retunes and reshuffles it.

"What is unique about my process, which I have tested extensively through computer modeling, is its ability to isolate and activate the codes for specific traits from other species. To create true, functioning chimeras."

"Hybrids," said the minister, as politely as if he hadn't already read and—she was certain—understood her report. The emperor's brother-in-law had a reputation for brilliance. "Tell me, can you create these chimeras from any species at all?"

"Theoretically, yes." Khira drew and released a breath, calmer now that she was being questioned on topics she knew so well. "I leave the potential benefits for others to determine, but no genetic material need be removed from or added to the host. The dormant traits are simply coaxed into expression from previously unexpressed segments of the chromosomes."

The minister tapped his lips with one finger, a sign of high excitement for one of his lofty caste. Khira's heart thumped faster as he reached into the breast pocket of his crimson robe and removed a small, clear data sphere. With a deft flick of his wrist, he rolled it like a marble down the long table.

"Could you do this?" he asked as she caught it.

Khira keyed the on switch, then blinked at the hologram that appeared. The image stole her breath.

"Your highness," she said once her lungs recovered. "You do me honor, but I couldn't possibly move straight from computer models to this! The number of variables affecting higher life forms are complex. The ethical issues alone would—"

The minister cut her off coolly. "I've been following your progress for some time, professor, and you've been running those models for the last six years, with increasingly good results. Have a bit more faith in your gifts than those hidebound idiots you work for. In any case, I wasn't suggesting you use a Yamish subject. A human would do. The races are genetically similar."

His lip curled slightly in distaste at this admission.

"But why this?" she asked, too shocked to guard her speech.

The minister shrugged. "Because this will interest people who matter. You know how bored the upper circles get. You have to admit, it would make a dramatic demonstration. Funding would pour in."

"Yes, but—"

A streak of royal blue flared through the minister's upper aura, a deliberate, if subtle, warning. *The blood of emperors flows in my veins,* it said. *What flows in yours?*

Khira shut her mouth as the minister leaned forward on his elbows, the royal blue now flowering delicately down his arms. It was the most astonishing display of etheric control she'd ever seen, but the minister was a picture of effortless complacence.

"If you wish to refuse our support," he said, "you are, of course, welcome to do so. I would, however, hate to see a promising career cut short. I hardly need say that, considering your background, you are unlikely to receive a second such opportunity. From anyone."

"You have been graciousness itself," Khira said numbly, because she had to say something. The minister's point was underscored by the presence of the cameras. He could not keep her refusal private even if he wished. Anyone might be watching. The rest of the royal cabinet. The emperor himself. A squad of trained assassins. Given the whispers she'd heard concerning the fate of other scientists who'd fallen out of favor, the last option wasn't as unlikely as she might have wished. Higher placed Yama than she had "disappeared." She didn't even have tenure yet.

Completely against her will, a fat bead of fear-sweat rolled down her spine.

"I would need extra safeguards," she said hesitantly. "Technology the university labs don't have. I would hate to . . . waste any subject, no matter what the race."

"You need only draw up a list."

Khira gripped the table's edge. Infinity help her. She wouldn't willingly kill anyone. She knew what to ask for to maximize a positive result, though she scarcely dared say the words. For a researcher as questionably bred as she to make this request was an incredible presumption. Her aura was jumping with terror, big yellow jitters she couldn't hide for the life of her.

Then again, the life of her was what she was gambling with.

"Yes?" the minister prompted.

"The Mount Excelsior Royal Labs," she gasped. "They'd have everything I need."

"Ah," said the minister, a sound of sudden comprehension. He leaned back in his chair. Amusement glittered in his eyes, probably due to her fear. Khira sat back herself and attempted to regulate her jagged breathing into something less uncouth.

"You know," he said. "If you weren't so patently terrified, I'd think you were a cunning bargainer. Most researchers wait decades to get lab time at the Mount. How long would you need to conclude your experiment?"

Khira shook her head in the hope of getting her brain to work. "Three days?"

It was the shortest amount of time in which she could conceive of accomplishing the bare minimum.

The minister's amusement deepened. "You can have three weeks and a budget I hesitate to share for fear you'll faint. I'll requisition a few black guards for you as well. You'll need them to procure your subject without incident. I'm sure no one wants any diplomatic complications to arise from this."

"No," Khira agreed hoarsely. The humans were not fond of having their people abducted—at least not officially.

She stared at her hands where they pressed the table, now white as marble down to their nails. She wasn't going to be killed, or ruined, or obliged to act as a murderer in the name of science. To top it off, she was going to have three weeks in the most advanced genetic facility on the planet. With that extraordinary knowledge coursing through her trembling muscles, she couldn't think of anything to do but stand and bow.

"Thank you," she said, addressing both the minister and the cameras. "I'll do my best to fulfill your expectations."

"We anticipate nothing less," the minister assured her—which wasn't exactly comforting.

Chapter 2

FOR a Yama, to descend into the Victorian capital of Avvar was akin to traveling back in time. Millennia had passed since Yamish-kind had been so primitive, and Khira sincerely doubted they'd ever been as dirty as humans.

The carriage in which she rode through the twisting, fog-shrouded streets was, thankfully, a Yamish vehicle masquerading as a human electric car. Though many humans still used horses for transportation, they had developed these contraptions in the last few years by repurposing Yamish technologies they'd obtained in the Avvar Accord.

Two generations had passed since that famous treaty, signed after humans stumbled upon the hidden cities of the Yama, thus ending her people's long and splendid isolation. Understandably, the Yama wanted nothing to do with their ridiculously emotional "discoverers," but the emperor made the best of a bad situation, ceding old technology to the humans in return for them allowing Yamish deportees to settle in Avvar's slums.

This was an improvement over letting Yamish rebels infect the general populace with their antihierarchical ideas. Additionally, helping Queen Victoria reign supreme over her neighbors ensured that human wars wouldn't spill into Yamish lands. The less the races interacted, the better for everyone.

Happily, Khira's faux electric carriage was in no danger of breaking down. It plowed through the mud and dung with no worse effect than the seeping of the stench inside the glass windows.

The air that carried the stench was frigid. For the first time, Khira felt sorry for the banished members of the lower class. The *rohn* didn't have it easy living here.

Her companions, the two black guards the minister had promised her, were dressed like *rohn* in plain gray robes and trousers—upper class *daimyo* being rare enough visitors to attract attention. The guards appeared at ease among the squalor of streets so narrow every turn put them at risk of scraping the walls. One guard operated the vehicle while the other sat beside her in back, but whether to protect or control her was hard to say. Neither guard had welcomed her insistence on accompanying them.

"You know what I need?" Khira repeated for the second time.

"Yes," said the guard who sat beside her, his awareness of the insult revealed by the subtle gustiness of his voice. "Adult male. Twenty-five to thirty. Healthy. Poor. No social ties."

"And you realize a healthy human will not be as vigorous as a healthy Yama?"

"Yes," said the driver. "Trust us, Dr. Forette. We have experience with these people. And we've done this sort of thing before."

Khira didn't apologize for asking. It was too important to be sure. The Blacks were an elite military regiment, answering directly to the emperor. Only the smartest, strongest, most loyal and ruthless Yama could hope to enter their ranks. The two who had been assigned to her seemed true to form—too true. Their blandly handsome faces were such mirrors of one another, she was certain they had been cloned from some previous assassin extraordinaire. Though she understood the desire for consistency among the royal guard, the geneticist in her was offended. Cloning was hardly the way to safeguard biodiversity.

Besides which, these two gave her the chills.

"This should do," said the driver, wrenching the wheel so hard the car bumped onto the pavement.

Khira flinched as a mud-coated dog yelped and ran away, but she gritted her teeth and said nothing. She was smart enough to know she was only as in charge as the emperor's guards let her be. Peering out through the noisome fog—the product of shortsighted humans continuing to burn coal in their factories—she saw they had pulled into a rubbish-strewn alley near a public house. Its sign rather grandiosely proclaimed it THE KING'S ARMS, though the area clearly had not seen any sort of king in centuries—having sunk from simply poor to demoralized. It was a good choice on her guards' part. The inhabitants of this place weren't likely to be missed. Gas lamps flickered gold behind the pub's greasy windows, luring a damp and hunched clientele inside.

Bundled as they were, it was hard to tell, but none looked like what she would have called healthy.

"Bother," she said. "I'm going to have to go in."

The guards exchanged a glance. "All right," said one. "But make it quick. You're not dressed for this."

"Five minutes," she promised. "If I don't see what I need by then, we'll go."

———

Harry Wirth, a.k.a. the King of the Costermongers, stared into the dregs of his beer and sighed. He propped his elbows on the end of The King's Arms bar, shoulder-to-shoulder with his fellow drinking men.

In truth, he had no reason to sigh. He'd completed the purchase of a house today, a three-story marble-front near Queen's Park. Just last week, he'd added another dozen carts to his fleet. It had been years since he'd gone hungry for any reason besides being too busy with work. His accountant's pretty daughter had let it be known she wouldn't mind walking out with him, and he suspected she'd marry him as well, if he asked.

He had everything he'd dreamed of as a half-starved workhouse boy. Every comfort. Every security. Every sign of respect he'd known how to want.

And what did he do to celebrate but jam his workman's cap on his head and shuffle back to his old, bad haunts.

He felt so empty he could have cried.

Instead, he signaled the barkeep for another pint.

It was too damn bad if he wasn't happy. He had what he'd always wanted, and that's what mattered. Tomorrow, he'd be back to business and forget the gaping hole that was growing inside his heart, forget he didn't love his accountant's daughter, forget he worked so hard he ended every night as tired as a dockworker. Most of all, he'd forget he didn't have a single friend to slap him on the back for his accomplishments. He was the boss. He was the *king*. That would damn well have to be enough.

"Hoo," said Old Dick the barman as he set the frothing mug in front of Harry. "Would ye look at that? We got some hoity-toity demons come slummin'."

Harry followed the old man's rheumy gaze and lost his breath in shock.

He didn't think the rest of the crowd had spotted her, but the most beautiful woman Harry had ever seen had just stepped inside the pub. He knew she had to be a Yama; her features were too perfect to be human, too delicate. Her skin was so pale and smooth she glowed, and her straight, satiny hair shone black as night. She was tall and slim, her figure wrapped in a floor-length, dove-gray mink. Harry's groin began to tighten in spite of knowing what she was.

Right then, she looked more angel than demon to him.

He watched her, too mesmerized to turn away. The hands that held her coat together wore long white kidskin gloves, probably to prevent her from accidentally touching any humans and being tainted by their energy. Her gaze scanned the crowd, her profile exquisite. He couldn't imagine she hoped to find anyone she knew here. Clearly, she hailed from her people's upper ranks, and The King's Arms—warm and bright though it was—wasn't clean enough for the lower ones. Yama of every class were fussy about such things, as Harry had cause to know.

The woman said something to one of the two male Yama beside her—servants, to judge by their dress. One servant shook his head and pointed in Harry's direction. Tension coiled in Harry's chest. He knew the woman was going to look at him . . . and then she did.

Her face was absolutely serene, a pool of lovely stillness nothing had—or could—ever ruffle. Her lips were red and pouting, her brows and lashes dark as coal against her alabaster skin. She blinked at him, and even though her eyes were the alien, rim-to-rim silver of all her kind, they jolted through him the same as if she were human.

He couldn't stop his reaction, no matter what his accountant's daughter might expect of him. His cock pushed against his woolen trousers in a slow, hard rise. Obeying instincts older than time, he straightened up from the bar and put his shoulders back. Her gaze slid down him and up again. Part of him knew he was displaying himself to her, was offering himself by means more primitive than words. *I'm good enough for you,* his pose was saying. *See how tall I am. See how strong. You want to go slumming? Give me a try.*

He removed his worn workman's cap and set it on the bar. Still she didn't look away. From the soles of his feet to his prickling scalp, his body pounded with desire. He'd never wanted a woman with this immediacy and force. He hadn't known he could.

The female demon's lips parted.

Now, he thought, his mind beyond logic. *Come to me.*

She blinked at him again, those thick black lashes sweeping over her inscrutable silver eyes.

Then, to his amazement—though, indeed, he shouldn't have been amazed—she turned to her male companions and gestured them ahead of her out the door.

"What now?" Khira asked her guards, doing her best to conceal the sense of off-balance oddness ticking in her breast.

The one who drove opened the motorcar's back door, holding it politely ajar for her. "Now we wait until he comes out."

Khira lifted her coat hem above the mud and stepped inside, her entrance followed closely by the second guard. Her shoes were ruined, but she hardly cared. She kept seeing the man . . . the *human* staring back at her.

He'd been so rough-looking—hypermasculine almost, with thick, shaggy light-brown hair and shoulders every bit as broad as those of her genetically tweaked guards. His harshly sculpted face had borne the shadow of a beard, a coarseness no Yamish male would have permitted. Within his baggy clothes, he was tall and strongly built. His strange human eyes were green beneath his heavy brows—like copper burning in a flame.

His expression when he met her gaze had been openly challenging. She shivered as she recalled it. She didn't think she'd want to approach this particular human alone.

Hidden by the weight of her cultured mink, her thighs hummed at the memory, as if his air of danger had actually aroused her. Khira shifted uncomfortably. If that were true, it wouldn't do at all. He was a subject, she a scientist. Desire had no place whatsoever in that relationship.

"Are you certain you can get him?" she asked the guard who'd remained on watch outside. "He looked strong."

"He's a human," the guard dismissed. "He'll never have a chance to fight. And if he did by chance resist, no one would notice in this weather."

The guard was right. The fog had thickened until she couldn't see the front of the motorcar. The few electric streetlights that hadn't been broken out by stones were mere confusion, their illumination petering out before it reached the ground. It was fortunate the car was equipped with global positioning scanners. They'd need them to navigate through this.

"Good," she said. "I want this acquisition to go smoothly."

Despite the firmness of her voice, something deep inside her didn't feel good at all.

———

Harry had never been one for overindulgence. He hated the idea of losing control and shaming himself. With the abrupt departure of the Yamish female—a cut direct if ever he'd seen one—the potential charms of sinking into a drunken stupor evaporated completely.

He was no Casanova, and he'd been turned down on occasion, but never so summarily.

Leaving his second pint untouched, Harry paid Old Dick, put on his cap, and shouldered mirthlessly from the Arms.

Maybe the walk to his new house would relax him enough to sleep. Maybe he'd forget he ever saw the beautiful demon.

He grimaced as the dank November air slapped his face. The fog, or "Grims," as Avvarians liked to call it, had been bad this week. The city's center smelled like the pit of hell, sulphur and sewage and who knew what else. Grateful for the barrier of his scarf, Harry pulled his coat collar up as well, but the chill wasn't all bad news. Cold weather meant good business in hot pies. As long as his employees could bear it, profits would be up.

He stepped off the pavement to cross the nearest alley, braced for the gritty, icy squelch of mud that swamped the cobbles underneath. His boots were up for the challenge—thick-soled army issue with stiff leather. The Grims swirled around his ankles like a hungry cat. He was lucky he knew this city like the back of his hand. Otherwise, he'd never find his way home.

"Hallo!" called a cultured male voice. "I say, could you help? I'm frightfully sorry to bother you, but we're lost."

Harry stopped and turned, waiting for the shadow the voice belonged to to come out of the alley.

"Thank you," said the as-yet-indistinguishable figure. "What with the fog, we've gotten turned a—"

Without warning, someone stepped directly behind Harry, too close for the proximity to be a casual mistake. An arm began to swing around Harry's neck. Almost before he realized he was being robbed, instincts from a hundred half-remembered street fights came to the fore. Twisting free of the choke hold, Harry stomped a foot that suddenly found itself in the wrong place.

The owner of the foot cursed as Harry followed up with a sharp backward jab of his elbow. He got ribs from the feel of it, and a satisfying rush of lost air, but then the first man stepped forward to join in.

"Want a fight then?" Harry said with an old, fierce joy, more than ready to roughhouse tonight. The man came closer. He was tall and moved like he was used to fighting himself. Harry didn't care. The instant the man took hold of Harry's collar, Harry put every ounce of his strength into ramming his thigh upward. Pretty as a picture, his kneecap connected with his attacker's groin, doubling him forward toward Harry's chest.

"Dose him," wheezed the sufferer to his partner. "Now!"

The other man had been gripping Harry by the arms, no doubt hoping to immobilize him. When he let one arm go, Harry cocked his fist and drew it back, fully expecting to be delivering a knockout blow to the man in front.

But Harry never got the chance to uncoil his punch. Something pierced his buttock with a quick, sharp pain, and every muscle he had instantaneously turned to water.

"Wha—" he slurred as the man in front snapped at the one in back to catch him.

"If he falls, we'll have that swill all over the car!"

Harry was duly caught, and lifted, and carried dangling like a drowned man over his attacker's shoulder. They were going into the alley. A black electric car resolved from the mist. Some automatic part of Harry's brain noted that it was a Falkham. A streetlamp glinted off the trademark winged Victory on the hood.

"Hey," he tried to protest as he was heaved into the dark back-seat, but all that came out was "h-h."

His heart began to pound too fast, fear coming over him all at once. This wasn't a robbery. He'd been drugged. He could feel his body; he could move his eyes and breathe, and that was it. A peculiar, quivering heat blossomed in his core, possibly from panic. He was as helpless to save himself as a kitten in a sack.

The Falkham's door was shoved shut behind him, its barrier pushing up his shoulders and head. When it closed, the metal made a sound he wasn't used to, a solid, resonant thump. Whatever this car was made of, it wasn't the usual tin.

Then a light sprang into being on the car's ceiling.

Harry's heart nearly stopped with shock. The demon woman sat before him. His feet almost touched her mink-covered knees. She was even more beautiful close up. On seeing him, the only change in her calm, smooth face was a widening of her silver eyes.

The men who'd attacked him must have been her *rohn* servants.

At the realization, something broke inside him, something he hadn't known was whole anymore. *She* had ordered those men to hurt him? *She* was responsible?

If she'd wanted to meet him, all she'd had to do was ask.

The two men slid into the front of the car from either side. The glimpse Harry got from the position his head was stuck in informed him they might be twins. Without a word, the driver revved the engine. Its powerful, quiet purr was as strange as the thunk of the door had been. The men must have been waiting for some sign, because the car remained where it was.

The woman leaned toward them, one gloved hand bracing on the back of their leather seat. "I thought you were only going to subdue him."

The driver twisted around to smirk at Harry. "He looks subdued to me."

Harry didn't know if it was the words that stunned the woman, or the singular sight of a Yama smirking, but she fell back. Her hands fisted in her fur as if she were trying to hide how angry she was. "What did you give him?" she asked levelly.

"Narcophane with a kicker," supplied the driver.

The woman cursed in her own language, which was when Harry realized they'd been speaking flawless Ohramese until then. Their accents were indistinguishable from any of his better-schooled countrymen. He wondered if they were so fluent in either tongue that they didn't care what they spoke. Worse, maybe they thought him too feeble for it to matter if he understood.

As if to confirm this, once she'd recovered from her temper's lapse, the woman continued in Ohramese. "You gave him a kicker? You know humans don't react to drugs like we do."

"Relax, Dr. Forette," soothed the man who wasn't driving. "We halved the dose. You'll be glad for it if we're stopped. He won't be wanting to escape even if he does get a chance."

The claim made no sense to Harry. He knew he'd fight like the devil to get away from them.

The woman's . . . the *doctor's* pouty lips had thinned. Her eyes turned back to him, running up and down. She didn't seem worried so much as taking inventory of his condition, but her gaze had a more personal effect. The quivery heat that had been forming a ball in his gut abruptly exploded, wave after wave of brandied warmth spreading through his limbs. His sex began to harden the same as if she'd rubbed it. He didn't think it was going to stop hardening, either. With every pump of his heart, his shaft surged longer.

Somehow she knew it. Her gaze fell and fastened on his groin. The way her servants had left him sprawled, he couldn't hide what was happening. Harry was no featherweight, and he was already big enough to show a hump. Her expression didn't change as she took this in, but a tinge of pink crept up her cheeks. To his dismay, that reaction was arousing, too.

"You can't sit like that," she said as if it were his fault. "You'll be on the floor the first time we turn."

With the strength for which her kind was famed, she pulled him upward to sit properly on the seat, swinging his legs around and placing his boots on the floor. Though he couldn't move, he felt everything. Every touch increased the lust thumping through his body, every whisper of her unbound hair. He was gasping from sexual overexcitement as his torso, unsupported by his muscles, began to slide toward the door.

Cursing softly, the demon hauled him back to her side. His head fell to her shoulder. The cool mink felt like heaven against his cheek, each strand a separate stroke of ecstasy along his nerves. He experienced an insane wish that he could strip naked and rub every inch of his pulsing body over that sleek, smooth fur—especially with her in it. Longing stabbed through him. He needed to be touched so badly, his vocal chords let out a mournful moan.

"GPS says our route is clear," the driver announced, which seemed to mean he was free to put the motorcar into gear. "We'll be at Paddington in ten minutes."

The wheels bumping down the curb jostled Harry closer to his captor. Her coat fell open to bare the curves of her bosom, each perfect, peach-sized breast snuggled into pale-yellow silk. She wore no corset beneath her Yamish outfit, and her nipples were swollen and slightly peaked. Had the cold done that, or was she excited? Either way, Harry's cock throbbed violently in his trousers. He discovered he could swallow—but only in time to moan again.

"Hurry," said the doctor, reaching briskly up to extinguish the ceiling light. "I think that 'kicker' is kicking in a bit faster than you expected!"

Chapter 3

A "kicker" was Yamish slang for a pharmaceutical aphrodisiac. The drugs came in different types, but the one Khira's guards had administered to the human obviously increased his sensitivity to and craving for oxytocin—a natural endorphin humans and Yama produced when they were touched. Add an arousal enhancer, and it was no wonder the human was feverish with desire.

Considering that the guards had also paralyzed most of his muscles, rendering it impossible for him to do anything about that desire, Khira concluded they had an inborn cruel streak—no doubt part of the reason the emperor had gone to the trouble of cloning them.

She tried stroking the human's cheek to calm him, but that simply made him break into a sweat.

"Paddington Station!" her driver announced, with an indecent ring of cheer. "Time to get this package stowed."

She and the other guard hefted the shaking human between them, dragging him along as if he were drunk. They left the ersatz motorcar on the street for some other agent to collect. Prohibited technology couldn't sit around. As quickly as they could with their boneless burden, they headed not for the station's main entrance, but through a long, weedy lot toward a dark siding. The atmosphere was clearer here, and their breath puffed white in the wintry air, the human's coming quick and short with his arousal. Khira fought not to swear. Right then, she was wishing she'd accepted anyone's "help" but these men's.

"Here's the carriage," said the driver, leaping up the stairs first. "We'll get him settled, and then I'll tell the engineer you're ready to hook up."

This time "carriage" meant a private railway car—though Khira saw as soon as she climbed in that it was another Yamish vehicle disguised as human. For that, she was grateful. At least they'd be traveling with a real bathroom and real heat. The furnishings looked comfortable, composed of a sitting compartment, a two-bunk sleeper, and the blessed W.C.

Polished brass gleamed on the fittings, a complement to the leather and the small Yamish-style smokeless fireplace. On the semicircular windows, parchment shades were pulled down. Khira was impressed. Whatever else the science minister intended for her future, he wasn't sending her second class.

The guards laid her acquisition on a tufted brown-velvet couch, showed her where to find supplies, and prepared to go.

"You're leaving?" she said, suddenly not so eager to have them gone.

"We're riding in the public cars," they explained, eerily in tandem. One of them smiled faintly and finished speaking for both. "In case we need to head off questions. Don't worry," he added, an outright insult, "we'll lock you in."

Lovely, she thought, meaning the opposite. A disturbing heat shimmied up her thighs. She and the sex-crazed human would be alone.

———

Khira stayed away from the human as long as her conscience allowed—though she did turn on the fire, pull off his boots, and tuck a pillow beneath his head. She knew he didn't need the blanket that draped the couch's back. Though shivers wracked his body, they weren't from the cold. The hump of his erection proclaimed how warm he was, tenting his loose wool trousers like a mute hammer to her guilt.

"It wasn't my choice," she whispered to the paneled walls in the sleeper where she was hiding, too restless to sit. "Of my own will, I wouldn't have done this to you."

Her will didn't matter. He was suffering, at least indirectly, because of her, helpless to ease himself in any way. Human or not, it wasn't fair to leave him like that.

She was allowing herself the indulgence of biting her knuckle, when she heard the clunk and rattle of their carriage being coupled onto the train. The car began to move, gradually picking up speed along the tracks. The rattling motion sent vibrations from her heels to her groin, obliging her to acknowledge that more was happening to her body than guilt or nerves. She was hot inside, pulsing and wet. Even as she admitted it, a rush of warm, creamy moisture slipped from her sex.

A second later, a moan trailed to her from the sitting room. It was the human. If she was bothered by these vibrations, how much more must they be torturing him?

She really couldn't put off going to him.

He watched her as she entered the sitting room, his eyes pleading silently. Too confused and miserable to glare, he didn't look dangerous now. He was shuddering, his erection even more pronounced than before. Her body tightened. If she didn't help him soon, she feared he'd go into convulsions.

Squaring her shoulders, she pulled on her long kid gloves. One of the many reasons humans were best avoided was the ease with which human etheric energy transferred to the Yama during skin-to-skin contact. This energy was a drug to Khira's people, better than coffee or chocolate or wine. Unfortunately, it also carried the taint of human emotion. Yama—especially the lower classes—might enjoy the invigorating effects of etheric force, but human emotions were perilous. Those Yama who weren't appropriately disgusted were susceptible to addiction, and a Yama who gave way to emotion might as well consign herself to banishment at once. Such a person would not be fit to live or work with. Khira had enough against her without risking that.

Prepared now, she crossed the room and stopped at his side. "It is all right," she said, bending to undo his waistcoat. "I'll make you feel better soon."

The moan that issued from him was surely trying to be words.

"I must remove *all* your clothes," she said. "Considering the state you're in, a simple hand manipulation isn't going to do. You need full body stimulation."

His strange green eyes went round, but of course he couldn't protest even if he wished. He panted as she propped him up to pull off his smock-like shirt. His chest was hairier than she was used to, and more heavily muscled. Beads stuck out from the center of his rosy nipples, as thick around as her smallest finger. The sight shouldn't have aroused her; it was too different, too obvious. Nonetheless, her sex closed hungrily on itself.

"I'll . . . open your trousers now," she said, carefully laying him back.

His erection pushed so forcefully against the wool that the fastenings were difficult to undo. He grunted as she finally freed them, and the full, hard length of him sprang up.

Having studied comparative physiology, Khira knew genital size varied widely in both races. This man qualified as well endowed in either. His organ was brutishly thick along all its length, girded by a net of dark, swollen veins. The huge head pounded like a heart from the blood that had forced its way into it and its lust-widened slit was weeping pre-ejaculate.

Unable to control her reaction, Khira licked her upper lip. She had to remind herself she couldn't touch his genitals this soon. The release wouldn't satisfy him unless she built up to it, and she was damned if she'd do this twice. Fighting temptation, she slid one gloved hand beneath his hips and lifted them, thus enabling her to drag his trousers down. As she wrestled them over his muscled thighs, she noticed his underthings were as damp as hers. He'd been seeping with excitement all this time.

"There," she said, her voice too husky to count as properly restrained. His naked body was incredible—hairy, tall, and beautifully formed. She'd been right to call him hypermasculine. The lush brown bush from which his cock was jutting was an utterly primitive display, one that spoke to parts of her that—clearly—weren't civilized at all.

As if to tease her, his nearer leg fell off the cushion, his foot striking the carpet with a thump. Khira didn't put it back. The heavy swell of his balls was bared. They were hairy, too. Ripe. She wanted, quite insanely, to cup them in her hands and squeeze.

"I'll just kneel, shall I?" she said, moving from the territory she longed to explore to a somewhat safer position near his chest. "I'll start at your head and work down." She shut her eyes against the image of the other head she was more than willing to work down. "Don't be anxious. All of this will feel good."

Good was not the word. What Harry felt as she massaged his scalp with her ten gloved fingers was an explosion of ecstasy. Wetness spurted from his cock, not come but the clear, sweet fluid that signaled its approach. If he'd had any brain to think with, he would have been embarrassed. He didn't though, and all he could do was wallow in the heavenly relief of finally being touched.

His skin felt as if it had been itching for this for hours. In fact, he might have been itching for it all his life. Naturally, he'd been with women, but those had been quick, practical encounters. No one had ever caressed him with their full attention, probably not even as a babe. Wards of the state got the minimum care to keep them alive.

As a result, her hands were a stronger drug than whatever they'd given him before. God help him, but if this Yama intended to keep him as a sex slave, she was making a persuasive case.

"Gl-" he managed to choke out, wanting the feel of her bare hands more than his next breath.

When she shook her head, her silky hair swept shiveringly across his chest. She rubbed that then, in slow, firm circles over his ribs, combing through his hair as her hands came closer to his nipples. She pinched them when she got there, pulling them out enough to sting. Sensation pulsated through him. He gasped as his cock spurted hard again.

"G- come," he grunted in warning.

"Sh," she said. "Not yet."

Her hands smoothed down his arms, her thumbs pressing forceful tingles across his palms. That felt so good a tear trickled from his eye. She squeezed his hip bones, his thighs, forcing each taut muscle to lift and relax. Then her warm, soft gloves cupped his scrotum.

His groan reverberated through his whole body.

She massaged his balls as if she didn't know the meaning of shyness. Maybe she didn't. Maybe her people approached sex differently. Whatever her inhibitions or lack thereof, pressure built inside him with frightening swiftness. He couldn't come before she touched his penis, he refused to for pride alone, but if she didn't stop squeezing him like that, he was going to.

"I'll help you last," she said, her voice softer than before. She gripped the skin at the top of his scrotum between her thumb and fingers and tugged firmly, something he had tried now and then himself when he wanted to slow down. She knew the trick of it better than he did. The pressure inside him eased a fraction, but not his maddening need for her hands on him.

"St-roke me," he pleaded, every syllable thick. "Cock."

Her eyes were startled to his, meeting them for the first time since she'd knelt down. Her pupils glittered, swollen disks of black in pools of silver ice. He couldn't help wondering what lay behind them. "You can't wait?"

"N—" was all his tightened throat let out.

"Very well," she said, and wrapped her fingers tight around his swollen root. She dragged them upward, her hold so snug he felt more hot fluid push from his slit.

God, he wanted to be inside her, holding her, fucking her, making her feel even half of what he felt now. His paralyzed body shook with pleasure and desire as the train clacked rhythmically on the tracks. Again, she pulled her hand tightly up him. He ached from the force she was using, from the incredible need to release the seed building up inside. Her grip slid over the rim of him, into the pre-come running from his crest.

He tensed, but, "Good," she said. "I can stroke you better if you're wet."

Her palm cupped the head, turning from side to side to oil her glove in his juice. The delicious feel of the leather rotating over those sensitive nerves made him drench her more. Her grip slid down easily, then up again faster. He thought back to his years in the workhouse and on the streets, when he would have given his eyeteeth for the smallest physical kindness. Now he had it, and it didn't mean a thing. Overcome by it all the same, another tear of bliss trickled from his eye.

The woman touched his cheek with her second hand, a tenderness at odds with her detached expression. He closed his eyes. He couldn't look at her, couldn't bare this soul-deep hunger for connection when she appeared so composed.

"Breathe," she said softly. "Breathe through the rise and the climax will be deeper. Breathe and you'll empty out."

The best he could do was gasp. Her hand was suddenly moving faster than a human's could. The friction of her strokes burned hotter than his blazing skin. He climbed the slope to coming until his body's anticipation hurt. His stones felt as if that's what they were made of. They pulled up urgently between his legs.

"Yes," she whispered. "Go."

She wrapped her second hand around his shaft, pushing both fists together at its center before pushing out again. His crown registered every finger that squeezed over it. She was stretching his cock in both directions. Her skill astounded him, not to mention the matter-of-fact manner in which she employed it—when all the while she nearly killed him with pleasure. Light flared behind his tightly shut eyelids a second before the climax tore out of him.

When he came, his hips jerked off the couch, joints and muscles straining without his control. Long, hot bursts of seed jetted and splashed down. He groaned as each brought him closer to complete relief, the sound harsh and guttural.

"There," she said, milking the last sweet spurts. Then she let go.

His organ sagged without her to hold it, as replete as it had formerly been desperate. He opened his eyes and looked at her, forgetting he hadn't wanted to. Her hand came out as if to stroke him one more time, but she pulled it back at the last moment and held it to her ribs. Her snug white glove was covered with his spunk, her heart pounding. He could see the quick vibration through her yellow robes. Whatever went on behind her alien silver eyes, she was not unmoved by what she'd done to him.

"Sor—" he said, wishing he could reach out to her. "You dint—"

"No." She stood, her movements crisp and graceful. "*I* don't need anything."

———

This might have been the biggest lie she had ever told, but she clung to it. The human was tired, relaxed from his orgasm and still weak from the narcophane. She covered him with the blanket and retreated to the sleeper and its monklike beds. Privacy did not help. His shape was branded on her brain. His muscles. His cock. The fountaining of his seed. At the end, she would have given anything to feel those things on her naked skin.

She stripped off her gloves, as if that would help her deny it. She would have to clean them before they could be worn again, but for the moment she just hugged herself, standing hot and restless in the center of the rattling room.

She would not masturbate, no matter how her sex pulsed and wept. She knew she'd never forgive herself if she gave in. Loss of control was her enemy, this attraction wrong in every way she could think of—wrong and dangerous.

A man who shed tears of pleasure was the last person the Forettes' daughter could afford to be drawn to.

Chapter 4

HARRY came awake hard and throbbing, as he very often did. His appetite for carnal gratification could be a nuisance. Most days, he would rather have gone straight out on his rounds than take care of it. Now his prick felt sore where the blanket chafed it. He tried to remember if he'd worked himself to release before he fell into bed. Had he drunk enough to forget? For that matter, had he drunk enough to make his house seem like it was shaking?

His eyes snapped open as the truth slammed back into him.

He was on a train going God knew where. He'd been kidnapped. And drugged. And a beautiful, black-haired demon had given him the wanking of his life.

His cock twitched hopefully at remembering that.

"Shut up," he muttered, then experimented with sitting up.

His legs felt like they were made of rubber, but they worked. He was alone in the train car's sitting room. It was the slate-gray hour before dawn, and he had to piss so badly he wasn't sure he could think about escaping until he did.

Luck was with him. He found a bathroom behind the first door he tried. It was a little satin jewel box with a flush commode. He refrained from flushing when he was done, suspecting the mechanism would make more noise than was good for him. Sadly, the bathroom's round window was too small for him to squeeze out of.

Resigned to doing this the hard way, he pulled on his trousers and grabbed his boots. He gave himself no time for second thoughts, but braced his trembling muscles and half-ran, half-threw his shoulder at the locked carriage door.

It burst open with a bang. He had an instant to notice how fast the landscape was racing backward before he fell—which he did for longer than he expected. Arms thrust out to catch himself, he hit a slope belly-first and slid. He was gasping when he finally stopped. The train had been running on a gravel grade maybe ten feet high. His chest was scraped raw from skidding down it, but other than that he was fine. Most important, the train was chugging on without him.

Shaking from delayed shock and fear, he pulled on his boots and got up. He'd landed in a rural village—in Jeruvia to judge by the shop signs. Unfortunately, he knew no more than five words of that language. He couldn't stay here. He wouldn't be able to ask for help or tell friend from foe. He looked back at the train, receding slowly along the tracks. The demon had to have heard him break the door. She was probably raising the alarm right now.

Run then, he thought, eyeing the woods beyond the town's last small cottages. Hopefully, between the dimness and the train taking time to stop, he'd find cover enough to hide.

———

Khira jerked awake the second the door banged open. The human had escaped. He had leaped from a moving train. She grabbed her tiny comm unit.

"Tell them to stop the train," she said as soon as the guard answered. "The human has escaped."

"I understand," he responded, for once all efficiency. "We'll get him as fast as we can."

She ran to the window to see if she could spot him. The figure she saw was small, but that had to be the human running and stumbling across open ground. She couldn't imagine how he was doing it. He should have been too wobbly to walk for another day. Her throat went tight at his determination. Even a lowly human treasured his freedom.

"I'm sorry," she whispered, stroking the chilly window as the train's brakes screamed. "If you knew the whole story, you'd know I have no choice but to bring you back."

She didn't know what explanation—or bribe—the guards had given the engineer, but they had the train stopped and the human back in their control within a quarter hour.

Khira joined them at the edge of the bare gray woods. Frost crunched on the fallen leaves, but the air smelled country-sweet. She dropped the satchel she was carrying and drew in a breath. The human was struggling violently between the guards, doing his level best to enlarge their knowledge of human swear words. The naked rage in his face was frightening.

"If it makes you feel any better," she said, "you couldn't have outrun them even if you weren't drugged. Yama have a mean racing speed of thirty miles per hour."

This didn't seem to soothe the human. He snapped his mouth shut, then immediately burst out again. "You have no right to hold me against my will! I'm a free citizen of Ohram, with a business to see to! Whatever you're trying to get from me—trust me, lady—I'm not giving it up!"

One of the guards stuffed a gag into the human's mouth. Evidently, he'd heard this speech before and dismissed the idea of this human having a "business" as easily as she did. Would a businessman have been drinking in that seedy pub? Would he be wearing such shabby clothes? The guard nodded at the satchel. "You removed the prohibited technology from the car?"

"Yes," she said, knowing just as he did that they couldn't return to the train even if they knocked their captive unconscious. One witness could be bribed to silence, but three Yama traveling with a human were bound to raise questions among a few hundred. "Can a transport collect us here?"

"Requested one already," said the other guard. "They'll be here before sunup. I doubt these villagers will see a thing." He jerked his chin at the human. "You want us to redose him?"

"No," she said, her body clenching at the thought of another round with him and the kicker. That idea appealed to her a bit too much. "Just put him in restraints. I want his system clear of drugs by the time we land at the Mount."

The silent arrival of the Yamish transport turned at least half of Harry's fury into awe. The flying vehicle—which Harry didn't notice until it hovered right above them—was the size of a four-horse lorry. Shaped like a chevron, its dull pewter metal matched the still-dark sky. It landed light as a feather on a stretch of winter-bleached glass.

Harry whistled as a section of its side rolled up to form a door. Everyone suspected the Yama had technology they weren't sharing, but no one knew it was as advanced as this. He almost forgot to struggle as the guards gripped him from either side and carried him into the, thankfully, well-heated vehicle.

Once inside, the guards strapped his legs, arms, and neck to a leather seat. The female demon situated herself beside him, as calm as if she saw people being strapped to chairs every day. Then the transport took off again. From the inside, the walls of the flying machine were transparent. Harry watched the ground fall away at a dizzying rate, the village and the train shrinking down to toys.

"Blimey," he breathed, unable to keep the exclamation in.

Interestingly, the lady demon looked as if she were trying to restrain a smile. Head down, she busied herself with what he soon discovered was a doctor's kit. It contained a salve that she dabbed gently over his abraded chest.

"Why are you doing this?" he asked in an undertone, sensing she was likelier to answer than the guards. They had buckled themselves into seats directly in front of him and the doctor. At the very front, in the curve of the chevron's nose, sat a uniformed male driver.

"You are injured," the doctor said, her gloved hand smoothing salve across his belly with a care that had his cock stretching. Harry tried to ignore the response.

"I mean, why have you kidnapped me?"

She pressed her full lips together and withdrew her hand. "You'll be fine. The utmost care is being taken for your safety."

"But I haven't agreed to come with you. You must know what you're doing is wrong."

She closed her kit and set it on the transparent floor of the vehicle. "You'll be fine," she repeated, and said no more for the remainder of the ride.

That ride carried them rapidly out of Jeruvia and over the North Sea. Harry gasped and gripped the arms of his chair at the sight of whitecaps so far below. The demons must be taking him to the Northland, to their home. He'd be surrounded by people who barely considered him a rational being.

He closed his eyes and began to pray silently. He'd gotten out of tight spots in his life before, but he could not imagine how he'd squeak out of this.

They flew for perhaps half an hour, during which time ice flows and families of whales appeared. Under other circumstances, Harry would have been enchanted. Today, he was hard-pressed to see how things could get worse.

In that, he underestimated his ill fortune. The transport came to a sudden, floating halt over a gigantic, craggy island of ice. The highest peak glittered like a diamond in the morning sun, its steep sides glowing blue and green from within. The transport descended until it alighted on a flat platform near the mountain's top. Men in smart black uniforms that matched their driver's scurried out in lockstep from a cave nearby.

Harry didn't have enough breath to whistle. There would be no running away from this.

"We're here," the doctor said, her hand coming out—unthinkingly, Harry assumed—to touch his knee. She was a picture of suppressed excitement as she leaned forward in her seat.

God help me, Harry prayed, because some absurd part of him was excited, too.

The human's mood was grim by the time the guards escorted him from the transport. He neither resisted nor tried to flee. Khira hoped he realized he had no chance of escape and was prepared to make the best of his situation. She was not, however, betting on it.

They reached the lab at the end of the tunnel without incident. Khira told the guards they could leave. Though the pair exchanged one of their clone looks, they complied.

Khira was relieved. The human had to learn to answer to her, with or without the emperor's men to back her up.

At the moment, he was running his hands in wonder across the shielded ice walls of his room. Mount Excelsior was a glacier, stabilized and adapted for lab use twenty years ago. All the lovely greens and blues of the ice mountain's former travels had been preserved. Even she, who had studied every spec she could get her hands on ahead of time, experienced a wash of exhilaration at being here. She was sorely tempted to run her hands across the walls herself.

That, or give in to her hunger to stroke the human's spine. He had left his shirt on the train, and his bare back was a wedge of thick, male muscle covered in silky skin. She regretted not getting the chance to touch it the night before, if only because it led to the equally spectacular rounds of his bum.

She had never had a man this strong-looking in her bed.

"The walls are warm," he marveled, beginning to turn. "I can see they're made of ice, but they're warm."

He caught her licking her upper lip. The nervous gesture exposed the dark forked marking on her tongue, the very marking that had led humans to label her kind demon. Though he didn't seem repelled, the human's face went still. He stared at her mouth, causing its surface to buzz oddly. Then he lifted his gaze to hers. She tried to read his emotions, but humans expressed themselves through their auras differently than her people did. All she registered was a sudden increase in his focus on her.

"You must be hungry," she said, feeling the need to distract him. "I will request you be brought a meal."

Perhaps a taste of superior Yamish cuisine would convince him he was better off where he was. She had no illusions that, just because he'd stopped struggling physically, his resistance was at an end. She could almost see the wheels turning in his mind as he paused to consider her.

"I'd like you to join me," he said.

This took her by surprise. "To join you."

"One thing I've learned is that if you can't get the better of someone in a fight, you have to bargain."

Her shoulders stiffened. "You have nothing to bargain with."

The bed sat in the center of the room. It was formed from a slab of clear Northlandic quartz, chosen for its light and sound conducting properties, and mounted on a shining, moveable frame. Khira did not appreciate the fact that she noticed it so starkly now, or that the human chose that moment to step to it and put his hands on the silver rail. They were big, capable hands with long fingers. Khira had seen that when he stroked the wall.

"You can tell me why you brought me here," he said. "Maybe I'll decide to cooperate."

Oh, she did not like his reasonable tone. It stank of strategy. In fact, it stank of a self-possession humans weren't supposed to have.

"I do not require your cooperation," she said coolly.

The human's slow, canny smile was almost enough to make her

believe that he could read auras, too, that he could see her hidden remorse and guilt.

"You may not *require* my cooperation, but I think you want it. You wouldn't have bothered to treat my injuries if that weren't true."

"That was simple civility. Any Yama would have done as much."

"Would they?" He crossed his arms to express his doubt.

Khira had been unjust. His chest was every bit as compelling as his back. The way its pectoral muscles bulged made her body feel all too warm. She was as wet as she'd been the previous night when she gave him ease. She grimaced as a creamy trickle slid down her thigh. Her voice was rough when she answered him.

"I admit my job would be easier if you weren't fighting me."

"So I'm a job."

She did not deign to confirm his guess. "You will not be harmed," she said instead.

At this, he shook his head. "Lady, I already have been. But I'm willing to overlook that if you'll break bread with me."

Breaking bread sounded like a ritual she shouldn't join, but he wasn't finished disarming her. "My name is Harry," he said and stuck out his hand.

She stared at it. She was familiar with the human tradition of shaking hands, but she'd removed her gloves the minute they landed. The things had been stained with salve and, before that, with his emissions. She'd tossed them into the first disposal unit they'd passed.

His eyebrows rose at her reluctance to reciprocate. "This is the part where you tell me your name."

He was only asking her to press palms. If she did not do it, he would think her afraid of this obvious attempt to forge a bond of sympathy. The shake would be a brief contact. Unless she pressed the whorl of energy above his heart, she wouldn't absorb much of his essence. If agreeing lulled him into complacency, what was the harm?

The harm was that she didn't know the harm, but she pushed the caution away.

"My name is Khira," she said and slid her hand into his.

Straightaway, she knew that touching him had been a mistake. Her body jerked as his energy surged across the barrier of their naked skin. Her nipples tightened so swiftly she felt as if they'd been pinched. Startled by the strength of the transfer, she couldn't gather herself enough to move.

"Khira," he repeated, stepping closer with his hand still clasping hers. "That's a pretty name."

Her sex was fluttering, tiny contractions that tugged her inner muscles into an even higher state of excitement. "Release my hand," she said hoarsely.

Rather than do so, the human—Harry—put his second hand over hers, surrounding it. "Your skin is warm, Khira. I was thinking it would be cold."

He was close enough for her to count his spiky eyelashes, close enough to map the green and gold striations in his human irises. There was barely an inch of difference in height between them, and to her surprise, the advantage was on his side. Her race was usually the taller one. As Harry's thighs brushed hers, Khira wondered where her vaunted "demon" strength had gone. She seemed unable to call on it as his energy poured into her. Her head was swimming, her body aching with desire. She found herself swaying toward him, and discovered his thighs weren't the only thing brushing her.

She didn't need to see his erection. She could tell it was as large and hard and thick as it had been the night before. She watched his face, mesmerized, as he licked his lips and inclined his head.

"What are you doing?" she whispered.

With the tip of his tongue, he touched the spot between the points of her upper lip. "Returning the favor you did for me."

When he sealed their mouths together, Khira lost her power to move. Everywhere their bare skin touched, her body basked in etheric force. Where they didn't touch, it crawled over her in hot, golden waves, seeping deliciously into her flesh until she felt as if someone had dosed *her* with an aphrodisiac.

Then, as if determined to make things worse, he pressed between her lips and stroked her tongue with his. His was a simple kiss: strong, direct, and absolutely wonderful. He sucked her as if he were feeding, embraced her as if she was dear. He couldn't have known what he was doing by touching her this way, but even if he did, Khira could not hold back. She threw her arms around his hot, silky back and drew on his mouth with all the strength she had feared she'd lost.

Immediately, his hand slid down her back to her bottom, tilting her pubis firmly over his erection. This felt so good she simply had to hitch her leg around his thigh. Harry groaned in approval. She *did* notice when he began to gather up her tunic, but was too desperate to keep kissing him to object. After some exploration, he found the hidden back clasp of her matching silk trousers. He undid it neatly and thrust his big hand within.

His palm met new, bare skin. Her head jerked back in reaction, but he followed the movement and caught her mouth to his again. His hand slid down her bottom cleavage to her sex.

Their heights were too close. He couldn't reach far enough to slide his fingers inside her. Realizing this at the same time she did, Harry turned her, hefted her higher, and pressed her spine to the warm ice wall. There his weight was able to hold her up.

He was panting when he unlatched himself from her mouth.

"Now," he said, "let's see how much you need this."

She was too far gone to mind him wanting to know. Two fingers slid inside her with a squelching sound, each radiating energy so sweet it almost made her come. She bit her lip and clutched his shoulders to keep her moan inside. She could have saved her strength. His breath hissed through his teeth as her eyes went briefly black, the Yamish sign of a sudden spike in sexual need.

"What the—?" he began to say, but she cut him off.

"Let me move," she said, squirming on his fingers, not wanting to explain.

"I'll move," he said a little shakily. "You just enjoy."

His hand was agile, more than she expected. She closed her eyes in bliss and self-concealment as he thrust those two glowing fingers in and out of her. Her trousers had fallen to her hips, and Harry now shoved her underthings down as well. When he pushed the bulge of his erection against her naked mound, the moan she'd been trying to restrain ripped out.

He knew what she wanted. Breathing hard, he spread her outer lips with the fingers that weren't inside her, baring her clitoris to the very welcome friction of his wool-covered cock. The effect of his movements was so powerful, juice gushed from her when she came.

"Lord," he said, her pubis beginning to slip in his hold.

She couldn't let him stop. She clamped her thighs around his waist and rocked herself hard and fast over his fingers. This time, she actually whimpered at her orgasm.

As good as it was, the climax wasn't enough to satisfy her. She knew that even as she allowed her legs to slide down his heaving sides. She knew it even more when he kissed her, deeply, sweetly, his now-wet hand sliding up her side to her breast. A moment later, his second hand rose as well. He covered both small mounds as he leaned into and rubbed his body over hers, as if every part of him needed to feel her. It was the warmest, most sensual caress she'd ever experienced. Her breasts were encompassed in his gently squeezing hold, and even with her tunic between them, her nipples burned. She wanted him so badly her knees trembled.

"Mm," he hummed against her mouth. "Keep touching me like that, and I might consent to be your sex slave."

Her hands were clamped on his warm, bare rump. Completely without her awareness, they had pushed inside his trousers to find more skin. She was so horrified at herself, she finally mustered the self-control to yank them back.

"I did not bring you here to be my sex slave!" she said, aghast. Her arms weren't working correctly yet. She pushed ineffectually at his hard, hairy chest, wishing she could be as offended by its solidity as she was by his smug amusement. Her temper snapped. "You . . . you are a human, a member of a deeply inferior race!"

At that, he pushed back from her himself. Khira had to grab her trousers to keep them from falling down, but he didn't laugh at her. Indeed, his face had gone stony.

"That's right," he said. "You Yama are smarter, stronger, faster, and just plain better in every way. The thing is, when you aren't shrinking back from humans in horror, you're leaning forward in fascination—like a cold, old man trying to warm his hands at a fire. Why is that, if my race is inferior?"

Stung by his words, and now secure in her clothes, Khira straightened her spine. "I really couldn't say. I am not a doctor of psychology."

"Then what are you a doctor of?"

He almost tricked her into answering. Khira pulled out her comm, judging it time to call the guards. Before she could, Harry put his hand over hers. Fresh, hot tingles swept from his palm, threatening to dissolve the strength she'd managed to gather. He seemed to have figured out what the communication device was for.

He leaned toward her, his musky scent much stronger and—to her dismay—much more agreeable to her nose than a Yamish man's.

"You don't need your guards to make me do what you want," he said, low and dark. "You have that power all by yourself."

She tried to pull her hand away but could not. She didn't understand this. She had drawn off what seemed like a considerable portion of his etheric force. He should have been the one who felt weak.

"You are trying to toy with my mind," she said, "to make me think of us as allies so I'll let you go."

"Why can't we be allies? You claim you don't intend to harm me."

"I don't, but there is nothing you can say or do that would convince me to set you free."

"Not even when you've finished what you've planned for me?"

"No," she said, and stubbornly set her jaw.

To her amazement, the human smiled crookedly. "Well, one out of two isn't a bad starting point."

"This isn't a negotiation!" Her exasperation caused her to raise her voice, a loss of face the human appeared not to notice.

"Yes it is, Khira," he corrected, with far more calm and sureness than she'd displayed. "As you'll discover when you try to get what you want from me."

She'd heard all the nonsense she could tolerate. His threats were empty. He had no power here—none! Composing herself with an effort, she twisted free from him and summoned the guards on her comm. They could keep him company while he ate. He'd see how well his smelly male wiles worked on them.

⸺⸺

The guards were laughing. Harry was eating at a square white table in his room, and they were laughing at everything he said. Khira watched them from the observation chamber and shook her head. Evidently, the guards' experience with humans had entailed them going more native than was advised.

Either that, or listening to Harry wax rhapsodic over his grilled swordfish was funnier than a scientist could comprehend.

She hoped Harry realized how dangerous his new friends were.

Shoving aside her annoyance, Khira pulled up the results of her initial scans on the viewing screen. As far as she could tell, Harry's energy signature was within normal parameters for a human. His aura showed minimal signs of depletion, no more than she would expect after a long day, and definitely not enough to account for her intense reaction to his touch. His testosterone levels were higher than males of her race, so perhaps his scent had sensitized her. Had he been Yamish, the fact that she liked his smell would have indicated they were genetically appropriate candidates for producing offspring. Since Harry wasn't Yamish, Khira didn't know what conclusion to draw.

You have *been ignoring your personal life,* she reminded herself. *Spending too many hours with your research.* Her strong attraction to the human, while unusual, might have been no more than her libido protesting its neglect.

She squirmed in her rolling, molded workchair, not convinced there was enough neglect in the world to account for her current state of neediness.

She signaled one of the guards with her comm, bringing him from his laughing slouch to review posture. Harry watched the transformation curiously.

"Let the human use the bathroom when he's done eating," she said. "Then strap him to the crystal bed."

It was time she initiated her experiment. The human would never understand who was in charge until she did.

———

Harry was relieved to discover that jokes comparing good food to sex amused males from all cultures. He'd sensed a bond with Khira as he pleasured her, a commonality of lust at the least, but her stiff withdrawal cast doubts on his chances of exploiting it. If the beautiful doctor refused to relent, he'd need a backup plan.

His hope to recruit the guards' aid vanished as soon as he saw their reaction to Khira's call. Their laughter stopped in an instant, impersonal coolness replacing it. When they strapped him naked onto the glassy bed, he didn't bother to struggle. Never mind his claim that Khira would never get what she wanted, she had the upper hand for now.

One of the guards, neither of whom he could tell apart, patted his shoulder before he left.

"You're lucky," he said. "Dr. Forette is brilliant—and highly motivated. This will go well."

The gesture seemed kind, and probably out of character, but Khira's "motivation" hardly addressed Harry's need for help to get out of here.

Sweat broke out on his forehead as the strange bed he was strapped to slowly tipped upright. A long, clear cylinder began descending from the ceiling, surrounding him on all sides. In its walls were embedded instruments whose function he could not guess.

"Hey!" he cried as one snaked out to suck a bit of blood from his arm.

"I cannot drug you," said the doctor's disembodied voice, seemingly in the tube with him. "These procedures require an unclouded mind. Please try to think calm thoughts."

"You try to think calm thoughts," he muttered. "You're not the one in here."

Without warning, spinning sunbursts of violet light shot out from a dozen of the tube's devices, followed by an eerie rising and falling wail. Every hair on Harry's body came to attention. Whatever the machine was doing, he wished it would stop. Both light and sound buzzed through his skin, penetrating tissues that should have been unreachable. His heart began to thunder inside his chest, and that scared him, too. He sincerely hoped he was too young to die of apoplectic fear.

Unbidden, a memory from his childhood rose. He'd been ten and so hungry he'd stolen a raw potato from the workhouse kitchen. Another boy had informed the matron, and, as punishment for his theft, Harry had spent two days locked in a dark closet. Though the experience nearly killed him, Harry had refused to cry. A few months later, he'd run away to live on the streets where, ironically, he'd eaten better than he had from "charitable" hands.

He'd had to sell a piece of his soul to do it, but that had simply taught him the value of doggedness.

This will be the same, he told himself. He pushed away the panic his lack of comprehension caused. The darkness and hunger he'd experienced in that closet he'd understood. But the differences between then and now didn't matter. He would be free.

This became his prayer as Khira's machine performed its mysterious operations. Instruments crawled over him on little metal legs, pricking him intermittently with needles. The violet sunbursts turned purple and blue and green. The unearthly music circled around him, murmuring sounds he almost thought were words. He saw things that weren't there. Clouds floating beneath him. The whispering tops of trees. Snowflakes crystallized from the water inside his cells, and then in structures even more miniscule, structures Harry didn't have names for.

Peace, the tiny, spiraling ladders soothed. *This song is perfecting us.*

Harry strove to ignore it all, repeating only *I will be free*, like the endless mantras he'd been told Yskutian monks performed. He would rather have confronted any danger with his fists, but if his head was all he had to work with, by God, his head was what he'd use.

Chapter 5

SHE'D thought there was nothing the human could do to stop her, but she'd been wrong. Twenty-four hours had passed, and none of her carefully planned modifications were taking effect. She'd increased the modulator's power as much as she dared. She had the genetic sequencer taking samples every fifteen minutes, but nothing achieved results. Each time his DNA looked like it was changing, the next test would reveal its codes had snapped back. Harry had gone into some sort of trance, and the interference from his brain waves was wreaking havoc with her programs.

The guards had been by the observation room no less than three times to check on how she was progressing—and to remind her that she had better make progress soon.

"We understand if you feel sorry for him," one had said. "The human is likeable. But that's no reason to go soft."

"If it helps," the second put in, "the future won't look bright for either of you if you fail."

Khira assured them she was neither "going soft," as they put it, nor about to fail. This was just a glitch that she would work out. These things happened to all researchers.

The minute they shut the door behind them, she put her head in her hands. She'd brought the human here to save him from mortal danger, and now he was in it up to his ears. The fact that she shared the danger didn't improve her mood.

Harry's unexpected stubbornness was narrowing her choices. She was going to have to do what her kind did best: wrap as pretty a package as she could around an outright lie.

As soon as Khira released the straps that bound him to the crystal bed, Harry sagged onto his knees. The state she found him in worsened her shame. His skin was pale and clammy, the purple circles beneath his eyes testifying to the fact that he had slept no more than she had. He stared at her, dull-eyed and breathing hard, like an ox who'd been led to slaughter only to find his end delayed.

A coil of cold, hard metal seemed to be twisting in Khira's chest. This was not what genetic science was supposed to be. In her heart, her chosen field was clean and beautiful. It was about possibilities.

Wrenched, she touched his pale, perspiring cheek with her glove. Harry flinched as if expecting worse. Khira dropped her hand.

"I'm ready to bargain," she said.

"You'll let me go?"

His voice sounded like gravel. Khira gathered her will to lie convincingly. "If you want to go, I'll release you after a year."

Harry barked out a laugh. He waved in the direction of the modulator, now retracted into the ceiling. "A year of this?"

"*This* will be over soon."

"I don't believe you," he said more bluntly than any Yama would.

Khira fought a blush even though her last statement had been true. "If you don't cooperate, those guards will kill you."

"I thought you didn't need my cooperation."

"I was wrong." She drew a breath to give herself time to decide. Maybe it was best to let him know what the problem was. "You're doing something in your head. It's interfering with my programs."

The stare he treated her to then was calculating. She could see his color coming back.

"Oh, please," she said, purposefully putting scorn into it. "Don't think you'll gain anything by continuing this obstruction. If my experiment fails, the guards will just get rid of you and snatch someone else."

Harry growled with animal frustration, then pulled her forcefully down to her knees with him. "How can you do this? I don't care how advanced you Yama are. I'm a person. Flesh and blood like you. How can you treat me like a specimen and still sleep at night?"

Her reaction was completely inappropriate. When he seized her face in his big, hard hands, heat coursed from the contact straight to her sex. Everything between her legs pulsed with hunger—her clitoris, her labia, the suddenly slick passage that led to her womb. She knew his fingers wouldn't quell her craving again. Only his cock could do that, only the hard, driving thickness that would lock their separate bodies into one.

Barriers cracked inside her, barriers that had been erected brick by brick since leaving her parents' care. Each had brought her closer to living up to the Yamish ideal. Each had helped her fit in. Now her protections crumbled around her. She began to cry and didn't know how to stop. The best she could do was cover her face.

"If they kill you," she said, aware that she was sobbing, "I may never sleep again. Please, *please* trust me when I say I'm trying to help."

Harry's hands had fallen away when she started crying. Now he gripped her shoulders and squeezed hard. Khira didn't think this was meant to be comforting. His gaze bored into hers.

"I need a token to prove that you aren't lying."

"Anything," she swore, trying to pull away from his hands. His energy was flowing into her, his human capacity for emotion. The continuing loss of control was more than she could stand. "I'll do anything you want."

"I want this." He gave her shoulders a shake. "I want the gloves off once and for all. I want you to bare what you've been working so hard to hide from me. I want to look into your soul when you make love to me."

She gasped, her tears stopping at his boldness. "I don't—"

"Save your breath. I know you want it as much as I do. I felt you dripping down my hand yesterday, and I can smell the lust on you now."

She could only smell him, and his scent was as heady as his touch. "That's an accidental side effect. Your etheric force is transferring to me."

"I've lived on the streets of Avvar. I've sold my life force to the *rohn* in exchange for money to keep me fed. As I recall, none of those Yama wanted to bed me."

"You lived on the streets?" Khira asked, struggling against the awful-wonderful weakness his closeness bred. "I thought you were a businessman."

"I am a businessman. I've fought my way up in the world since then."

She believed him. Pride had brought his chin up, and confidence shone in his gold-green eyes. He wasn't ashamed of what he'd had to do; he'd accepted it. This assertion of his power—male and professional—was restoring him to himself. Khira wished she *were* a doctor of psychology. Maybe then she'd know if his recovery would increase her chance of gaining his compliance.

"To have overcome such obstacles is impressive," she ventured, stalling for time. Her hands had risen unconsciously to his chest, but they were hardly pushing him off. "I would have thought you'd want nothing to do with my kind."

"Khira," he growled, the sound sending fingers of arousal deep into her. "I believe we've established I have no problem being close to you. Now say yes or no."

"I can't," she confessed. "I can't do either."

He kissed her, hard at first and then slow and deep. He groaned into her mouth as his tongue swept her upper palate. Oh, she loved the rumbling sounds he made. Her hands curled helplessly into his chest hair. She wanted her gloves off, too—probably more than he did.

"Say yes," he growled, and kissed her deeper yet, each thrust of his tongue a searing imitation of what he wanted her to agree to.

Khira's head bent back with pleasure from imagining it. "Yes," she whispered. "Yes."

—————

Harry had been hardening ever since he'd caught her to him for a blistering kiss. At her answer, his cock jolted up so forcefully, it might have been trying to punch through her clothes. She'd said *yes*. He was going to have her.

Too impatient to wait, he reached for her right hand and peeled its long glove off—this one black satin. Trapping her wrist, he brought her palm to his mouth to kiss. She watched him, unable to take her eyes off his. When he finished the kiss with a lick, her shiver had him pulling her hand to his groin.

"Touch me," he said. "Wrap those demon fingers around my cock."

She was panting as she did it, and, Lord, it felt good. His cock swelled in her hold, and her eyes went black. The air between them shimmered like a summer day.

"Tell me what that means," he said, "when your eyes go dark."

"It means—" She paused for breath. "It means I'm very excited. It means my arousal level jumped from what it was before."

Harry's arousal jumped enough for both of them. "Touching me arouses you."

"Yes, though I can't explain why my reaction is so intense."

He smiled at the plaintive note in her voice. "I'm glad," he murmured next to her ear, unable to resist nuzzling her silken hair. "I want us to touch each other all over."

"I could—" She swallowed. "I could take off my clothes."

"Why don't you let me?" he suggested and reached for the side tie to her pretty black-and-gold wrap tunic.

Her hand was still on him, as if his cock were her personal lifeline. He had to ease her fingers free before he could peel the embroidered garment over her head. He was glad the Yama had such strange ideas about what constituted appropriate women's garb. It was very easy to take off. The breasts he'd only felt through her clothes up till now were as lovely as he'd expected, delicate, up-tilted handfuls with red nipples. He bent to suckle one pointed tip and thrilled to her strong shudder.

Khira tore the second glove off herself.

"I can't take it," she said, her hands forking through his hair to clutch him closer. "I need you inside me now."

She pushed away, her strength surprising him. She stood to shove her trousers and underthings down her legs. Harry didn't mean to, but he gaped up at her when she was done. He had never seen a naked woman who looked like she did. Human fashion tended toward curves and softness, and Khira's body was a thoroughbred's—lean and strong and ready to race. Awed, he smoothed his hands up her thighs, the muscles as easy to see as a man's. Reaching the top, he spread his fingers across her mound.

"You're smooth here."

His thumb curled gently over her vulva, and she covered his hand with hers. "We remove our hair."

Her face was still, her Yamish mask. *She's afraid of how I'll see her nakedness,* he thought. The guess made it easy to bend forward, easy to press his lips to that bare triangle of skin. Though he saw no outward change, he sensed her relax.

"You're beautiful," he said. "May I kiss you here?"

She drew a quick breath and nodded. He parted her, baring her reddened pleasure peak to his mouth. He thought he had never looked forward to tasting a woman more, to watching how she reacted. Her fingers bit into his shoulders when he sucked the swollen button against his tongue, not seeming to mind that his day-old beard must be scratching her. Or perhaps she liked the feeling. She made no sound, but her body seemed to moan silently. Half a minute later, she tore herself away. He looked up at her. Her eyes were black again before they cleared.

His body clenched to realize how much he was exciting her.

"You want me inside you," he said, the knowledge sure in his mind. He'd been steadying himself on her hips. He felt them trembling as she mouthed *yes*. He sat back on his heels and spread his knees. His cock thrust up in blatant invitation, as eager to get on with this as she was. "Come down to me."

He reached up to help her join him on the floor, their fingers fitting naturally. As soon as she released his hands, he lifted her, cupping her tight little bottom to bring her up his thighs. Her hair curtained down his arms in a black whisper. He closed his eyes, just for a moment, as her soft, satiny mound slid to a rest against his erection. It had been a long time since he'd had a woman. He wasn't sure how long he could last with one he wanted this badly, but he bloody well wasn't going to stop because of that.

When he opened his eyes again, her silver gaze was waiting for his. Her hand fluttered down to cover his pulsing tip. He knew it was weeping from the way her palm slid around.

She looked down at what she held. "I didn't know you would be this big without the drugs."

"I won't hurt you."

"You couldn't. I'm stronger than a human woman. Even inside."

"Show me," he challenged with a smile that drew her lips to brush his. She must have enjoyed the contact. Her cheek turned from side to side in his short whiskers.

"I want you to kiss me when I take you."

She said it like a confession, and he had to laugh. He didn't think he'd ever been *taken* before.

"Why does that amuse you?" she asked.

He kissed her rather than answer, pushing deep into her mouth, stroking her sleek, wet tongue until it answered his. His body was too hungry for more talking; besides which, that pouting mouth of hers was made for kissing, the one sensual feature on her smooth Yamish face.

Apparently, she had more sensual features he couldn't see. Even as they fed on each other's mouths, she rose to her knees and tipped his erection toward her. She fit it against her entrance before slowly, torturously, pressing down on him. From kissing her vulva, he knew she was aroused, but the incredible, devastating sensation of her pushing that tight, hot wetness over his cock brought him to the edge. He didn't expect her to fit all of him—she was built too lean—but when he thought she'd taken all she could, she closed her eyes in concentration and something shifted inside of her, making room.

"God, yes," he gasped as the last hard inch of him was engulfed.

This time she smiled, a tentative curve—for all he knew, the first deliberate smile of her life. Her hands roved down his back to caress his rear. He'd never known a woman this bold about sex. His balls felt unnervingly ready to explode.

"Don't rush," he pleaded, despite his body's urging to do just that.

"Oh, no," she agreed throatily, her thighs beginning to tighten for her first rise. "This is far too good to rush."

———

Khira had little choice but to admit it: This was what she had been wanting from the moment she saw the human in that seedy pub. To ride his maleness. To take his human fire into her. She ran greedy hands over every part of him she could reach, wallowing in the drugging evidence of their difference, letting her body grow so needy she knew there'd be no turning back.

"Fuck," he breathed as she made her inner muscles ripple over him. Khira tensed, but, "Do that again," he demanded.

She hid her thrill of pleasure in his corded neck, gripping him even tighter a second time. The idea that he could dictate to her was foolish, but she liked him trying all the same.

"Oh, yes," he said. "That's wonderful."

The tension in him shifted, his cock pressing up higher inside of her. His hand slid from her hip to cup the back of her skull. "I'm tipping you back now. Don't let go."

He laid her beneath him as carefully as if she were glass, then braced above her on straightened arms. She could tell he liked this position, and she certainly didn't mind once he moved again. His hips beat more freely against her, no faster than the pace she had set but with an extra push at the end to reach deeper. He watched his cock go in and out of her—wet, thick, red from friction and excitement. The sight clearly wound him up. He groaned quietly with need.

"Do it," she said, her hands rubbing urging circles around his hips. Her body was as eager to go as his. "Take me as hard and fast as you want. Trust me, you won't come before I do."

He looked at her. "Trust you," he repeated with a muffled laugh. "You have no idea how close I am."

She didn't have to argue. Her body did it for her. His body stroked in one more time, and she came apart, the orgasm strong. She made a choked and helpless whimper as her neck arched up.

"All right," she dimly heard him say. "Hard and fast it is."

It was hard and fast and *loud*, not only from their bodies slapping together, but from his groans and gasps and muttered curses of delight. The sounds, so foreign to her experience, pushed her over a second time. His thrusts turned wild then, his expression pained. Desperate for more, she pulled at him with all her inner muscles' strength.

"God," he said, slamming into her so hard the crown of his penis seemed to jolt her heart. "God, God—"

His words dissolved into a long, hoarse cry. This was the end for him. His testicles slapped her buttocks with the final quickening of his thrusts. He came with his body clenched to his toes, straining, shooting, his lips pulled back from his teeth in an orgasmic snarl.

Khira wasn't prepared for what his peak did to her. The flow of energy from him to her was already strong, and she'd forgotten it would flare with climax. Ecstasy seized her as his sun-bright aura flooded into her. Her very fingertips seemed to come. She moaned at the forceful spasms, utterly unable to hold the exclamation in. On and on it went, until she struggled to comprehend how she could hold so much pleasure. Harry must have felt it, too. He shuddered one last time into her.

"Ahh," he sighed, long and low, sagging onto her. His body relaxed as completely as it had previously been coiled. "Khira, that was sweet."

Acting the gentleman, though there was no need, he rolled onto his back with her on top of him. His hand stroked lazily down her hair. Happily, the floor was sealed and warm like the walls. She squirmed into a more comfortable position atop his chest, which roused him momentarily.

"Do you want more, love?" he asked, his palm sliding meaningfully around her left buttock.

She blinked, her eyes stinging unexpectedly at his endearment. She reminded herself that anyone could be "love" to one of Victoria's citizens. And that, as a dignified Yama, she wasn't supposed to enjoy such things.

"No," she said, snuggling her blushing face into the crook of his neck. "I am content."

Humming, he wriggled his back against the floor as if his shoulders itched. "I am as well. Just be sure to wake me when you want to do this again."

———

Khira waited until he was sleeping soundly. Then she picked him up and carried him to her room. Her chamber wasn't much different— also stark and white—but the bed was more comfortable.

She laid him in it gently, not troubled by his weight, but unused to carrying anything this large and limp. Harry could rest here until tomorrow when, hopefully, whatever bee he'd had in his brain would be forgotten, and she could continue with the business of saving his life.

What that saved life would be like she didn't want to think. She'd protect him as much as she could with whatever power her knowledge gave her. More than that, she couldn't do.

Harry rolled onto his side in sleep, his big, muscular body oddly vulnerable. Khira grabbed a soft, white blanket to cover him. Before she could spread it, her gaze was arrested by two blazing red stripes that had appeared along his shoulder blades.

"God," she whispered, unthinkingly echoing his human prayer. Her hand went out. Her procedures *were* working. The modulator's DNA-altering frequencies must have gotten stored in his aura. When he'd dropped his mental guards to have sex with her, they'd been able to take effect.

Khira pulled her hand back without touching the inflamed lines. His shoulder muscles were shifting configuration, new bones forming beneath the skin. When she cocked her ear close to his back, tiny popping noises could be heard. In spite of all that remained to concern her, triumph bloomed in her breast. She had done it. She had brought a dormant portion of his genes to life. She dragged a chair to his bedside, unable to keep her eyes off the unfolding change.

Harry murmured and moved uncomfortably. Khira stroked his arm to soothe him, though she doubted he'd wake up. The human body had built-in safeguards to stress. Ask too much of it, and it would burrow into unconsciousness to heal, or, in this case, to grow. He'd probably sleep like a baby until this was done.

"Rest," she murmured, pulling the blanket over his legs. She'd retrieve her medical kit soon. With luck, she'd be too busy easing his transformation to worry about how she'd break the news to him when he woke.

Chapter 6

FOR once, Harry wasn't sorry to come awake with his cock as hard as bone. He lay sprawled on his back, propped on a stack of pillows over which an even softer throw had been draped. He knew this wasn't the bed in his room; it was far too comfortable. Best of all, a mouth he recognized as Khira's even with his eyes closed was doing its best to swallow his aching prick. She was bent down over him, kneeling between his legs.

She must have seen his cock rouse ahead of him.

He moaned, his hand combing down the silken spill of her hair. "I was wishing you would do this that first night."

In truth, he'd been wishing he could wake up like this his whole adult life. Her mouth was strong, that dark, forked marking not the only difference in her tongue. Inhumanly agile, it flickered up the ridge of flesh beneath his shaft with a quickness that had his hips squirming uncontrollably off the bed. He gasped and gripped the curving leanness of her upper arms, needing something to hold on to that wouldn't entail jamming himself down her throat. Wisely, she held down his thighs when she applied that vibratory flutter to his swollen crown. The pointed tip of her tongue drew a circle of intense sensation around the well-stretched helmet, until he feared the next time she sucked all of him upward, he would explode.

"You'd better stop if you want to join me," he managed to warn her, his eyes screwed shut with near-orgasmic enjoyment.

She didn't say a word. She cupped his testicles in one warm hand, shifted her attentions to an even more sensitive spot beneath his rim, and trilled her tongue again. Harry knew what her action meant. She intended him to finish in her mouth.

If he hadn't been gritting his teeth too tightly to speak, he would have thanked her. That she would be this warm to him, when she'd already given him what he asked, touched him deeply. In his experience, no woman let a man spend in her mouth unless she really wanted to. In spite of everything Khira had put him through, this gratified him more than anything had in some time.

That happiness—or at least his lust—continued to increase even when she finished her little tongue trick. She licked him once for good measure from root to rim, slid her palms up the muscles of his belly, then pushed the ring of her lips down his throbbing length. Having reached her limit, she sucked wetly, tightly up again.

After all her teasing, the feeling was incredible. Tears of pleasure squeezed from his eyes, while at the same time the oddest pressure knotted in his back, as if he were lying on a muscle wrong. He couldn't worry about it. Khira was pushing down on his shaft again. Her subsequent upward pull had his body tingling from head to toe.

When her fingernails scratched lightly through his chest hair, he felt as if his body had turned into one big cock.

"One more," he tried to say through his strangled throat.

Khira was already there. The next downstroke tensed him like a bowstring, and the sucking, tonguing upstroke shot him into ecstasy so abruptly that an actual twang of release jolted through his groin. Her head came down again, warmth wrapping warmth as his climax squeezed from him in a series of deep contractions. Dimly, he felt her kiss his penis as she slipped away. Though sorry it was over, he'd never been so satisfied in his life.

When his brain recovered its powers of higher observation, he realized the odd pressure on his back was gone. Indeed, he felt pleasantly floaty all over.

"What the—?" Khira exclaimed.

Her hands were gripping his hips from an angle he didn't understand. Too replete to puzzle out why her hold seemed wrong, he opened his eyes lazily.

He was suspended in the air above her head. He blinked, dumbfounded. Was this some new Yamish technology? He craned his neck to see Khira and tilted, still floating, to the vertical. Khira's hands were now planted indignantly on her waist. She was naked, which was rather nice.

"You're not supposed to be able to do that!" she snapped.

Harry couldn't help but grin at her. As he did, something rustled behind him, something big. He looked around to see what it was and gasped. A huge pair of wings was unfolding behind him: brown, feathered wings whose tops nearly brushed the warm ice ceiling.

"Ack!" he said, thinking some monstrous Yamish bird had been set on him. He began to twist, trying to get away, but only plummeted to the floor.

"Ow!" he said as his knees cracked the smooth surface.

Khira was at his side in an instant. The wings had followed him down. He swatted them in a panic, his arms weirdly heavy, as if he'd been drugged again. Khira grabbed his hands.

"Stop it," she said. "They're yours. You grew them. You can't beat them off."

"Oh, *God*." He didn't want to believe her, but she was stroking the wing on his right. He could feel her fingers moving gently down each feather.

"See," she soothed, moving behind him to pet the wings as a pair. "You're all right."

The caress felt perversely nice, but his fear was stronger. "What did you do to me?"

"Well, I didn't hurt you. I just . . . altered you a bit."

"A bit!" His response was a half-choked burst of outrage.

Khira's voice turned prim. "I didn't think you'd be able to fly. Your wings were supposed to be just for show. Birds have hollow bones. Your body should be too heavy to lift off. Then again, people say the same of honeybees."

"Oh, then everything's all right!"

She was still fondling his feathers, too distracted to pay his sarcasm any mind. Of course, he was feeling distracted, too. Those wings must have had a lot of sensually connected nerves. Absolutely against his will, he made a cooing noise, his back relaxing utterly beneath her touch. Despite its recent pleasuring, his cock began to lift.

"Khira," he growled a second before his body lifted off as well, not unlike a hot air balloon.

Startled, he flapped his new wings and nearly went careening face-first into the wall. He caught himself on his hands and tried a gentler motion. This time, he wafted perfectly over Khira's head. He laughed, forgetting his rather insane troubles in the unexpected delight of flying. The laugh sent him bobbing up another foot, with barely an effort from his wings.

"Oh, no," Khira said and covered her mouth.

"Don't say 'oh, no,' " he scolded teasingly from the ceiling. "What you did may be unforgivable, but it's fun."

"But, clearly, you're flying because you're happy! The shift in your emotions must have changed your vibration, and faster vibrations mean lighter molecules—like steam rising." She paced back and forth beneath him, muttering about *unpredictable correlated traits* and *shouldn't have turned that damn modulator up so high.* "They'll all want to fly!" she cried up at him.

Her deduction may have been right, because her distress sobered him enough to touch down.

"Who'll want to fly?" he asked from the floor.

"The *daimyo.* The bored royals the science minister thought would be a market for my procedure. If they buy wings, they'll want to use them, and they'll only be able to if they throw off every discipline our kind holds dear. Harry, this is a disaster!"

She clutched his arms. His wings seemed only partly under his control, so he wasn't positive how he did it, but his pinions curled around her in a sort of hug. "I admit, this isn't a change I would have invited into my life, but—"

"They'll want to fly," she insisted, cutting him off. "They'll want to laugh and be emotional like humans. The fabric of high society will fall apart. The emperor will never, *ever* lend his blessing to that. He'll do anything to destroy the evidence of what I've done."

Her face was white with horror, her lips tinged blue. Harry dropped his wings, brushing the hollow of her cheek with his thumb instead. Khira shook his comfort off. "We have to get you out of here."

"What?"

"Now. Before the guards find out what happened."

Harry pressed a fist to his chest, unaccountably disappointed that he wouldn't have the year with her she'd said she required. He tried to make sense of the feeling as he watched her bustle naked about the chamber, stuffing bricks of who-knew-what into a small silk bag.

"These are medical rations," she explained, though he hadn't asked. "Very high protein. You'll need extra energy for flying."

"Flying?" She expected him to *fly* out of here?

She threw him a pair of trousers, which Harry automatically pulled on. "You'll have to manage without a shirt. We don't have time to rig anything to fit around your wings."

"Khira, we're in the middle of the ocean."

"There's an island ten miles east of here, and the mainland isn't more than twenty beyond that. Once you reach it, if you just keep flying south, you'll hit human lands."

"This is crazy. I can't fly home. Even if I could, what would people think when they saw this?"

He spread both arms and wings, but Khira's jaw clenched

stubbornly. "Maybe one of your human doctors can remove them. Anyway, I thought you wanted to be free. Surely you don't intend to throw your chance away."

Dressed herself now, she grabbed his hand and pulled him to the door. Rather than push the button that slid it open, she peered at a lighted glass square on the adjacent wall, on which walked tiny, moving pictures of the lab's workers. Harry's mind was too numb to register this new wonder.

"The corridor is clear," she said. "We can slip into the service tunnels at the end."

They ran pell-mell down the empty corridor. Harry was surprised he could keep up with Khira, given the Yama's supposed thirty-miles-per-hour racing speed. He ducked into the small hatched tunnel no more than two paces after her. Like everything else, the tunnel had been carved out of the glacier's ice, its walls glowing softly blue. A single low metal rail ran along the center of its floor, possibly a guide for carts.

Khira was already hunched inside. She reached past him to close the hatch, the brush of her arm illogically welcome. "I don't think these tunnels have sensors. We can crawl from here to the landing pad where they leave supplies."

None of this meant much to Harry, but he crawled after her, learning quickly to tuck his wings close so his feathers wouldn't bump the walls. He felt surprisingly good, considering what he'd been through—anxious and confused, maybe, but not tired. His thoughts were just coherent enough to hope Khira wasn't going to get into trouble for helping him escape.

You're getting out of here, he reminded himself. He hadn't asked Khira to abduct him. The beautiful mad demon scientist could look out for herself.

"No one will hear your name from me," he promised, worried all the same. "My government won't be bringing actions against yours."

Khira blinked at him over her shoulder. "That would be kind of you," she said after a moment's hesitation. "But let me see you off safely first."

Five more minutes of crawling brought them to a second hatch. Khira pressed her ear to it, apparently heard nothing to alarm her, and pulled the lever to open it. Fresh, cold air burst inward, whipping Khira's hair and leaving Harry glad for the coverage of his wings. He might be a freak of nature, but at least he wouldn't freeze to death.

Khira climbed out onto a different, smaller landing pad from the one where they'd arrived. A large flying car, this one shaped like a hornet, sat unattended on the flattened ice.

"Quick," she whispered, waving him after her.

They used the cover of assorted other mysterious equipment to scurry around a corner to a narrow ledge. When he saw the view, Harry clutched a jut of ice to save him from dizziness. He'd forgotten how high up they were.

"You can take off from here," Khira said. Seemingly unaffected by vertigo or cold, she handed him the bag of medical rations and pointed to a black, snow-covered mountain rising from the ocean opposite their perch. "There's the island. Once you land there, your human eyes should be able to see the mainland."

Harry tied the little sack of food around his wrist. More than anything, he wanted to kiss the careful blankness from her face. He knew he ought to be ecstatic about leaving, but he couldn't help thinking his and Khira's paths weren't supposed to part this way. He realized he'd never felt so connected to another person, nor could the rare pleasure they had shared explain it all.

In one heartbreaking flash, he saw the truth of her: that she was bright and lonely and gave too much to her work. That she wanted to be kind, but was afraid to most of the time. That she was proud, but not too proud to bend when her conscience demanded it.

These things were true of him as well. Different though they were, she matched him.

"I can't do this," he said hoarsely.

She laid her palm on his chest, a flush of color creeping up her forearm from his energy. "You have to. Things won't go well for you if you stay. Now be happy. Fly and be free again."

He gazed into her shining eyes and watched her bite her trembling lower lip. A moment earlier, he'd thought her face was blank, but from the look of her now, she hung a breath away from tears.

Perhaps he wasn't the only one who sensed how well they'd fit.

"Khira," he said, soft with wonder, but she shook her head and made a shooing motion with her hands.

"Be happy," she reminded him.

Harry couldn't say he was happy, but some emotion rose in him, so fine and strong it lifted him off his feet. The regret that blazed in her silver eyes filled every empty spot he'd ever had with warmth.

"Go," she said, shooing him again.

He went reluctantly, lifting his strange new wings and trying not to dwell on how sad he was to be leaving her. Driving his wings strongly downward, he shot forward, his heart too full to have room for fear.

She wants this for me, he told himself. *I should go.*

He'd flown twenty yards from the ledge when shouts from behind him had him spinning round. As he struggled not to roll arse over teakettle, a bolt of what looked like liquid lightning streaked by his head, missing it by inches. Khira's guards had found them out. The twins were kneeling near the escape hatch with long, fat guns braced on their shoulders, presumably guns that shot lightning bolts. Harry dodged another volley with a maneuver so unthinking it had to be the work of the instincts that came with his wings. He looked at Khira, still unseen on the ledge. She waved frantically, urging him onward while he had the chance. One of the guards spotted her movement.

Harry didn't have to be told this was bad. He was already speeding toward her when she screamed. A chunk of ice had just exploded in her face. The second guard had stopped shooting at Harry to target her.

"Arms up!" Harry shouted as he swooped down.

He caught her to him without touching down, only scraping one wing at the last moment. Luckily, the injury wasn't to his flight feathers. He turned with Khira pressed to his chest and pounded the air with his wings. Khira's hair wrapped him like a cloak as they soared away.

"Harry," she gasped, clutching his torso with all her limbs.

Harry couldn't answer, even to soothe her. He was breathing too hard from their conjoined weight.

"Go left!" she cried a second before another bolt blazed to their right. This caught a feather close enough to singe. "Oh, please, you have to go faster. Those plasma rifles are deadly!"

Harry tried to go faster, but he was feeling heavier himself. He had to think of something less grim than dying, or they'd both end up plummeting.

"Tell me . . . you love me," he panted, not caring how pathetic he sounded. "And if you don't, for God's sake lie."

"I do," she said, almost without a pause. "I didn't realize it, but I think I must!"

The dismay in her voice convinced him; amused him, too. As if by magic, strength surged through him, not just in his wings but every part of him. The feel of the air scudding beneath him was suddenly absolutely right—as if he'd been meant to fly all his life. When another flash from the electric weapon jagged a foot away, he almost laughed.

"Hang on," he said, driving them determinedly forward again. "I think this calls for evasive maneuvers."

Though Khira shrieked when he began to take them, a moment later she kissed his chest. "I love you," she repeated. "Please don't make me lose last night's dinner before we're safe."

"I love you, too," he said, and stole one sweet moment to kiss her hair.

Khira and Harry had one advantage. Their head start enabled them
to find a concealed cave to hide in on the next island—before the
lab could scramble a search squadron. They sat there now, side by
side and backs to the wall. Harry had wrapped one wing around
her, which had to the most peculiar comfort Khira had ever been
snuggled in.

It was also an arousing comfort. Her body buzzed from having
clung to him while they flew, and their continuing closeness didn't
help. If Harry hadn't been so justifiably preoccupied with matters of
survival, and likely in need of conserving his strength, she suspected
she would have spent every minute before nightfall having sex with
him. They planned to continue their journey then, because Harry
had discovered that, in addition to possessing owl's wings, he could
also see in the dark. Yamish pilots were equipped for night vision,
too, but at least Khira and Harry would be more difficult to spot.

With the arctic wind blasting around them while Harry flew,
any heat signature they generated should be obscured.

"We can't go south," he said, swiping crumbs from his meal bar
onto the floor. "Every aircar we saw was searching in that direction. They must assume I'm trying to get home."

"They must assume I know better than to stop you. Any Yama
we asked for help would surely turn us in."

"*Any* Yama?" Harry asked, obviously doubting this. "Don't
you have family?"

"Yes," Khira admitted—rather grumpily.

Harry peered at her uncharacteristic frown.

"Oh, all right," she surrendered. "We'll go to my parents."

"If you're afraid they won't help us . . ."

"They'll help us," she predicted darkly. "Believe me, they'll be
delighted to."

———

Harry wasn't sure how much longer he could keep going. Holding
Khira was wonderful, but he'd been flying for hours, and his

muscles burned. The stars no longer enthralled him, the magic of flight was old, and Khira's meal bars tasted like pasteboard. If it hadn't been essential that they get as close to safety as they could before dawn, Harry would have begged a halt. Instead, he tried to suck more air into his aching lungs.

Happy thoughts, he urged himself, but the best he could do was imagine how long he was going to sleep with Khira in his arms when this was over.

"You're tired," she murmured, one hand stroking sympathetically along his side. He was grateful that she was strong. At least he didn't have worry about her losing her grip on him.

"I'm fine," he said against her temple. "Though maybe if you stopped squirming, I wouldn't have to fight to keep my balance."

The heat of her blush was palpable against his chest.

"Sorry," she mumbled, writhing even as she apologized. "I'll do my best."

It took Harry a second to realize what was wrong. "Oh, Lord," he said, his own heat beginning to rise despite his fatigue. "You want to make love."

"I don't! I mean, I do. I've been holding you all this time, and your etheric force keeps seeping into me no matter how tired you are, but I know you need your strength for flying."

"Are you wet?" Harry's voice dropped an octave to ask this.

"What good would it do for me to answer that?"

Rather than argue, he slid his hand around her bottom to touch the seam of her trousers. They were drenched, her cream kept warm by its proximity to her body. She moaned when he brushed her mons with his fingertips. He could feel the swollen bump of her pleasure bud as her nipples pebbled against his chest. Suddenly, his wings didn't feel so tired. Knowing how much she wanted him, and had been wanting him all this time, was giving him a second wind.

"Let's do it," he said. "Let's have sex."

"Harry, we can't. You're tired, and it will drain you. Even if it wouldn't, we really shouldn't stop."

"Who said anything about stopping?"

She shuddered in his hold, her temperature abruptly torrid. This was enough of an answer for him.

"Take off one leg of your trousers," he ordered. "If you open mine at the front, we should be able to get me inside."

"Harry . . ."

"Khira." He squeezed her squirming bottom and beat his wings harder. "Remember the last time I had a climax? That was the first time I lifted off. Maybe this is what I need to perk me up. I know you can feel how willing I am."

She moaned again, loudly, as he rolled the bulge of his erection against her mound. The treatment fattened him even more, leaving him breathless in a different way. Khira cursed, but he didn't care. She had unhitched one leg from his waist and was quickly wrenching off that side of her trousers.

"You have to believe me," she panted. "I wouldn't be risking this unless I were completely desperate."

He loved that she was desperate, loved that she slung her leg back around him, grabbed his prick, and shoved it greedily inside her quim—which had to be a hundred times as hot as the surrounding air. Harry's wings momentarily lost their coordination. He swerved sharply left before his overloaded senses recovered.

"It's fine," he assured her as he straightened their path again. "I can fly. You—God—you pull up me, and I'll push in."

As it turned out, his wings did this for him. Every downbeat drove him deep into her body's clasp, until he'd have sworn the pleasure had him stretching inches longer than usual. She had to do that shifting trick with her sheath to let his full length in. She began coming in minutes, not once but repeatedly, crying out at each climax and begging him to go on. She was not a Yama then, but just a woman, and Harry reveled in her need. His cock was soaked with her juices, slick as butter and hard as steel. He hardly knew where he was flying, only that no power on earth could make him want to stop.

This felt better than any experience, of any sort, that he had ever had. She was fire in his arms, in his soul. When she came again, spasming hard around him, he wasn't completely sure the pleasure wasn't his.

His body knew differently. His hips began to snap faster, doubling the speed of his wings. He realized his balls had rucked up against his body, preparing—rather imminently—to eject their stored burden.

"I have to," he warned her, gripping her bottom to sling her to his root. "I have to come now."

Her head arched back with her groan, but it wasn't a groan of protest. She was tightening yet again, hard enough to make him see stars that weren't hanging in the sky. Half a heartbeat was all it took. His seed burst from him like holy fire. He felt them soar upward dizzyingly fast. Rosy lights shimmered around them, flaring, blending, until they formed one shared blanket of energy. It was an orgasm sweet enough to nearly kill a man.

Happily, it didn't. Harry came back to his proper mind when they drifted, entirely without exertion on his part, through a wispy cloud. Tiny ice crystals tinkled against their skin.

"Oh, Harry." Khira's nose nuzzled his neck. "That was nice."

He laughed and took control of their flight, angling them down to warmer air currents. Evidently, they'd been making love for some time. The horizon was growing lighter, and, wonder of wonders, he thought he saw the ring of seven grassy hills Khira had told him to watch for. A miniature castle sat within their shallow bowl, looking very much like something from the human Dark Ages. The oddity that crouched behind it he had seen only once in an illustration. If memory served, it was called a geodesic dome.

Harry experienced a shiver of excitement no amount of uncertainty about his future could quell. Whatever else came of this adventure, he was going to see secrets few humans had.

"I think we're here," he said.

"Good," Khira responded sleepily. "I need a nap."

Chapter 7

THEY did not go directly to her parents' estate. After all these years away, Khira needed time to gather her defenses. Instead, they napped in a sheltered hollow near Forette lands, with Harry on his back and Khira wrapped in his wings, lulled into relaxation by the humming bees. Thanks to her father's genius, this area had its own microclimate. The springlike temperatures saved them from shivering.

Khira woke when Harry stirred beneath her. She wanted to purr at the way his hand immediately smoothed her hair down her spine. Embarrassing though it was to admit, she could get used to human tenderness.

"Khira," he said, his voice still thick with sleep. "There's something I need to know. How can I be strong enough to do what I did last night? Just how much did you change me?"

Khira knew he meant the flying and not the sex, but still had to fight the blood rushing to her cheeks. The few extra adjustments she'd made to him had not been part of her assignment.

"As long as I was working on you," she said, "I corrected some . . . inefficiencies. In your muscles. And your cardiovascular system. You mustn't have been taking good enough care of yourself. Your heart had some problems. I wanted you to have a good, long life, and if we happened to be separated in the future, I wanted to be sure you could defend yourself."

"Then I'm as strong as a Yama now?"

"You do appear to be, though—clearly—you've manifested a few more changes than I expected."

He sat up with her in his arms, the better to think about this, or perhaps just to shake the circulation back into his wings. She thought he might comment on her taking liberties with his insides, however well meaning, but when he returned his burning gaze to hers, he had other matters on his mind.

"Khira, no one ever said they loved me before."

"I thought humans said that all the time."

"Not the ones who knew me. My mother died the day I was born. I never knew who my father was. Strangers took care of me until I ran off. The people I've met since have kept their distance. I suppose I'm not the warmest person they know."

Khira knew warmth was culturally relative, but this took her aback. Hadn't Harry let down his guard with anyone but her? She petted his naked shoulder and then the soft cream-colored down beneath the feathers of his right wing. His eyes closed briefly with pleasure. She sensed emotion in him, deeper than any that had sounded in his voice or shone in his eyes, deeper perhaps than any Yama would have strength to face. He had been lonely, achingly so, among people who did not regard isolation as their common lot. Aching for him herself, Khira tried to say the right thing.

"It hurt that no one said they loved you."

Harry shrugged. "Sometimes it did."

More than sometimes, she thought. "I'll tell you again," she promised rashly. "If you want me to."

"I don't want you to lie. Not anymore."

"I didn't lie the last time. If this feeling inside me isn't love, no Yama knows what love is. I risked everything I valued to ensure your safety."

"Including your life."

"Well, I wasn't certain the guards would kill me. I only thought they might."

Something about the way she said this caused him to laugh. She realized she didn't mind. The sound seemed natural, even pleasant, coming from him. His eyes were shining now, as they hadn't when he admitted to being hurt. Harry allowed tears to rise from pleasure or amusement, but not for pity of himself.

"I hope you'll tell me you love me again," he said, "any time you'd like."

Khira nodded, hoping this response was acceptable. A Yama would have been insulted to receive far subtler professions of fondness more than once a week. She wondered if, as a human, Harry would find once a day too much. She suspected she wasn't going to wish to say it any less.

"There's something I need to warn you about," she said, done with putting it off. "Before we reach my old home." She pulled in a breath and let her confession out in a rush. "My parents belong to a sect called the Laughing Yama, which was formed not long after humans encountered us. They believe laughter strengthens their minds and bodies. When I was a child, every day, for half an hour, my parents would send me to my room to laugh."

Harry's brows were raised with suppressed humor. "They sent you to your room to *laugh*?"

"I expect that doesn't sound bad to you, but it branded me as different, and among the Yama, being different isn't tolerated well. If my parents hadn't been members of the aristocracy, and certified geniuses, the emperor would have banished them. As it is, certain doors will never open to me because of them."

Harry looked at her kindly. "I'm sorry for that. I'm sorry for anything that hurts you."

Khira waved his sympathy away, though in truth it felt nice. "The past doesn't matter. You won't dislike them. They're decent people, and they're virtually guaranteed to like you—which is fortunate since we may have to stay with them for a while."

"Virtually guaranteed?" He puffed his chest. "I like the sound of that."

She didn't explain that they were going to like him because all Laughing Yama liked humans—or thought they should. Most had never met one in the flesh. More important to her was that Harry didn't appear put off by the prospect of being stuck with her. This suggested that the love he'd expressed was not a passing state. The tension that had been gripping Khira's throat eased just enough to let her heart rise into it.

Khira hadn't mentioned her family was rich. Then again, conceivably, among her people, living in castles was commonplace. The knocker Harry had taken hold of dropped to the thick wood door with a hollow boom. He felt, quite distinctly, that he was stepping from his proper place. For Khira's sake he hid his insecurity. Yama or not, she looked nervous enough for both of them.

After two long minutes, during which he fought not to fidget, the giant door swung silently open. A tall, slender woman stood behind it in a flowing, red silk gown—also Medieval in style. Apart from her silver hair, she looked very much like Khira. With widened eyes, she took in the tableau before her: the rough-faced, winged human standing shoulder to shoulder with her rumpled and estranged daughter. To Harry's surprise, she did not enfold Khira in her arms, but spoke as if they'd seen each other the day before.

"Good heavens!" she exclaimed, her inflection nearly human. "What have you done to this man?"

Khira bristled in a highly muted Yamish way. "Why do you assume it was me?"

"Because I know you, daughter. You feel compelled to do the impossible just to prove you can. But, please, both of you come in.

I am Brinmythra Forette—Dr. Forette, if you like. Welcome to our home." She bowed, the palms of her hands pressed together before her breasts. Then she added, rather oddly, "Hahahahaha."

The laugh was less convincing than her *good heavens*, but Harry assumed it related to her philosophical persuasion. He bowed back as smoothly as he was able to, what with the extra weight on his back. "Pleased to meet you, Dr. Forette. I'm Harry Wirth."

As he stepped into the great hall behind Khira's mother, two silver-faced servants in old-fashioned human livery bowed to them.

"Don't mind the androids," Khira's mother said. "They're just prototypes."

Harry jerked his brows at Khira for an explanation. She mouthed *later* silently, but her mother turned in time to catch the exchange.

She had stopped beneath a suit of armor that hung suspended from the vaulted ceiling. It seemed to be serving in place of a chandelier. An electric light had been installed inside it, and golden rays shot out from the chinks. Evidently, not all the decorating choices here were human.

"Do you know," Khira's mother said, her head tilted thoughtfully to the side. "You two have complementary auras, truly a perfect match. I never knew that could happen between the races. Considering Harry has all that lovely etheric force, the two of you must have an interesting time in bed."

"*Mother,*" Khira said.

Her mother looked innocent. "Is there some reason I shouldn't mention this? Your father and I were the same, though naturally we're both Yamish. I doubt she'll be able to drain you," she added to Harry in an aside. "Mates with matching auras tend to form energy circuits."

"Mother is an expert in auric systems," Khira explained through slightly gritted teeth. "And robotics. And please don't take her seriously when she calls us 'mates.'"

"Wouldn't dream of it," Harry said, though he knew his grin

was telling Khira differently. She was far too flustered not to have thought of them being *mates* herself, a term he suspected meant spouses rather than friends. That concept appealed to him a good deal more than he might have guessed.

Khira was wondering if this reunion could get any more awkward, when her father burst into the great hall from a back chamber. Per usual, his hair was standing out in great white tufts. He was half a foot taller than Harry and spindly as a stork, the trait for height occasionally being exaggerated in the upper ranks.

"Hahahahaha," he said, the formal laugh of greeting coming out a pant. "Good Lord, Khira, I told the minister you weren't here!"

"What minister?" asked Khira's mother as Khira—in spite of a lifetime schooling herself out of bad childhood habits—squeezed Harry's hand in alarm. More shameful, she wasn't one bit sorry when he returned the grip reassuringly.

Khira's father straightened his tunic. "It's the emperor's minister of science. He set his transport down in my tomatoes! He didn't say so, but I got the impression Khira was in trouble. Maybe she and this, er, winged human ought to hide in the dungeon. Hello, by the way," he added to Harry. "I'm Dr. Forette. Always pleased to meet a member of the race who was born knowing how to laugh. Hahahahaha!"

"Er, the honor's mine," Harry said before turning his confused face to Khira. "*Should* we hide?"

Khira put her hands on his ribs and let his energy flow into her. Her mother had always excelled at reading auras. Khira wasn't surprised that she'd seen her and Harry's complementary patterns when Khira had not. Now, knowing she couldn't weaken him—his etheric force would simply flow back to him again—she enjoyed the warmth and steadiness the contact lent.

"The minister has already guessed we're here," Khira said. "He's compiled a file on me. I suppose he knew better than I did who I'd turn to. It might be best just to speak with him."

"No, no, no!" her father broke in, waving his long, thin hands. "Those inner circle bastards trick everyone."

Khira knew why he was upset. Her parents, who had little head for contracts, had gotten the short end of more than one deal with the royals.

"You taught me I couldn't run from my problems," she reminded him. "You said they'd only run after me. At least I know he's not here to kill me. He'd have hired someone else for that. Maybe we can work out an amnesty."

"An amnesty for what?" demanded Khira's mother, but Khira had no time to explain.

"Wait with my parents," she said to Harry, pressing both his hands to her heart. "If the minister sees you, he'll only be reminded of what I've done."

"I'll send the androids," her mother offered before Harry could object to being left behind. "If the minister tries to intimidate you, they'll wrestle him to the ground."

"I thought they were prototypes."

"They're *good* prototypes," she emphasized.

Rather than laugh, because the robots were probably a hair's-breadth from perfect, Khira gave her mother the sort of hug neither had gotten into the habit of exchanging.

"Oh, my," her mother said, unsurely patting her daughter's shoulder, thus giving Khira the singular satisfaction of having been, for once, more eccentric than her parents.

———

The emperor's minister of science wasn't one to beat around the bush. He waited on the marble path beside her father's pansy beds, glittering in his gold-edged blue robes. Her father's geodesic weather dome rose behind him, lightning flickering in its upper reaches as some experiment played out.

The minister raised his brows at the two bewigged silver androids tramping behind her, but must have decided they weren't a threat. His own guards stood in the distance beside his aircar. As soon as Khira reached him, he spoke.

"Congratulations, Dr. Forette. You passed the test. The emperor didn't think you would, but I was certain."

Khira was convinced he'd intended to steal her breath, but she'd had too many shocks of late to lose it easily. "How can I have passed?" she asked, with nearly royal aplomb. "I ran away with my subject."

The minister almost smiled. "True, but the experiment itself succeeded brilliantly—despite the unfortunate side effect. And my apologies for the guards trying to shoot you. They hadn't been apprised of all the . . . subtleties of the situation. Whether you realize it or not, Dr. Forette, you have proven yourself the premiere geneticist working today. Not since ancient times has a true chimera been created. The emperor would like to finance a lab for you. Here, if you like. Your parents' land seems suitably isolated."

Khira suspected this wasn't a suggestion, but chose to treat it as if it were. "What, exactly, would I be doing in my lab?"

"Seeing if you can undo the damage that was done to Yamish royals during earlier genetic trials."

"How much earlier?" she asked, immediately wondering if there were secret records to which she could obtain access.

The minister gazed placidly at her face, no doubt able to read her rising interest. "If I said three thousand years, would it frighten you? No, I didn't think so. It's true. The myths of our bygone history do not lie. The so-called ancient Yama were every bit as advanced as we are today. Now, after millennia of inbreeding among themselves, the royals are paying the price for those earlier scientists' genius."

"Paying how?"

The minister waved at a passing dragonfly. "We can discuss details later. I assure you, however, that from here on, your only subjects will be consenting Yamish adults."

"I'd want a written contract."

"I thought you might." The corners of the minister's mouth twitched. "You will, of course, have to induce the human to stay here. We can't have him talking to or being seen by others. I presume you have some means by which you could reconcile him to his lot."

Her bare toes curled uncomfortably into the grass, her shoes having fallen off during the previous night's flight. "I believe I do."

I hope I do, is what she thought.

The minister may have sensed her uncertainty. "The only other option is to amputate his wings and perform a memory wipe, the technology for which—as you know—is somewhat barbaric."

Khira said nothing. No way in creation would she subject Harry's wonderful mind and heart to that. She wanted him to remain exactly what and who he was.

Amazingly, the minister seemed uncomfortable with her silence. "Well, then," he said after a pause. "It seems we are essentially in agreement. I'd like to add that I'm pleased to have avoided ordering you killed. Your brain is a national treasure. I might wish you had a different familial derivation, but perhaps true originality needs original soil. Your parents certainly have proven theirs."

Khira bowed, feeling as if he had unwittingly given her a gift with this compliment. Maybe it was time she made peace with her upbringing. Maybe it was going to bring her more rewards than she'd dreamed. Aloud, she said, "I look forward to meeting with your lawyers."

The minister bowed elegantly back and returned without further formalities to his transport.

Until it lifted off, Khira refrained from sighing relief.

———

Harry had never been as content as he was at this moment. He and Khira sat in a sheltered courtyard within the castle, holding hands on a small stone bench, behind which roses as big as soup bowls shed their scent. Khira had told him, word for word, what the minister had said. Unless Harry wished to do himself and her great harm, his life as he'd known it had to be over. Astonishing as it sounded, he couldn't have been happier.

He lifted Khira's knuckles to his mouth for a gentle kiss and asked a question that had been preying on his mind. "Was there really a problem with my heart?"

She'd been staring at her new slippers, but now she looked at him. Her gaze was different than it had been when they first met, still serene, but somehow open—as if she were now willing to let him see what he could find within. "I was wondering when you'd ask me that. Yes, your heart had a weakness. It wouldn't have killed you for another decade, but that seemed too soon to me nonetheless."

"So you fixed it."

A tiny pucker appeared between her brows. "The thought of you dying young disturbed me. I suppose I should have realized you'd already engaged my affections."

"Because you found me so irresistible while I lay paralyzed with my prick gone begging, and even more so when I jumped off a moving train to get away from you."

"Those circumstances did intensify your pull on me."

"I'm glad," he said, because if he hadn't, he would have laughed.

"You won't mind . . . living out here?" she asked shyly.

He kissed her forehead. "I fought all my life to get where I was when you found me: safe, respected, financially secure—everything I'd dreamed of as an orphaned boy. The night you walked into that pub, I'd finally realized it wasn't enough. I didn't need things, or security. They left me empty. What I needed was someone to give my heart."

Khira turned her head away. Harry didn't think this was because he was saying things she disliked hearing, though he did lighten his tone. "I won't miss being lonely," he added, "and I won't mind living in a place this peaceful and clean. Not being the king of the costermongers might cause me a pang now and then, but I expect I'll find some way to earn my keep."

"The *king*?" Khira repeated faintly, which made him smile. "Harry, I really must apologize for misjudging you so completely when we first met."

"No need, love. Appearances can be deceiving." His grin broadened. "For my part, I thought you no less than a queen."

"Oh, no!" she protested. "My family's position among the *daimyo* is very modest: strictly lower upper class. Apart from our ingenuity, the Forette line has very little leverage. That's why I hoped you might consent to—" Khira cleared her throat as if it were tight. "My parents *are* in dire need of business advice."

"Are they? Well, if they wish to employ me, I hope they're prepared to amass more leverage than they have now. When I take charge of a business, I do it right." Harry rubbed his newly shaven chin. "I trust it's all right to confess I like them."

Khira couldn't repress her grimace completely. "I imagine their character is more what you're accustomed to than mine."

"Not at all!" he assured her, chuckling. "Just think, though, if you *shared* your parents with me, tolerating them might seem less of a burden."

"It's true you've never had parents," she said judiciously. "You might enjoy any sort, no matter how peculiar."

"Plus, sharing parents seems like a thing mates should do."

Khira narrowed her eyes. "'Mates' means married, Harry."

He genuinely enjoyed smiling at her. "I suspected as much."

She said nothing as to whether marrying him would be welcome, but beneath the thumb he was using to caress her wrist, he felt her pulse racing. She scooted closer, until her entire arm was pressed to his ribs. Harry's pulse picked up as well. He knew what this kind of contact could lead to.

Self-conscious about the erection growing at his groin, Harry glanced up the nearest castle wall. Khira's mother had the maids inventing shirts with wingholes behind the upper windows, and Khira's father kept walking out on the parapet to wave. Maybe tonight, once her parents stopped fussing over them, he and Khira could sneak out of the castle and try making love while flying again. The hope of doing that made him much better than resigned to keeping his new appendages.

Perhaps Khira was entertaining similar ideas. When he wrapped his wing and arm around her, she snuggled her head into his shoulder.

"Mother was right about one thing," she admitted. "I do feel compelled to do things to prove I can. When I get my lab, I might have to see if I can grow myself a pair of wings."

"Ah," Harry said, his heart expanding like a heat wave inside his chest. Then and there he knew, even if Khira didn't, that she had as good as accepted him. God, he loved her, odd Yamish ways and all. Though his eyes were pricking with emotion, he managed to speak calmly. "You know, you will have to hone a few new skills before you can keep *up* with me, so to speak."

"Yes," Khira agreed, her lovely face a picture of determination. "I'll have to learn to laugh as well as you!"

Angel and the Hellraiser

Vickie Taylor

Chapter 1

DEATH was a fickle bitch, and Zane Halvorson flirted with her every chance he got.

Okay, so maybe firing a flare gun into his parachute while he was still four hundred feet above his landing zone, and staring up in awe as the fragile nylon disintegrated into ash a little more quickly than he'd calculated had been closer to insanity than showmanship. What the hell? He was an aerial stuntman. He got paid to defy death. To make the crowd scream and mothers cover their children's eyes to keep them from being traumatized for life by his twice-weekly, seemingly inevitable, gory demise.

Never let it be said that Zane Halvorson didn't give people their money's worth.

If one of his stunts did actually manage to kill him, at least he'd die in a manner of his own choosing. On his own terms. Terms that seemed to finally be coming to fruition on a sunny Sunday afternoon at the central New Mexico Boat and Air Show, as the short-lived glory of the flaming parachute gag dumped him in the lake next to the airfield, well short of his planned drop on the tarmac.

Tempting fate on a regular basis the way he did, he wasn't surprised to find himself sinking to a dark, watery grave at the bottom of Lake Mitchell. Drifting to his death with a auburn-haired beauty he'd never seen before floating serenely at his side, however, was quite a jolt.

The current fanned a halo of dark, wavy locks around her head. The sunlight glaring off the surface of the water surrounded her in an ethereal glow, like she was some kind of goddess. Her eyes were deep-sea green, and held such tranquility that just gazing into them filled him with peace. Acceptance.

The last bit of oxygen he'd hoarded in his lungs during his descent escaped and gurgled toward the surface in a column of bubbles, and he watched with a kind of detached curiosity. He felt odd. There should have been pain. He'd hit the water at far too high a speed to not be injured. There should have been panic as the weight of his waterlogged jumpsuit dragged him down, and the cords of his demolished parachute tangled around his arms and legs, ending his struggle to kick and swim his way to the surface, to air.

But there was no panic. No pain. There was only a gentle touch of the mystery woman's fingers to his cheek, and comfort, as if someone had tucked a soft blanket around his shoulders on a cold night. That and a slight tingling in his hands and legs as his extremities slowly went numb.

His eyelids grew heavy and slid half-closed. The lake pulsed like a living thing around him, its heartbeat thrumming low and steady in his ears. The woman beside him floated closer, and her nearness enveloped him in warmth.

Who are you? he asked, hearing the words as clearly as if he'd spoken them, though—hell—that wasn't possible. He was underwater. He was drowning. Maybe he was already dead, though he didn't feel dead. He felt . . . satisfied for the first time in a long time. And a little confused.

I'm an angel, she answered in the same freaky speechless communication.

An angel?

Sent to you by God.

Yep. Definitely dead.

With a concerted effort, he pried his eyelids back open a fraction. They were deep in the lake now, darkness closing around them. Yet the light still surrounded her, bouncing off the particles in the murky water in a strange pattern that spread behind her back like . . . wings.

He slammed his eyelids shut. Who was he kidding? There was no celestial being coming for Zane Halvorson. After a life of beer drinking, bar brawling, and hell-raising recklessness, he was more likely to spend his eternal days breathing fire than angel dust.

His mouth twisted into a wry grin. *'Fraid there's been some mistake,* he drawled in his thoughts.

No. A gentle smile graced the corners of her mouth. *I'm here for you. Only you.*

He felt her fingers working at the buckles of his harness, and the cumbersome equipment fell away. Instantly he felt buoyant, lighter in body and in soul. Next, her hands moved to the zipper of his jumpsuit.

Okay, normally, a beautiful chick undressing him and professing that she was here only for him would be a real turn-on. An irresistible turn-on, even.

Today, dying at the bottom of this godforsaken lake, it pissed him off.

No. He pushed her hands away.

She arched back, her delicate brows pulling together. Her arms swirled at her sides, holding her stationary in the water. *But I've come to save you.*

To save him? God had sent an angel. To save him. The irony of it burned. The warmth that had suffused him suddenly banked to an uncomfortable heat. Rage. *Don't you get it? I don't want to be saved.*

He'd no sooner thought the last word than a current with the strength of a tsunami slammed into him. The jet stream propelled him up with such force that he felt as if the skin might be ripped from his body. His internal organs plummeted to the bottom of his abdomen. He was a bullet streaking across an open plain, a rocket in the night sky, an untamed creature of the sea, streaking from the dark depths toward the surface, toward the sun. Toward life.

———

She had a name.

A moment ago, she had simply *been*. A benevolent life force on a mission for humanity, she had existed as energy, as light and imagination, a small piece of the energy, light and imagination that was the universe, and now she was Rosemary D'Amica, photographer for the *Las Nueces Times*. She had shape. She had form. She had a name.

She had a body.

She ran her trembling hands down her sides, feeling the strength of the ribs beneath her skin, the curve of her waist, the flare of her hips. She tipped her chin down to catch sight of her own heaving chest, her pebbled forearms, and shivered.

God, no!

Being forced to take human form was always a possibility in her job. She'd just hoped she could avoid it. . . .

The sunlight assaulted her eyes, and she flung a hand up in front of her face to ward off the brightness. She was on a boat. The roar of the engine, the slap of waves against the hull, and the simultaneously inhaled breaths of hundreds of air-show onlookers on the shore beat against her eardrums. The cotton tank top and denim shorts she wore chaffed at her skin. The bitter tang of fear stung her tongue.

"Roll him over!" A voice pierced her mind like a needle. She wasn't used to physical sensation. Until a few seconds ago, she'd existed in a place of quiet, of peace. The light, the sound, overwhelmed her. It was all too much, too loud, too sudden.

She clapped her hands over her ears, but the voice drilled through.

"Roll him on his side. Do it now, Rosemary!"

Through squinted eyes, she glanced up at the man yelling at her as he piloted the boat toward shore full-throttle. John Murphy, she realized. Part-time staff reporter for the *Times*. She knew his name the same way she knew her own. The way she knew where she lived and where she worked. In the blink of an eye, this life had been created for her and all the mortals who would swear they had known her all their lives. Part of the grand plan, whatever that was, designed by a higher power. Much higher.

Following John's gaze, she looked around and realized she was on her knees on the deck of the small boat, crouched over the body of Zane Halvorson. Water dripped from her chin to his still chest.

Coughing as her own burning lungs came to grips with the sudden availability of—and need for—oxygen, she rolled the lifeless man to his side and looked back to John.

"Slap him between the shoulder blades!"

"What?" Violence wasn't in the angel handbook.

"Make him cough up the water. Try to get him breathing!"

Shaken by her lack of understanding of corporeal matters, she did as she was told and hit the heel of her hand on Zane's back, then looked back to John.

"Is he breathing?"

She splayed one hand across the cool, damp chest, and lowered her ear next to the man's mouth, but couldn't hear or feel anything. "I don't think so!"

"All right." John measured the distance to shore with a glance, then turned back to her and shouted. "Rescue breathing."

"What?"

"Mouth to mouth. CPR!"

At first Rosemary had no idea what he was talking about, but the knowledge flooded her mind the same way all the details of the mortal existence that had been built for her had. She rolled Zane to his back, then checked for respiration and pulse. His heart was beating, but he wasn't breathing.

As if she'd practiced a thousand times, she tipped his head back, pinched his nose and blew two quick breaths into his mouth, then rolled him to his side, thumped his back and checked for respiration again.

Feeling her senses heighten even more as adrenaline pumped into her system, she raised a desperate glance to John. "Nothing!"

"Try again! Keep trying!"

The boat's engine revved until they sounded as if they might snap like a wire strung too tight. Rosemary ignored the painful whine, focused on her task. Roll. Breathe. Roll. Slap. Roll. Breathe. Roll. Slap.

Her stomach lurched as the boat hit the dock hard enough to send her skidding across the deck, grasping the shoulder of the unconscious man beside her to keep him from toppling overboard.

Silence descended with a force as deafening as the clamor that had brutalized her only minutes ago. She could feel the dying vibration of the engine as John cut the motor. The held breath of the people watching from shore.

All of her concentration narrowed into Zane Halvorson. Roll. Breathe. Roll. Slap. Roll—

He coughed. More accurately, his whole body spasmed. Streams of lake water jetted out of his mouth as his hands clutched protectively over his stomach and his knees drew up to his chest.

After a few moments, Zane's eyes opened. Huge, dark pupils sucked her in like a vacuum. A moment of recognition passed from his eyes to hers, then a hint of inquiry and finally narrow-eyed suspicion. Off to her side, John picked up her camera and snapped off shot after shot of the two of them. Her chest clenched around each gasping breath—Zane's and hers—until he finally seemed to realize where he was, how many people were watching.

His gaze still locked on hers, he reached out and grasped her fingers. His lips curved in a deliberate smile as he rolled up to his knees and raised their joined hands toward the sky in a gesture of triumph for the crowd.

"Woooooo-hooooooo!" he hollered, and as one, the crowd let out a deafening cheer.

The noise and the light crashed in on Rosemary again. Dizzy and queasy from the onslaught, she tried to pull back, away, but Zane held her tight.

His smile widened, but before she'd recovered enough to read the intent swirling in his hazel eyes, he slipped an arm behind her shoulders and draped her backward in his embrace. His mouth followed her down, and his lips captured hers in a kiss that had her fingers fisting in the wet fabric of his jumpsuit and her muscles turning to jelly.

It was over as quickly as it began. He raised his head, waving at the crowd while she hung in his arms, breathless and helpless, like a worm on a hook. Once again the crowd cheered.

"A little CPR of my own," he announced, quieting the people gathered around the dock as he pulled her upright, grinned at her and gestured toward her with his hand and a slight bow of his head. "For my guardian angel!"

Chapter 2

ROSEMARY padded through her second-story apartment, absorbing sensory details with every step—the feel of the smooth hardwood beneath her bare feet, the ticking of the mantel clock over the false fireplace, green and blue flashes of light streaming through the sun catcher in the kitchen window. She'd been in this human form, this body, for twenty-four hours now, and still everything seemed too bright, too loud, too hot or too cold.

How long had it been since she'd felt, tasted, touched in the way of mortals?

She couldn't say. Time didn't exist in her plane of existence. There was no past to regret, no future to anticipate. She just *was*, moment to moment.

She didn't know how long it had been since she'd last been in human form, but she did know the world had not been like this. So crowded, so noisy.

The thought of facing the modern world this way, with all of her human feelings and fears intact, was nearly enough to send her scurrying back to bed and under a cocoon of covers where it was quiet and dark. Safe.

But hiding wasn't going to get her back where she belonged. She was stuck here until she finished the job she'd come to do, and that meant facing the world—and Zane Halvorson.

It happened this way, occasionally. People weren't always ready to accept the gift she offered. They had issues.

Zane Halvorson seemed to have more issues than most. *Guardian angel?* She was called many names by many people in different parts of the world, but that was a new one.

Sighing, she stopped her pacing before a maple cabinet that displayed an antique china collection with pattern of delicate blue and yellow flowers. A small dish of candies sat on the hutch. Curious, she lifted the lid and cautiously placed a small green square on the tip of her tongue.

Mmmmmmm. Her eyelids drifted down, and she smiled, remembering. Party mints. The sweet and creamy kind that melted in the mouth.

So maybe not everything about the human existence was as odious as she'd first thought. She could get through it. She knew where to find him and she knew what needed to be done. The trick would be to stay focused. Work quickly. She'd be out of here in no time. For if she knew one thing, it was that death would visit Zane Halvorson again.

Soon.

———

The sound of beer bottles clinking and pool balls clacking was all a man needed to soothe what ailed him—at least in the Zane Halvorson book of medicine. One step into the Oasis, his favorite dive, and he felt like he'd dropped a twenty-pound pack off his back. All around the room friendly faces raised beers and pool cues in greeting.

His gray-haired pilot and the designated dirty old man of the aerial-show crew, Jasper, broke away from a conversation that was surely leading to a deep and meaningful one-night stand with the new waitress and sidled over. "'Bout time you got here, Z. How you doing? Feeling all right?"

"I'm good." Actually he was a little shaken. Not so much by almost dying, but the whole angel-of-the-deep thing had him freaked out.

She'd been on a boat near where he'd splashed down in the lake and jumped in to rescue him. He'd caught a few glimpses of her in the water before he'd lost consciousness. Anything else he thought he remembered was probably just oxygen deprivation screwing with his memory. His mind was a frightening place on a good day. On a bad one . . . hell, he didn't even want to think about the possibilities.

Jasper clamped a hand on his shoulder and propelled him across the barroom. "Come on, you gotta see this. Jimmie is cleaning house on the tables tonight."

Zane shook himself from the memory of sinking in cold, dark water. "Yeah, in a minute. Let me get a drink."

Jasper toddled away. "Hurry it up. You're missing a show. Kid's got a gift, I tell you."

Zane sidled toward the bar. Jimmie had a gift all right. For losing every cent he won on the pool table in the backroom poker party that would start up in about an hour.

He smiled. It was good to be home.

With his elbows propped on the scarred wood bar, one boot planted on the brass rail near the floor, and hips leaning against a leather-covered stool, Zane waited for Pete, the bartender, to finish the highball he was mixing. While Zane waited he looked around the room, sinking into the familiarity of the place as he picked out all the regulars among the sea of new faces in town for the air and boat show. Dan and Mike were in a heated conversation over who deserved to be this year's baseball MVP. Kyle was working the crowd. Joey was wrapped around his girlfriend in the booth behind—

Her.

She sat by herself at the little table tucked into the farthest corner, head down and both hands wrapped around a glass, almost as if she hoped no one would notice her.

His guardian angel.

He took a moment to study her unawares. He hadn't really gotten a good look at her yesterday before the paramedics had stormed the boat and hauled him off to the emergency room. He just had that impression of wild, dark hair and deep green eyes—the kind of gorgeous that could hit a guy like a punch in the gut if he wasn't careful. He hadn't had a chance to talk to her at all.

He wasn't sure he wanted to.

How fucked-up was that? She'd saved his life. Then there was the whole dramatic kiss thing, which he really ought to apologize for. But even though his brain said to get off his ass and go talk to her, his boots—

Aw, hell. One of the speedboat jockeys had her in his sights and was about to make a move. Zane intercepted the guy before he got out whatever clichéd line he was about to drop on her.

Holding the speed freak back with a casual palm planted on the man's chest, Zane dropped into the chair across from her. "Mind if I sit?"

She raised her head. "No. Although next time it might be nice if you asked before you actually sat."

"I can leave."

She flicked a glance up at the speedboat guy who was still hovering with a hopeful gleam in his eyes, then met Zane's gaze levelly. "No, you can't."

"Cheeky. I like that." He nodded toward her empty glass. "What're you drinking?"

"Water."

Wineing, he held up two fingers to the waitress, and a moment later Sheila deposited two longnecks and a bowl of popcorn and pretzels on the table, greeted Zane with a playful bump of her hip on his shoulder, and then left without a word.

Zane pushed one of the bottles to the woman across the table. "Better than water."

She just wrapped her hands around the bottle the way she had her glass and watched him down his first swig.

"So, you're a photographer. For the *Times*."

"Yes. You saw the paper this morning, huh?"

"Kind of hard to miss that big headline '*Times* Photographer Saves Parachutist.' Not to mention the picture of us . . . you know."

"Ah, yes. The picture." She picked at the label on the beer bottle with her fingernails, but she had yet to take a drink, he realized.

"Yeah. About that kiss. I mean, it was just for show. Had to do something to reassure the crowd. I'm sorry if—"

"What in the world were you thinking, setting your parachute on fire like that?" she interrupted.

Okay, so she didn't want to talk about the kiss. He was relieved, actually. He'd consider that his apology was accepted.

He shrugged. "It's an old gag. It's been done plenty of times before."

"And the people who did this gag before, they lived to tell about it?"

"Mostly."

"Is the money really worth risking your life for? Or do you just do it for the thrill?"

He leaned back and hooked one arm over the back of his chair. "Yes to both."

"Sure it's not just some kind of death wish?"

"For two people who hardly know each other, this conversation is getting awfully personal."

She pursed her lips a moment, then spoke softly. "I breathed life from my lungs into yours yesterday. I'd hardly say we're strangers."

He narrowed his eyes. His heartbeat quickened and his breathing deepened. He wanted to look away, but he couldn't seem to break the connection between them. For a moment, he felt that same odd, floaty sensation he'd experienced in the lake yesterday.

"You want to know the truth?" he heard himself saying without consciously deciding to speak. "The money's good and I like the rush. But there's a third reason. I do it for the kids. You know, the ones who come to the show with the parents who want them to grow up to be computer engineers or lawyers. The ones who are afraid to dream because they don't think they're smart enough or good enough or . . . whatever crap has been pounded into their heads."

He wiped his palm on the thigh of his jeans. "I can see them down there, holding their breath while I fall. Then when I hit the ground and later they come running up for autographs—I can see it in their eyes. They know anything is possible if you're not afraid to try. They believe they can fly."

The Army had taught him to jump out of airplanes, but when they hadn't wanted him anymore, he'd taught himself to make a life doing what he loved most. He'd decided to pass on to a new generation the courage and the love of freedom that had made him an Army Airborne jump master for twelve years.

Zane realized his hand was fisted on his thigh and forcibly relaxed his fingers.

Rosemary was quiet a moment, processing his heartfelt confession, he supposed. She dipped her fingers tentatively into the popcorn bowl, as if afraid it might burn her, pulled out a piece and popped it into her mouth. "Salty," she said, cocking her head to one side like she'd never tasted popcorn before. "Good."

She reached for a handful. "Kids or no kids, you have to know someday it could end badly. I guess you're prepared to go out that way, without any warning. You've got your affairs in order."

"I don't really have many affairs to order," he drawled. Strange conversations that kept taking blind curves way too fast had a way of bringing out the good 'ol Texas boy accent. Tended to slow things down.

"So there's not some big thing left undone that you want to do before you die? Some great goal to meet? Some terrible wrong you need to right?"

"No." This conversation was seriously starting to give him the creeps, and still he couldn't help but be intrigued by her. By why she cared about any of this. "I gather you're not much of a risk taker."

"I'm here, aren't I?" She arched one fine eyebrow inquisitively, and there it was. The sucker-punch gorgeous look nearly knocked the breath out of him even though he'd been prepared for it. At least he thought he'd been prepared for it.

He leaned across the table toward her. "You know, it's the strangest thing. When I was underwater . . . drowning . . . I could have sworn you talked to me."

"What did I say?"

"That you were an angel."

Just the tips of her mouth curved up. "Maybe I am."

And maybe he was the devil in blue jeans. God knew, he suddenly felt horny enough to be.

The suggestion that they go somewhere more private to talk— among other things—had almost reached his mouth when a hand clapped him on the back. "Z, buddy. Sorry to interrupt the reunion, ma'am." Jasper nodded at Rosemary, then looked back at Zane. "You gotta come with me. Kyle just put out a hundred big ones for all takers that he can beat you off-road, in the desert. Night course."

Zane heard Jasper, but his eyes were all for Rosemary. "I'm kinda busy right now."

"Zane. It's a *hundred* big ones. And the little toad's running his mouth about how your confidence is shook, after yesterday and all."

Indecision warred within him until a solution made him smile. He stood and held out his hand to Rosemary. "You want to understand why I do the things I do? Come with me."

Chapter 3

"W HAT is that?" Rosemary had trailed along willingly enough with her hand still clasped firmly in Zane's until she saw the gargantuan . . . behemoth parked at the edge of the lot outside the Oasis.

"It's a truck," he answered, tugging her forward when she held back. "A four-by-four."

It looked more like a tank. It was midnight blue, one of those short-bed deals, with roll bars framing the cab, a chrome exhaust pipe and tires . . . the top of the tires hit her waist-high. She'd need a stepladder to climb into the thing, or so she thought until Zane opened the passenger-side door, spanned her waist with his big hands and lifted her inside as if she weighed no more than a cloud.

The monster sounded like a tank, too, when Zane turned on the ignition and revved the engine. When the diesel roar had receded to an angry growl, he turned his head toward her and threw her a grin. "Buckle up for safety."

"Where are we going?" she asked, fumbling with the latch on the seat belt. She wasn't at all sure this was a good idea. Not at all.

"For a ride in the desert."

"I don't think—"

"Come on, it'll be fun. It's a nice night, and the stars are out."

She glanced up, unimpressed. The stars were much more impressive when they surrounded you rather than just floating overhead. She licked her lips, about to unbuckle the seat belt and bail out when a red Jeep Wrangler—Kyle's, she supposed—whipped by them on the driver's side, its horn beeping like the Road Runner as it passed.

"Damn. He cheats!"

"Zane, you're not going to ra—"

The big truck lurched as he threw it in gear and stomped on the accelerator. Her head snapped back and her hands automatically clutched whatever they could find—the center console and the door handle.

"What're you *doing*?"

"Reason number four for doing what I do, sweetheart. The most important reason of all. It's called *living*. Full throttle. Every second of every day."

She swallowed hard as gravel spun out beneath the truck's tires and they peeled out after the Jeep, plunging into the darkness, guided only by two spindly beams of light. "At the moment I'm more concerned about dying."

That couldn't happen, right? She wasn't even really alive, after all. This was just a shell she was inhabiting temporarily until she finished her work here and everything got back to normal.

No way. It couldn't happen.

She squeaked as the truck bounced off the edge of the parking lot and across a dune of sand. Despite the seat belt, her body was ejected from the seat, then jerked left, then right as the rear wheels fishtailed, biting into the shifting sand for purchase.

Zane laughed, his attention focused on the cloud of sand ahead of him that had been churned up by Kyle's Jeep.

"Zane, please!"

"Just hang on, Rosie. We've almost got him!"

Rosie? No one called her Rosie.

They careened over another sand dune, the front wheels popping up first, then the back end, flying so high she felt like they might flip into a somersault at any moment. Her fingers dug deeper into the leather-grained handle on the door.

"This is crazy!" she yelled, but Zane was hunched over the steering wheel, driving blindly into the sandstorm ahead. Seconds later, the view out the windshield cleared as they pulled alongside the Jeep.

"There you are, you little bastard! Thought you could beat me by jumping the start line, did you?" He flipped Kyle the universal sign of disdain and gunned the truck even harder. The engine shuddered and the truck edged ahead of the Jeep by a bumper, and then a quarter panel.

Rosemary finally managed to bring a full breath into her lungs—until she looked into the dimly lit desert ahead and spotted what looked like the edge of the world. She screamed. "Zane, stop!"

He only clutched the steering wheel and grinned. The truck flew over the edge of the arroyo and down the embankment, bouncing and jouncing so hard that the steel frame of the truck groaned in protest.

"Are you crazy?" she yelled over the din.

He glanced away from the path in front of him long enough to chastise her with a look. His eyes beamed with excitement. "Relax. We're fine. And we're winning."

The Jeep surged in front of them and dived right into the narrow bed-runoff canal. Zane countered by zigging left, throwing her right, and she made the mistake of looking out the passenger window. The desert landscape passed in a nauseating blur of dunes and cacti, glittering eyes as nocturnal critters skittered out of their path, and churning sand. Every bump jolted her upset stomach and aggravated her pounding head. The movement and noise and scattered bits of light was too much for her—she'd barely gotten to the point where she could enjoy popcorn, for heaven's sake. Every jolt was like a hammer blow to her body. Every crunch of the tires and grinding gear was like an ice pick in her ears. Her senses couldn't take this kind of stimulation.

Biting back her rising bile, she switched her hand grip from the door to the handle over the window. "Zane, please!"

He was too intent on the path ahead, if there was any path, to spare her a glance. "We're almost there."

"The race is lost. He is beating you."

"I've got him right where I want him. Right . . . here!"

The Jeep turned down a narrow track to the right, then swiveled left. Zane passed the point where he'd turned, then yanked the steering wheel right and gunned the truck up an impossibly steep incline. Gravity forced Rosemary's spine against the seatback. She heard the tires spinning, grasping for purchase on the steep slope. The engine whined in protest.

"We're not going to make it!" Oh God, they were going to flip over backward.

Even as she thought it, the truck's front tires peeled over the edge of the canal. The frame bottomed out for a fraction of a second, and then they were airborne, flying without wings. Just before she squeezed her eyes shut, Rosemary saw the hood of the Jeep, its roof just a meter beneath the truck's big tires, still winding its way out of the gulley, and she screamed.

Her chest was still burning, yet to draw in a new breath when they pulled into the parking lot alongside the Oasis. Zane turned the truck off, jumped out and spun around the front of the hood whistling, tossing the keys and grabbing them out of the air before he reached her door and offered her a hand out.

Slapping his arm away, she stumbled out of the truck, her head still spinning and her heart pounding.

He frowned. "You okay?"

She jabbed him in the chest with her index finger. "You. You. Are. Insane!"

He shook his head. "It was just a little race."

"A little race? You— We—" Her voice failed her, so she made an arcing, flying motion with her hand, her eyes wide.

He crossed his arms over his chest and chuckled. "A little rattled, are we?"

"Rattled? Why, you— You want to see rattled? I'll show you rattled!" Zane Halvorson could be damned for all she cared. There was only so much an angel could take.

She felt the well of power within her. Like the buffer in some kind of massive generator, the energy built up in her body, sizzled from her heart to her fingertips. She raised her hands, already feeling the lightning sizzling toward her fingertips, ready to strike out. But before the first bolt left her hands, a wind kicked up, blowing her hair in front of her eyes and whispering urgently in her ear.

Zane threw his arm in front of his face to protect his eyes from the blowing sand. Rosemary dropped her hands and clenched her fists at her sides, then turned and stomped toward the bar.

"Rosie, wait!" he called behind her, but she gritted her teeth and marched on without turning back.

When Saint Peter whistled, even she didn't dare refuse the call.

Rosemary sat on the last stool at the end of the bar, hunched over a half-empty glass until the last of the Oasis's patrons called it a night.

"Careful there," Pete said, swabbing his way down the bar toward her with a damp cloth. "Or I'll have to be calling a cab to get you home."

She looked up at her mentor, confused. "It's ice water."

"It's not the drink I'm worried about." His eyes sparkled when he smiled, and the wings of the eagle tattoo on his bicep fluttered as he slung the dishcloth over his shoulder and stepped her way. "Friends don't let friends drive depressed."

She ducked her head again. "I'm not depressed. I'm just—" She sighed. "I *hate* this."

"Being human?"

"I don't know how people stay sane in this form." She plunked her elbows on the bar and propped her chin in her hands. "All the ups and downs and noise and people. It's . . . chaotic."

"It's life."

"Life is highly overrated."

"Says the Angel of Death."

She looked up at Saint Peter through eyes bleary with exhaustion. That was another thing. She never got tired in her true form. The Angel of Death never needed a nap.

She rubbed her temples. "This guy has a death wish, Pete."

"Then why is he still alive?"

"I was hoping you could tell me."

Pete finished cleaning the bar and began to straighten the open bottles in the liquor bin, making sure each was securely corked. "The usual, I suspect. Unresolved issues."

She snorted. "Yeah, like the fact that he's an adrenaline junkie."

"This you've decided after what, a whole hour in his company?"

"That's about fifty-eight minutes longer than I needed."

Saint Peter stopped his cleaning and leaned over to her across the bar. "Does the phrase 'Judge not, lest ye be judged' ring any bells with you?"

She dropped her gaze, a rush of heat flooding her cheeks. By the heavens, it wasn't just the sensory overload anymore, but in the last few hours all these human emotions had begun to surface, as well. How was she supposed to do her job with all these feelings distracting her? One minute she wanted to laugh, the next she wanted to cry. And when she stared into Zane Halvorson's hazel eyes for too long, a whole other set of wants altogether began to make itself known.

She slumped back in her chair. "So what am I supposed to do, Pete? Stalk the guy until he finally figures out what's wrong with his life so that he can die?"

Pete went back to his work, turning his back to her. "Perhaps."

She studied his expression in the mirror behind the bar and knew there was something he wasn't telling her. "Or perhaps not," she guessed, then mumbled, "I have other work."

"You have only the task He gives you."

Embarrassment rose again in her cheeks. "I just want to go home."

"Then you need to complete your task."

"You know I can't affect the outcome one way or another. Only He decides who lives and who dies. I'm just here to bring home the ones He chooses. Why would He keep me here like this, waiting for this one man to resolve his issues?"

Pete set down the glass he'd been drying and met her gaze in the mirror. "Perhaps you should consider that Zane Halvorson is not the one with issues to be resolved."

An hour later, Rosemary stumbled through her dark apartment and fell spread-eagle on the bed.

What did Peter mean, that perhaps Zane Halvorson wasn't the one with issues? Of course the man had issues. He'd jumped out of a perfectly good airplane and set his own parachute on fire, for goodness sake.

She pulled pillows up to either side of her head to drown out the ticking of the clock and the rumble of cars on the street below.

She would just have to wait him out, that's all. Stay close to him. Sooner or later Zane Halvorson would die, and the Angel of Death would be there to save his soul. Then she could go back where she belonged.

End of story.

Chapter 4

ZANE stood on the landing outside Rosemary's door and resisted the urge to tug at his collar. Jesus, he wasn't some kid picking up his date for the junior prom. Just because he'd put on a shirt that actually had buttons for once didn't mean anything. Nothing at all.

He was only here to apologize. He'd been a little rough on her last night at the Oasis. Sometimes he forgot that not everyone liked to risk life and limb for a hundred-dollar bet and bragging rights. Some people preferred a slower pace. Time to smell the roses, or whatever.

He didn't understand those people, but he knew they existed, nevertheless.

Oh, hell. Who was he kidding? He was here because he wanted to see her again.

His dark-haired angel intrigued him on a lot of levels. The ones south of his waistband were easy to understand. She definitely had a look about her. Sexy and innocent, world-wise and naïve all at the same time. She had that fresh kind of face that didn't need makeup, a body that didn't need designer dresses to look good.

Some of those other levels, though, weren't so easy to explain. Like the whole guardian angel thing. He didn't believe in the "angels among us" propaganda, but she had saved his life. He figured that created some kind of bond between them.

He was curious about her. Since he'd been a kid, he'd liked to take things apart and put them back together again to see how they worked. Bicycles, toasters, engines—he always had to know what made them tick.

Now he wanted to know what made Rosemary D'Amica tick.

Pulling his shoulders back, he pasted a pleasant smile on his face and rang the bell. A moment later she answered, and the sight of her erased every word of his carefully rehearsed apology from his mind.

"Um," he said.

Her feet were bare, as were her legs up to the fringe of her cut-off denim shorts. She wore an old football jersey that fell off one shoulder, and her wild curls spilled out of a ponytail that looked like it had been caught in a windstorm. In the crook of her arm she held a pint of Ben and Jerry's double fudge chocolate ice cream with a soup spoon sticking out of the open tub.

He grinned. "Breakfast of champions, huh?"

Good going, Romeo. Way to make points.

"I, uh, I wasn't expecting company." She dropped the ice cream on an entry table and turned back to the doorway, looking at him quizzically. "What are you doing here?"

"Brought you something." He pulled the bouquet of daisies from behind his back and held them out for her.

Her eyes widened as she took them. "Why?"

"I'm sorry about last night. I got a little carried away with the whole race thing." He peered over her shoulder. "Can I come in?"

After only a brief hesitation, she stood aside and ushered him over the threshold. In the kitchen, she put the daisies in a vase in the middle of a butcher block table and gestured him toward a chair. He sat while she retrieved her double fudge chocolate from the entryway.

"Isn't nine a.m. a little early for ice cream?"

She hugged the tub protectively. "It's never too early for chocolate. I never tasted any until yesterday. I think I'm addicted. You want some? I can get another spoon."

"No, thanks. You never tasted chocolate?"

"Mmm," she said, spooning a bite into her mouth. "I've led a very sheltered life. So you were saying? About the race?"

"Yeah." He traced a finger over the beak of a hummingbird embroidered into a navy blue placemat in front of him, and his mouth watered as Rosemary's lips closed over another bite of ice cream. "We goof off sometimes," he said, looking away. "Just letting off steam, you know? I shouldn't have dragged you into it, though. It can be a little intense."

"Intense is one word for it. Crazy would be another that comes to mind."

"You think what I do is nuts. I get that. But in reality, every stunt I do is planned out, every detail. My team is the best, and we take every precaution to make the show safe."

She waggled her spoon at him. "So I ended up fishing you out of the lake . . . why, exactly?"

"I miscalculated the burn rate on the chute. Look, I didn't say there isn't some element of risk. But if you really want to know why I do what I do, then come see for yourself. Come out to the airfield and let me show you how much preparation goes into every stunt."

"Okay."

He opened his mouth, but managed to stop the argument he was about to make just in time. "Really?"

"Really."

He narrowed his eyes. That was way too easy. "Why?"

"Actually, I was talking to my editor at the paper this morning. I told him a little bit about what you said—making kids believe they can fly and all—and he wants to do a story on you. Sort of a follow-up to the accident piece. And he's agreed to let me write it. This could be my big break."

"Well, I wouldn't want to get in the way of that. It's a date, then."

The spoon froze halfway to her mouth.

"Well, not a date, exactly," he corrected. "More like a . . . a . . ." He lost his train of thought as she ate her ice cream and pulled the spoon out of her mouth slowly between closed lips, wiping away every hint of chocolate. Except for the smudge left at the corner of her mouth.

"A business meeting," she said.

"Yeah. Sure." He swallowed, working hard to pull his gaze away from the chocolate smear. "Business. I should go now." Before he did something stupid, like taking care of that little dab of chocolate on her lips—by tasting it for himself.

He stood and headed for the door without looking back. She followed and leaned against the jamb as he stepped outside. If he hadn't turned around to say good-bye, he might have gotten away clean. But no, suddenly he had to be Mr. Manners.

Aw, hell. He lowered his head toward hers, until he could feel her breath on his cheek and see the individual flecks of green in her wide eyes. With his heart thunking against his breastbone, he blew out a deep breath, and lifted his hand. "You've got a—" He motioned toward her face.

He moved to wipe the tiny daub of ice cream away, but her hand got there first. She frowned, looking for somewhere to wipe the mess, and with his gaze still locked on hers, he took her fingers in his and brought them to his lips. Gently he nuzzled away the chocolate, then released her.

Her hand hovered in midair, as if she hadn't realized he'd let her go.

"So. I'll see you this afternoon." His voice sounded rough all of a sudden.

"This afternoon." She still hadn't moved.

He smiled to himself as he turned and left, checking his watch as he jogged down the steps. He had to get to the airfield. He had a hangar to clean up and a crew to browbeat into being on their best behavior.

Most of all, he had to figure out how he was going to pull his head together enough to perform an aerial stunt this afternoon, when all he could think about was the taste of chocolate and Rosemary D'Amica on his lips.

———

"Hello? Earth to Rosie!"

Rosemary felt someone tapping on her shoulder and turned to hear Zane's muffled call. "What? Oh." She pulled out the plastic earplugs she'd bought at a drugstore on her way to the airfield.

"Sorry about that," she said, shrugging. "All the engine noise and such. Have to protect the old eardrums." Actually it wasn't just the engines, but the crying children and their cheering parents, the hawking of the hot-dog vendors, the blare of the loudspeaker that bothered her. She was still having a hard time adjusting to the constant noise. She hadn't realized that the noise had abated when they'd left the field and walked into the hangar.

Zane guided her over to a vintage biplane and she walked along the fuselage, trailing her hand across the riveted metal.

"It gets a little loud out there sometimes," he said, "but I doubt it's anything that'll do you any permanent damage."

"Better safe than sorry."

"So some people say."

"Not a theory you subscribe to, I take it."

"There is such a thing as being too cautious. Missing out on some of the best moments life has to offer just because they involve a little risk."

Near the front of the plane, Rosemary climbed the stepladder and peered into the rear cockpit.

"Go on," Zane said behind her. "Climb in."

In the copilot's seat, she tried to imagine soaring a thousand feet up with nothing beneath her but air. The thought brought goose bumps to her arms.

"So what's on the bill for you today?" she asked. "Hurling yourself out of a perfectly good airplane with nothing but a bed sheet to slow your fall? Shackle your hands and feet like Houdini and see if you can escape the locks in time to pull your parachute cord?"

" 'Fraid not—although that last one is not a bad idea." He patted the side of the biplane like a favorite pet. "It's Louise's turn. Wing-walking day."

"While the plane is flying. Wing walking." She pointed forward and to the left of her seat. "Out there."

"That's generally where the wings are, yes."

"You really should have your head examined, you know that?"

He swung up onto the wing to demonstrate. "Look, it's not that bad. I have these struts here to hold on to. And when Jasper gets ready to do the barrel rolls, I slide my feet into these straps here on the lower wing."

"Barrel rolls?"

"Yeah, we do a few acrobatics while I'm out. Slow and easy, though, nothing—"

She held up her hand to stop him. "I really don't think I want to know." The turkey dog he'd bought her for lunch wasn't sitting well on her stomach, and this conversation wasn't helping.

Smiling, he grabbed her hand and pulled. "Come on. I'm closing the show tonight, so I've got a couple of hours before I have to get ready. Let's go walk around."

She let him lead her around the aircraft on display and listened patiently while he lectured her on wing design, air speed and avionics. Surprisingly, she found if she focused on his voice, the background noise didn't disturb her as much as it had before. And she enjoyed listening to him. To her, they were just a bunch of airplanes, but he was like a kid in a candy store. His eyes lit up as he made an airplane shape with his hand and flew it around, even making engine noises as he explained the concepts of bank, pitch and roll to her.

Everywhere he went, people watched him. He'd been right about the kids, she realized. They stared at him in awe, and a few of the braver ones even ran up and asked for his autograph.

Amused, she noticed the children weren't the only ones staring openly. Rosemary caught a fair number of young women ogling him as well, especially at his backside as he walked away from them. Not that she blamed them. He did fill out those worn jeans quite nicely—

She caught herself and stamped out that thought before her own gaze wandered into forbidden territory. *What was she thinking?*

The Angel of Death should not be lusting after the soul she'd come to collect.

All too soon the afternoon wound down and it was time for the last stunt—Zane's wing walk.

Her stomach quivered unhappily as he climbed into Louise's second seat behind Jasper, his pilot, and gave the thumbs-up. It protested significantly more vehemently when the yellow biplane soared over the upturned faces of the air-show crowd and a figure clad in black coveralls and goggles climbed out onto the left wing. He waved and they cheered, and her breath stalled as he ambled along the rear edge of the wing all the way to the tip, where he held on to a strut with one hand, braced his feet and bowed dramatically backward off the tip of the wing, before levering himself up and proceeding down the front edge of the wing as if he were strolling down a country lane.

The plane made a large loop at the edge of the airfield. Zane crossed over Louise's fuselage and repeated his performance on the right wing.

When Zane was headed back toward the cockpit, Rosemary finally dared suck in a lungful of air, thinking the show must be almost over. Until he stopped halfway up the wing and stretched his arms out to the struts on either side of him.

Jasper climbed to a higher altitude, then eased the biplane into a slow, spiraling roll to the left. The crowd gasped. Rosemary covered her mouth with her hand, afraid to look and yet unable to close her eyes.

When Louise had leveled out, Jasper executed the same maneuver in the other direction and the crowd let out an approving roar.

And then the unimaginable happened. Halfway through the roll, while the airplane was upside down, a black dot separated from the plane's wing and tumbled through the sky, end over end.

Oh, God. Oh, no. Oh, God!

Zane had fallen.

Chapter 5

U H-OH." Kyle, one of Zane's mechanics, stood to Rosemary's right, his hands jingling change in the pocket of his coveralls.

The second mechanic, Jimmie stood on her other side in a similar position. "Looks bad for the Z-man."

Oh, God. This couldn't be happening. She hadn't been called. If Zane was going to die now, she had to be there.

She bent her head and started to run, but strong hands on her arms held her back. "Let me go!" She slapped at the mechanics.

"Wait for it," Kyle said, watching Zane's body tumble headlong toward a horrific death.

Jimmie cracked his gum.

A moment later something fluttered alongside Zane's falling form, then a rainbow of color exploded above his head with an audible *phhhhhhummpf.*

A parachute. *Oh, thank God.*

Rosemary doubled over and pressed a fist to her chest.

"Ah, disaster averted once again," Kyle said dryly.

Jimmie cracked his gum again.

Realization setting in, she straightened and turned her head from one man to the other. Flames rushed up her neck to her cheeks. "You knew. You knew and you didn't tell me!"

Jimmie hunched his shoulders. "Well, what'd be the fun in that?"

"Fun! You think that was fun?"

Kyle and Jimmie shared a look.

"You know, I think I've got a carburetor to clean," Kyle said.

"And I—" Jimmie bit his lip. "I'm sure I got something to do. Must be somethin'," he mumbled as the two of them turned tail and ran.

Chickens. They shouldn't have bothered. They weren't the ones in danger.

Zane Halvorson, on the other hand, was in serious trouble. Unresolved issues or not, when he got back here, she was going to kill him.

———

"Thanks for the ride, Mac." Zane grabbed his gear bag and swung his legs out of the ATV that had been sent out to the field to pick him up.

"Anytime, man," Mac called, but Zane didn't turn to acknowledge him.

He was frozen in place by an icy green stare. Rosemary's body language screamed *furious*. Her arms were crossed over her chest, her hips cocked out to one side and she was tapping her foot.

"What?" he asked.

"Did you think that was funny, Zane? Was it a big joke—make the gullible reporter think you really fell? And could you have mentioned that you wear a parachute when you do this little stunt?"

He sighed and started toward her, albeit with a little less swagger to his gait. "It's the shock value that sells the gag."

"You about shocked me into a heart attack!"

He dropped his bag in front of her and shook his head. "Look, I honestly just didn't think to tell you I was going to take a dive for the tourists. Everybody around here knows the routine. Besides, I told the guys to stick close to you. Surely you saw that they weren't too upset."

"'The guys'? By that you mean your little junior birdmen? They were having too much fun watching me nearly pass out to clue me in."

Zane rolled his head back and shot an exasperated look at the two young mechanics watching them through the office window. When they scurried away, he turned back to Rosie, reached out and took both of her arms and slid his hands down to hers. She stiffened at his touch, but didn't pull away. Hopefully that was a good sign.

"I'm sorry I scared you. But hey—" He winked at her. "I had my guardian angel looking out for me, right?"

Her eyes narrowed dangerously. He sighed and let go of her hands. "I know what I'm doing out there, Rosie. You've got to trust me."

"*Trust you?* Helloooooooo! Pulled you out of the lake. Mouth-to-mouth, remember?"

"You are never going to let me live that down, are you?"

"No."

He hung his head for a moment, and then looked up at her, trying to figure a way out of the hole he'd dug himself. Her dark curls were even more tousled than normal, as if she'd run her hands through them. Repeatedly. Her cheeks were flushed and her lips were pressed into a straight line with little crinkles at the corners.

Damn, she was cute when she was angry. So cute that his own annoyance faded, and he chuckled, then laughed outright. "Okay, I guess I deserve that."

Behind him he heard Louise taxiing into the hangar. He cocked his head toward the bird and told Rosemary, "Come on, I got just the thing to help you put the whole ordeal behind you."

She narrowed her eyes. "What?"

"Come fly with me." He called up to the cockpit, "Leave her running, Jasper."

"You taking her out?" the pilot called.

"Yes."

"No, I don't think so." She backpedaled as Jasper climbed out of the front seat and Zane rolled the staircase up to the second seat for her.

"Come on, it'll be fun. Just you, me, Louise and the open sky. We've still got plenty of daylight left. I bet you've never seen the desert from three thousand feet, have you?"

"No, I haven't."

He held his hand out to her. "Let's go, then. I know just the spot I want to show you, where the dirt turns red as—"

She finally relaxed her uncrossed arms, and instead wrung her hands in front of her.

"What's wrong?" he asked.

"I—I've never flown in an airplane before."

That took him by surprise. "You weren't kidding when you said you'd led a sheltered life, were you?"

"No. Actually sometimes I feel like I haven't lived at all." She gave the airplane a long look, and then tipped her chin up. "Maybe it's time to change that."

———

Rosemary had to admit, Zane had been right. Once her initial bout of nerves had worn off, she'd loved every minute of her flight over the desert, even the few minutes when he'd switched off the engines and they'd glided, nothing but the air currents beneath them holding them aloft.

The sunset was indescribable. So many colors, so vivid. Vibrant, like the man who had talked her into taking that magic carpet ride.

She watched him now from her table at the Oasis where she sat with a spiral notebook in front of her, purportedly scribbling notes for her newspaper article. He was kicked back against a windowsill, long legs stretched out in front of him and a beer bottle in his hand, watching his crew, who were caught up in some game she didn't fully understand, but that seemed to involve playing pool with blindfolds on and drinking shots every time the other team hit one of their balls into a pocket. He laughed at something one of them said, and winced as Jimmie and Kyle each downed their third shot in under fifteen minutes. Thankfully, the table was clear of balls and, judging by the handing off of blindfolds, it was time to switch teams.

Zane strolled over to her table, turned a chair around and straddled the seat, hooking his arms over the back and resting his chin on his forearms. He took a swig of the beer he'd been nursing all night and nodded toward her notebook. "Making any progress?"

She wrinkled her nose. "Not really. The guys look like they're having fun."

"They can afford to let their hair down a little. Tomorrow's our off day."

"No stunts?"

"No. Air show runs Sunday through Saturday, with Wednesday off to give everyone a chance to rest up and maintenance their equipment."

Inwardly she breathed a sigh of relief that he wouldn't be performing tomorrow. Zane Halvorson was the most alive man she'd ever seen. Knowing that life would be over soon, and that she'd have some part in its end, even if it was only to carry his soul on to a new plane of existence, wasn't sitting with her the way it once had.

Until Zane, she'd always believed that life on Earth was a mostly painful and unhappy experience. Sure, there were moments of joy, sometimes even true love, but she never doubted she was taking them to a better place. She never understood why some of them clung so tenaciously to their lives here. Why they grieved for each other so when a soul moved on.

Finally, maybe, she was beginning to understand.

Zane took another sip of his beer and she realized she was staring at him. And he was staring right back. Awareness left tingly little tracks up her arms and all the way down to her toes, an odd sensation, but not altogether unpleasant. In fact, she rather liked it.

"You had a good time in the air today," he said.

"I already told you three times that I did."

"Just making sure. Because I've got some really big fun planned for us tomorrow."

She wasn't sure she liked the sound of that. "What kind of fun?"

"Today you flew with me. Tomorrow you jump with me."

She jerked as if she'd stuck her finger in a light socket. "Oh, no. *Hell*, no."

"Hell, yes. Tandem jump. You'll be strapped to me, and I'll do all the work. You'll just be along for the ride."

"Not going to happen, flyboy."

"I'll give you a lesson in the morning, we'll jump in the afternoon. You'll be perfectly safe."

"Lak—"

He held up one finger to silence her. "Don't say it. We'll land squarely on terra firma. I promise. You'll love it. It's the closest thing there is to heaven on Earth."

She drew a shaky breath, her resistance fading. This was crazy, but it was also exhilarating. Her stomach was already in knots just thinking about jumping out of an airplane. But she was the one who'd decided to give this living thing a try as long as she was stuck in human form. It was like once she'd begun to sense and to feel, a door had been flung open, and that door couldn't be closed again. She craved new experiences.

Did he say she'd be strapped to him?

Who knew? This jumping thing might have all kinds of possibilities.

"I'll think about it," she said.

He grinned and before it turned into a gloat, she plucked the beer bottle from his hand and took a swig.

The alcohol tried to come back up as fast as it went down. She coughed and waved her hand in front of her open mouth to cool her burning throat.

"Let me guess," he drawled. "Never drank beer before, either."

Her composure regained, she spun on her heel with a haughty *"Hmpf,"* and went off to see about joining the boys in a game of blindfold pool.

There were lots of things she'd never done before, but before this week was up she just might try every one of them.

Chapter 6

WHAT *in heaven's name had she been thinking?*

The wind from the open door of the plane buffeted her. The vibration of the engines only added to the shaking her body was doing on its own. She was holding on to the strap riveted into the wall beside the door so tightly that she would probably need pliers to pry her fingers off.

Zane straightened up from where he'd been checking every buckle, clip, strap and carabiner on their combined gear for the third—no, fourth—time. "You ready?"

"No." Was that her voice? It sounded like a Saturday morning cartoon character.

"Come 'ere." His arms circled her waist and drew her flush against him.

They were strapped together, her back to his chest. She could feel the slow beat of his heart between her shoulder blades. His hips against her backside. The hard muscles of his thighs against her legs. She let herself sag against him, increasing the contact until there was no part of them that wasn't touching. Molding to the other's shape.

"Breathe slow and deep," he murmured in her ear just loud enough to be heard over the wind and engines. "In and out."

While her respiration gradually evened out, he tucked his chin in the crook of her neck and kept talking. "You're going to be fine. I've done this hundreds of times. Maybe thousands."

"Really?" There, she didn't squeak quite as bad that time.

"Twelve years Army Airborne. Seven of them as a jumpmaster. I've taught more people how to hurl themselves out of airplanes than you'll find in most small cities."

She groaned. Did he have to use the word *hurl*?

Breathe. In. Out.

A light went on over the cockpit door.

"What's that?" she asked, tensing again.

"Drop zone." Still holding her around the waist with one arm, he stroked the curve of her waist and her hip with the other. "Are you ready now?"

"Just do it already," she answered, squeezing her eyes shut. "Because if you're waiting for me to say 'yes,' it's not going to happen."

"Okay, here we go." She let him scoot her closer to the open door. "Just remember what I showed you in the classroom. Relax and let me do all the work."

She nodded, her eyes still closed, but unable to shut out the image in her mind of the patchwork landscape and tiny buildings so far below. Too far below.

Teetering on the brink of the doorway, Zane stopped them once more. With a hand on her chin he turned her head and she opened her eyes to meet his gaze.

"One more thing," he said. "Don't forget to breathe."

With that last word he pitched forward, tipping her out of the plane and into the most terrifying moment of her life.

The initial blast of the wind was almost bruising in its force. She wanted to curl up in a ball to escape it, but Zane's instructions echoed in her mind. *Extend your arms and your legs. Arch your back a little. Keep your head up.*

Moving jerkily, sometimes flailing against the air currents, she worked to find the position, while her heart tried to pound its way out of her chest.

"Don't fight it."

She jolted at the sound of Zane's voice in her ears. She'd forgotten there were radio headsets in their helmets.

"Don't try to control it. Don't try to hold on to the air," he said. "Let the air hold you."

She tried, willing her muscles to relax, and gradually the ride smoothed out. Her initial panic faded and she opened her eyes.

"Oh, my. It's beautiful!" Falling through clear blue sky, totally unencumbered. Totally free.

"I told you you'd love it."

"How fast are we going?"

"You sure you want to know?"

"No." Laughter bubbled up in her chest, borne of sheer joy. "It's . . . amazing."

"You've got about fifteen more seconds to enjoy it. Then we're going to deploy canopy. I'll give you a three count, and you'll feel a sharp pull. Remember not to brace against it. Just go with the motion."

She gave Zane a thumbs-up, content to spend her last few seconds of free fall in silence, memorizing the feeling so that she would never forget.

"Three. Two. One. Deploying canopy."

As he'd warned, their direction changed suddenly, but Rosemary hardly even blinked. She was too busy smiling to be afraid.

Their mad dash toward the ground became a leisurely excursion. She felt like a child on a playground swing set, floating this way and then that. Back and forth and ever downward.

It was over far too soon. Zane guided them to the ground so softly they could have been stepping off a curb instead of hitting the ground from thousands of feet in the air. They could easily have walked right out of the landing, but Zane's arms snaked around her waist and pulled her to the grass in a gentle roll anyway.

When she found herself on her back, on top of him, with his hands not so tightly wrapped around her any longer, but roaming restlessly over her stomach, her rib cage, and occasionally grazing higher, she began to suspect his motives. When a pair of moist lips nipped at the back of her neck, she knew exactly what his motives were.

"Hey, no fair," she said. She couldn't reach much of him in this position.

He chuckled and pulled his hands away long enough to make quick work of the rat's nest of straps and buckles and cords entangling them, then flipped her over so that they lay chest to chest.

That was better, she thought, pulling her helmet off and pressing her lips to the hollow of his throat. Much better.

He let her explore for a while. Pulling the neck of his jumpsuit aside, she pressed kisses down the length of his collarbone, then up the tendons on top of his shoulder, up his neck to the underside of his jaw. All the while his mouth was on an expedition of its own, plundering the side of her neck and the sensitive spot behind her ear.

"God, you taste so good," he murmured, and her pulse leaped at the scrape of breath and lips and teeth over her carotid.

Eventually their meanderings brought them face-to-face, and their mouths danced at first, searching for the right position, the perfect angle, then their lips fused, sealed in a bond of give and take, conquest and surrender, then a melding of two into one. A communion.

The kiss evolved as they shifted restlessly against each other. It changed. It advanced and retreated and surrendered only when their need for oxygen became greater than the desire to tease and touch and taste.

Rosemary sagged against Zane, panting. He shifted one of his legs between hers, raising his knee until his thigh pressed against her intimately.

She moaned, the friction between her legs adding one more ache to the long list of demands her body was making—all of which could only be met by the man lying beneath her.

Carefully she levered herself up on her elbows and laid her

hands on either side of his head. His chest heaved against her breasts, setting off another delicious tingle. "Zane?"

"Hmm."

"Can we do it again?"

He opened his eyes halfway. "Mm-hmm. Soon as I catch my breath."

She giggled. "I meant the parachute jump."

"Oh." Was that disappointment in his voice? "You bet. Anytime."

Across the field, Rosemary saw Mac headed toward them on the ATV. Zane rolled his gaze that way, too, then lifted his head and kissed her long and hard until they could hear the whine of the engine close by. Finally he eased his head back and tucked a curl behind her ear.

"Meanwhile," he said, "what do you say we take this free fall somewhere a little more private?"

———

Zane splashed some water on his face, then leaned on the bathroom sink and faced himself in the mirror.

What the hell are you doing?

"Exactly what you think I'm doing," he grumbled almost silently.

You can't. It isn't right. It isn't fair.

"Life isn't fair."

So it's okay for you to hurt her because you don't like the way your life is going.

"I'm perfectly happy with the way my life is going. It's the way it's going to end that I'm pissed off about."

Will dragging her into your troubles change that? You have no future to offer her.

"I'll break it off after the air show. Once she's done her story. She never has to know."

She'll still be hurt.

"She'll be hurt if I back out now."

Not as badly.

"Dammit! What do you want from me?"

Keep your voice down.

Zane glanced nervously at the door, hoping she hadn't heard anything. All he needed was questions about who he'd been talking to.

What are you going to do?

He scrubbed his hands over his face and shook his head. "Hell if I know."

Indecision churning in his gut, he pasted on a grim smile and stepped out of the bathroom.

"Took you long enough. I was beginning to get worried about you in there." Rosemary sat on the edge of his bed, biting her lower lip. Her legs were crossed and her hands were clenched in her lap. He'd never seen her look so nervous.

It was normal to be a little anxious the first time with someone, but she trusted him, he thought. And there was no doubt their attraction was genuine—

Realization hit him like a lightning bolt from heaven.

What were the chances that a woman who had never tasted chocolate or drunk a beer until this week had ever . . . ?

Slim to none, he was afraid.

Damn, as if this wasn't hard enough.

He sat next to her, close but not touching. She searched his face with her eyes, questioning.

"Look, Rosemary. I was thinking. Maybe this isn't the best time—"

Her hands clamped together even tighter in her lap. "Did I do something wrong?"

"No. God, no. Hell, no." Christ, if this didn't kill him, nothing would.

She lurched off the bed, almost stumbling in her hurry to get away from him. "Sure, well. Yeah. I mean if it's not a good time, then we should reschedule. How does a week from Tuesday sound? Maybe you need to get your calendar and check. Or maybe you were thinking of something a little further out. Like *not in this lifetime*."

She scooped up her jacket and tried to jam her feet into the sneakers she'd kicked off like she was trying to kick the stuffing out of something. Or someone. Oh yeah, she was a virgin all right.

Zane had to bite back a grin. Her embarrassment had morphed to anger in record time, giving credence to the old saying that hell hath no fury . . .

Color flooded her cheeks and her hair lashed her cheeks as she whipped her head around. The angrier she got, the more beautiful she looked.

How the hell had a woman like her reached this point in her life without sleeping with anyone? She must have had men knocking at her door night and day.

Maybe someone had hurt her before she'd gotten to that point. The way he just had.

He sighed. "I'm sorry, Rosie. There's just some stuff going on in my life right now—"

She turned on him, one shoe on, one shoe off and eyes like twin green flames. "Oh, stuff going on in your life. I'd love to say I understand, but I really can't since I've never actually had a life, have I?"

He scrunched his face, confused. "What?"

"Never mind." She bent down and picked up the sneaker she couldn't get on. "You're right. I'm sure it would never work out between us. I mean I'm—"

He grabbed her wrist as she straightened. Waited for her to raise her head and look at him. Damn, he hated seeing the hurt swimming in her green eyes just beneath the fury. Hated that he had put it there, and that he was going to make it worse.

"Rosie, I'm dying."

Her lips pursed, her mouth slightly open. For a moment, neither of them breathed.

"What?" she finally asked, the word coming out on a rush of breath.

"That's why I left the Army. Medical discharge." He let go of her wrist and took a slow breath. "Three years ago I was diagnosed with a brain tumor. Radiation and chemotherapy didn't work. I went into surgery three times, and they finally got it all, but by then the damage to the blood vessels in the area couldn't be repaired. I have a hundred little aneurysms in my head just waiting to explode. And when one of them goes, they tell me, it will be like a string of firecrackers, only a little slower. Within a few hours, a day at most, they'll all go."

He didn't think she even realized she was shaking her head, denying his words even as she heard them. "That can't be— You can't—"

"Last time I saw the doc, he said he didn't think I'd make it another six months." Zane managed a weak smile for her benefit. "That was five and a half months ago."

Chapter 7

W HY didn't you tell me?" Rosemary knew she was out of line—not just with the question, but with the tone of voice in which she'd asked it. No one talked to Saint Peter that way, but she wasn't sorry. She felt like she'd just woken up from millennia of sleep. For the first time in her existence, she had begun to question what she did, and why.

Across the bar, Zane and his crew broke into a fit of laughter as Zane turned away from a swimsuit-model calendar they'd tacked to the wall and then threw a dart over his shoulder.

Rosemary smiled. At least there were no blindfolds involved tonight.

"That's ten points!" Zane declared, studying his hit.

"No way!" Kyle called.

"I got her thumb!" Apparently certain body parts were worth higher scores than others.

A dark-haired man in black jeans and a leather jacket shouldered Zane out of the way. "Let me show you how it's done, old man."

The new guy looked familiar to Rosemary, but she couldn't place him. "Who is that?" she asked Peter.

"Name's Trey MacAllister. He's a wheel man. Heard Zane is thinking about adding some ground work to his show, needs a stunt driver. The deal is, if he can beat Zane at backward darts, he's hired. If not . . ." Peter shrugged.

Rosemary shook her head. Only Zane would substitute a game for an employment interview.

As if he knew she was thinking about him, Zane turned to her from across the room. The look he sent her was quickly shuttered, but not before she'd read the pain there. The longing. The same feelings echoed inside her.

He broke the eye contact suddenly, and stumbled into a chair as he reached to pour himself a beer from the pitcher on the table.

"I don't think the wheel man's going to have much trouble winning himself a job. Our boy's been hitting the brew hard tonight." Peter's voice was heavy with resignation. "Guess I can't blame him."

Rosemary turned back to her mentor, fighting back the moisture in her eyes. "Why didn't you tell me Zane thinks he's going to die?"

"He *is* going to die."

"He thinks he's going to die of a brain aneurysm. That's why he does the crazy things he does. He doesn't think he has anything to lose."

"Maybe he doesn't."

"What about *time*? No doctor can know for sure when it's going to happen. He could have days, weeks, maybe even months left."

Peter checked sideways up and down the bar, as if to be sure none of his other patrons were close enough to overhear, then leaned toward Rosemary across the bar. "I thought you were the one who didn't understand why people fought so hard to stay here, to hang on when there was a better place waiting for them on the other side."

Her shoulders sagged. "Maybe I did feel that way, once. But I hate to see him give up even a minute of what he has left. He just . . . *lives* more than any human I've ever seen."

Every second. Full throttle. That's what he'd told her. Now she knew why. He didn't think he had many seconds left. And that belief was going to drive him into killing himself in some stupid stunt.

Peter peered at her over the rim of the glass he was wiping dry. "What about you? How are you finding mortal existence?"

"I want to go home," she said. Life hurt sometimes, as she'd found out firsthand earlier today in Zane's bedroom. Still, she didn't blame him. "But not at his expense."

Peter made a noncommittal noise. "It's not our choice. You know that. When it's time, it's time."

"I don't think I can do it." She swept a stray lock of hair behind her ear and looked up at Peter through her lashes. "I can't take him."

"You have to."

"What if I don't?" She raised her head and met his gaze squarely. "What if this one time, I say *no*?"

Peter's silvered eyebrows drew down even as his gaze lifted, traveled back to the pool tables, and Zane's new wheel man. He wiped the glass in his hand hard enough to shatter it.

At first, she thought his anger was directed at her. Then she followed his gaze across the room, and a cold pool spread through her chest.

The new guy clapped Zane on the back and laughed at something one of them had said. He had the rakish dark hair and easy smile of a charmer, but when he turned his gaze back toward her and Peter, as if he felt their gazes on him, his dark eyes were empty, bottomless wells.

Rosemary's skin prickled as she recognized him—not the mortal body he currently inhabited, but the evil inside him. His purpose on Earth was the same as hers—he was a shepherd of souls from this realm of existence to the next. Only when he gathered a person's essence, he took it to a much darker place.

"If you don't take Zane's soul," Peter said in a rough tone she rarely heard him use, "someone else will."

Rosemary tried to stay away from the air show on Thursday—tried, and failed. Zane had made his choices, and they didn't include her. Today's stunt wasn't a dangerous one, a formation skydive with a local team he'd worked with before, and it had gone off without a hitch. The airfield was closing down for the day. There was really no reason for her to be here.

Except that she couldn't stay away.

She hadn't slept well, knowing that one of the Fallen, a dark angel, had taken up residence so close to Zane, and this heavy-limbed, blurry-eyed feeling that came with exhaustion had her fighting to hold on to any semblance of objectivity about death—Zane's death—even more than usual.

Zane's hangar was cool compared to the evening heat outside. Kyle and Jimmie had the biplane's cover opened and were standing with tools in hands over her, but seemed to be more focused on a discussion going on in the office than the engine. Through half-open mini-blinds, Rosemary saw two figures behind the glass. Since they were shouting, it wasn't hard to identify them as Jasper and Zane.

"I didn't ask for your opinion on this stunt, Jasper!"

"That's the point, Zane. You didn't ask because you know it's crazy. I'm not letting you do this."

Rosemary glanced at Kyle and Jimmie. "What's going on?"

The boys shrugged as one. "Been at it like this all afternoon," Kyle said. "I've never seen them so mad at each other."

Jimmie shoved his greasy hands into the pockets of his coveralls. "It's the new guy's fault. Jasper don't like the stunt him and Zane worked up. Says it's too risky."

Rosemary's heart rolled over. It wasn't beyond one of the Fallen to put ideas in a human's head that would guarantee a soul to be available soon. Ideas like an impossible stunt.

A third figure moved out of the shadows in the office. Rosemary's jaw tensed. *Trey MacAllister.* The dark angel spoke too quietly to be heard, but Rosemary knew how insidious the Fallen's strategy could be. He would plant the seeds of distrust, drive the two long-term friends apart.

Clenching her fists until her fingernails dug into her palms, she marched toward the office.

"I'm not doing it, Z. I'm not flying this stunt."

"Fine!" Zane dragged a hand through his hair as Rosemary opened the office door. "You think I can't replace one washed-up pilot? I'll have someone else on board before you make it out of the parking lot."

Zane's statement drew Rosemary up short just inside the office. Surely he realized how hurtful his words had been. Jasper rasped his hand over a day's gray beard stubble. "You do that," he said quietly, and shouldered his way out without looking back.

"Jasper, wait!" she called, but his footsteps echoed across the hangar without pause.

She turned back to Zane in disbelief. "What are you doing? He's your best friend!"

The hard mask that was Zane's face slipped for a moment, revealing a wash of emotion, but then snapped back in place when Trey spoke up.

"I know a couple of pilots. I could check if they're available tomorrow," he said.

Never taking his eyes off Rosemary, Zane said "I'd appreciate that."

After Trey stepped past her with a triumphant look, Zane closed the door behind him.

"I didn't expect to see you back here," he said quietly, as if all the fight in him had been used up.

"I didn't expect to be back here."

He wandered across the room to his desk, looking lost. "So why are you?"

Because she really wasn't sure why she'd come herself, she ignored the question. "What are you doing, Zane?"

"Doing about what?"

"Hiring a guy because he was able to beat you at darts—when you were drunk and he wasn't, I might add."

"Hey, his resume is great and his references all checked out." The cocky grin he flashed didn't fool her. "The darts were just a formality."

"So you're going to throw away a friend who has stood by you for years for a good resume and references?"

Zane's grin fell. "Jasper will come back when he cools off. He always does."

She shook her head. "Whatever you're planning, don't do it, Zane."

"It's just a gag. It'll come off, no problem."

"Are you sure you want it to?"

A muscle ticked in his jaw. "I'm not trying to kill myself, Rosemary."

She wasn't so sure, but she held her tongue until he finally quit picking at his desk blotter and raised his hazel gaze to hers, the fake grin back in place.

"Besides, if anything goes wrong, my guardian angel will be there to protect me, right?"

"No." Rosemary shook her head slowly, sadly. "No, she won't be."

She left before she gave in, before she told him too much, before she begged. Kyle and Jimmie called to her as she passed, but she hurried on by, wiping her eyes before anyone could see her tears.

Outside, a hand grabbed her arm and swung her around. Trey MacAllister twiddled a straw in his mouth, the dark voids of his eyes boring into her.

"The more you try to talk him out of it, the more determined he'll be to do it," the dark angel said.

"I know."

"Good. Just so we're clear. He's mine."

Rosemary yanked her arm free. "Go to hell."

Trey smiled. "Plan to. Saturday, as soon as I'm done here."

He strolled away, and Rosemary had to lean against the corrugated tin hangar for support.

Oh, God. On Saturday, Zane was going to die.

Chapter 8

"GIVE me some more altitude!"

What the hell was he doing?

Zane stood just inside the door to his jump plane, and wondered if the multiple aneurysms in his brain had somehow robbed him of common sense. Or maybe the part of his brain responsible for self-preservation had been removed with the tumor.

He had a pilot whose name he didn't even know at the controls of his plane and a wheel man he had never worked with in the cab of a semi below. A semi that would squash Zane like a bug on a windshield if it weren't perfectly controlled.

He also had several thousand people on the ground below, looking up and waiting to be thrilled on a beautiful Saturday afternoon. Too late to back out now. He'd been paid, and he'd damned well deliver, even if the only two that really mattered to him—Rosemary and Jasper—weren't among the spectators.

He'd expected either or both of them to show up in the hangar before he taxied out, but it didn't happen. He might have expected it to take a bit longer with Jasper, the stubborn old man, but Rosemary . . . he'd really needed to see her. To know he wasn't alone.

Silly superstitious idea, he knew, but he really had come to think of her as his guardian angel. She made him feel safe.

He'd find both of them afterward, he promised himself. He'd make things right.

Taking a deep breath, he stepped out of the airplane, and tumbled into position for the free fall. He couldn't see Trey's truck yet, but when he reached one thousand feet, he would key his radio, and the semi would begin a lumbering trek down the airfield's west runway. By the time Zane lined up on it, it would be traveling fifty miles per hour.

He would have to maintain a fast descent himself to keep up. But the real trick would be releasing his chute at exactly the right moment—the moment before his feet touched the padded deck of the truck's flatbed trailer. A fraction of a second too soon, and he'd fall like a rock, missing the padding and going *splat* on the concrete instead. Too late, and the wind resistance on the chute would tumble him off the back of the truck, which would be about as fun as leaping off a speeding train.

What the *hell* was he thinking when he agreed to this?

One thousand feet. He could see the truck now. It pulled out and slowly built up speed as he steered left and right, lining up on the flatbed.

Five hundred feet. Two-fifty. One hundred.

His heart crashed in his chest. He let go of the fear, the noise, the bright sunlight in his eyes, and narrowed his focus to two things: his feet and the X marking his landing spot on the flatbed.

He needed more speed; the truck was outrunning him. He eased up on the braking of his chute and felt the pull as his speed increased.

At ten feet, he centered himself over the landing zone, said a quick prayer and reached for the clasp that would release his parachute.

As he pulled the clasp, the truck's brake lights flashed on.

"No!" He had time only for that single thought, that single syllable, before his momentum carried him off his landing spot and into the back of the cab of the truck. He hit with a grunt, and pain exploded in his ribs, his back, his head. He tasted blood in his mouth and felt it running down his throat when he was yanked violently to the side.

Something was dragging him toward the edge of the flatbed. Abstractly, as if it were happening to someone else, he looked up and realized that one of his arms was tangled in the cords of the parachute that had not blown completely free. The other ends of the cords had dropped down beneath the truck and wrapped around an axle.

In seconds, he, too, would be pulled beneath the massive wheels.

Pushing her way to the front of the crowd lined up along the fence outside the airstrip, Rosemary spotted a familiar gray head and weathered face.

"Jasper? Jasper!" She waved and shouldered past a big man with binoculars trained on the sky to stand beside Zane's pilot—former pilot. "I didn't think you'd be here."

Jasper cast a worried glance at the sky. "Damn fool kid."

"I know. I'm worried about him, too." She rubbed the older man's shoulder. "Can he really land a jump on the back of a speeding truck?"

Jasper clenched his fingers in the chain link when the loudspeaker barked out the jumper was away. "Yeah, he prob'ly could. It's something he's thought about doing for a long time. On a perfect day, with the right team and a lot of time spent working out the details, he's good enough to do it."

She frowned. "I take it you don't think today's that day."

"He threw this together too fast. They're not ready. And he's been a little . . . off . . . lately." He kicked at the grass.

"He's had symptoms from the aneurysms?"

Jasper's gaze snapped up. "He told you?"

Rosemary nodded.

"He's been having headaches and such. It's why he ended up in the drink with you the other day. He'd never have miscalculated the burn on that parachute if he'd been feeling right."

Rosemary felt as if she'd swallowed a stone. It sunk slowly to the pit of her stomach. "He doesn't think he'll be around long enough to get another shot at this."

And she was beginning to wonder if he might be right.

Zane's parachute came into sight, and both she and Jasper pressed closer to the fence for the best view of the truck as it ambled down the runway. Zane pulled on his steering cables and zigged left, then right.

"Come on, kid," Jasper grumbled. "Line 'er up."

She put one hand over his on the chain link as Zane drifted closer to the bed of the truck. As his feet were about to touch, she held her breath and squeezed Jasper's hand until her knuckles went white.

For a second, it seemed he would land the jump perfectly, and then all hell broke loose. The truck slowed, and Zane kept going forward until he hit the back of the semi with a *thud*, and slumped to the bed of the trailer. The sound of fabric ripping could be heard even over the truck's engine, and Zane was slowly dragged toward the edge, and then disappeared underneath the behemoth vehicle.

High-pitched screams from the crowd mixed with the squeal of the truck's brakes. Before Rosemary knew what he was doing, Jasper started to scale the six-foot fence.

"Oh, God. Oh, Jesus. Christ." He pulled Rosemary up the chain link with him.

Together they ran across the field and onto the runway. The truck had finally stopped. Trey MacAllister had gotten out of the-cab and disappeared under the front wheels of the trailer. By the time Rosemary and Jasper got there, they were both breathing heavily.

"I still don't see him!" she panted. "Do you see him?"

Jasper shook his head, his face pale. A knife appeared in his hand, pulled from a sheath on his belt, and he dove under the trailer. From somewhere in the distance, Rosemary heard the wail of sirens as she ducked down after him.

The darkness disoriented her for a moment while her eyes adjusted. She smelled grease and rubber and her own fear. Her heart threatened to kick out of her chest before she was able to make out Zane on the ground, his right arm tangled in parachute cord and stretched up toward the axle. Jasper hacked at it with his knife while Trey MacAllister leaned over Zane, a hand on his chest as if to comfort him.

Rosemary knew better.

With one great lunge she shoved MacAllister back on his heels. "Get away from him!"

Trey grunted at the impact. "Hey!"

Rosemary fumbled on the ground for Zane, pulled his head into her lap. Blood smeared his face from his nose to his chin. "He can't be dead. He's not dead."

Her hands shook so badly she couldn't find a pulse, which only increased her panic. "Please don't be dead."

"N't dead." Zane's weak voice was music to her ears. When she looked down, his sleepy hazel eyes were the most beautiful sight she'd ever seen.

Trey crawled an arm's-length closer. "You can't just cut in—"

"Get out of here!" she snapped, tightening her hold on Zane and rocking slightly. "Get out and don't ever come back!"

Jasper finally cut through the parachute cords, and lowered Zane's right arm down to this side. Then he held up the knife, the tip pointed toward Trey's chin. "The lady said, 'Git'!"

Mumbling a curse, Trey backed away. Rosemary could hear

doors slamming and the sound of boots on pavement, and knew the medics had arrived.

One corner of Zane's mouth kinked up weakly as she rocked him. "Gr'dian ang'l," he slurred happily, looking up at her, and then his eyelids drooped closed.

Chapter 9

"YOU should be in the hospital," Jasper grumbled as he helped Zane up the stairs to his apartment. On the landing, Rosemary fumbled with Zane's keys, trying to find the one to unlock the door.

"No way," Zane argued, gently pushing Jasper's arm away. He sounded stronger. "Hate those places. Sleep in my own bed."

"Uh-huh," Jasper said, and caught Zane as he stumbled on the top step. "If you can get there without falling on your face, that is."

"I'm fine. Just a little groggy from the pain meds."

Amazingly, the worst of his injuries from the fall had been a strained shoulder and a broken nose. The ER had released him, despite Jasper's vocal protests.

How he had avoided being crushed under the truck's wheels, God only knew. All Rosemary knew was that he hadn't died today after all, and as she'd recently come to understand, every day on Earth was to be cherished.

As she and Jasper led Zane to his bedroom, she got a good look at his apartment. It was masculine and efficient, decorated in navy blues and deep greens. There wasn't an abundance of belongings sitting around. Not that it was stark by any means, but everything had a place and served a purpose.

The only indulgence might have been the king-size bed with its polished posts and cozy down comforter folded at the footboard. When Zane stretched out, Jasper plumped the pillows while Rosemary leaned over and began to untie his shoes.

Zane cringed and pulled his legs up. "All right, enough with the hovering. I'm fine."

Jasper eyed Rosemary at the end of the bed spreading the comforter over Zane and tucking it around his legs. He lifted one eyebrow. "I can see that." He smiled at her, then turned back to Zane. "You behave for once. Do what the lady tells you. And you take care of my boy," he added for Rosemary.

"Always," she promised.

Once they were alone, Rosemary wasn't quite sure what to do with herself. "Are you hungry? I could make you some soup."

He wrinkled his nose. "Soup?"

"You really should eat."

"I was thinking more like steak, baked potato, salad. I've got some great Greek dressing I bet you'd like. I'll do the meat if you handle the rest." Like that, he was out of bed again, and she sighed. The man never stopped.

In the kitchen, while the steaks sizzled in the broiler and the microwave hummed as the potatoes cooked, Zane reached for a bottle of wine.

She stopped him with a hand on her arm. "Not a good idea while you're on painkillers."

He patted her on the head. "Just getting some for you, Mom."

Dinner passed companionably and the wine went to her head. With her belly full and a light buzz, she didn't know how long they'd been sitting in silence until she finally became aware that he was staring at her, bemusement and some other emotion she couldn't define etched in his expression.

She looked down to see if she'd dribbled salad dressing down her shirt. "Something wrong?"

"No. Everything is perfect." His voice had a husky edge that chafed over her nerve endings, making her whole body tingle.

Suddenly restless, she jumped to her feet, collected the dishes, deposited them in the sink and started rinsing. She jolted when a pair of strong arms wrapped around her from behind, and a broad chest pressed to her back. "You don't have to do that," his voice rumbled in her ear. His warm breath bathed her neck. "I'll get them tomorrow."

"There's no reason to—"

"Shhhhh." He pulled her hair over her shoulder to hang down her chest and then traced a single fingertip down her spine from her hairline to her nape, triggering a string of explosions as he passed over each vertebrae. Involuntarily, she audibly gasped for air.

"Scared?" he whispered as his lips replaced his fingertip.

"Yes."

"Me, too." Was that his . . . tongue curling over her spine now? "Want to stop?"

She shook her head in the negative. Speech was beyond her for the moment.

"Good."

He turned her in his arms and his mouth covered hers, soft and moist and unrelenting. He was perpetual motion, always adjusting, always seeking, always giving, and she followed his lead, accepting all that he offered and softly demanding more. When both their chests were heaving, he abandoned her lips to kiss a trail down her neck and murmured, "You know all I have to offer is one day at a time."

She let her head fall back to give him better access. "I'll take it."

He slid his hands down her sides to her hips and back up again, catching the hem of her shirt and sliding his hands beneath until his thumbs brushed the undersides of her breasts. "All I could think about during that damn jump today was that I didn't want to die without ever having a chance to do this."

She arched her back, bringing her harder against him, and tunneled her fingers through the waves of his hair. "I don't want you to die at all."

He stripped her shirt off and ran his hands up her rib cage again.

This time when he reached her chest, he palmed her breasts and lifted them, bringing his mouth down at the same time to kiss the swells.

If Rosemary thought she had experienced the gamut of human sensation this past week, she'd been mistaken. Nothing, nothing she'd seen, heard, tasted, smelled or touched compared to this. It was as if her very blood had become electrically charged. Everywhere her pulse beat, her body tingled.

Zane's hips met hers, pushed against her rhythmically. The counter bit into her back giving her no retreat. No relief from the pressure, and the tingle became a burn.

With the current inside her sizzling hotter with every nip on her breast, every touch on her neck, her ribs, her stomach, she forgot about retreat and went on the offensive. Sliding her hands over his shoulders and down his arms, she hooked her fingers in the belt loops of his jeans and pushed, stepping forward as he walked backward so that they never lost that luscious contact.

His shirt came off in the living room, and she explored miles of smooth skin and hard muscle with her fingertips. Her pants were lost in the hallway and she discovered what delicious friction denim made against bare skin. By the time they made it to the bedroom, they were down to just their underwear, and those didn't last long. Zane gave an appreciative smile for the black lace—or maybe it was for what lay underneath—when he flipped off her bra and tossed it on the nightstand.

Finally unencumbered, they lay on his big bed, their bodies entwined, enmeshed so that one was indistinguishable from the other.

Rosemary gasped at each new nerve he discovered. Each new sense he titillated. She remembered how sensitive she'd been to too many stimuli when she'd first taken on this human body, how she'd feared she would drown in the sensations. Now all she wanted to do was dive in headfirst.

She made a game out of eliciting the same responses in him that he won from her. Everywhere he stroked her body, she stroked his. Everywhere he kissed, she kissed, carefully avoiding the little white bandage across the bridge of his nose. Every nibble was returned with equal fervor. Before long he glowed with a fine sheen of sweat and her skin glowed as if she had a fever. She spread her legs and hooked one knee around his hips seeking the contact that would be the final bridging of their two bodies into one.

He rolled gingerly onto his back, protecting his sore shoulder as he pulled her on top, and brushed back the damp hair that was stuck to her forehead. "You've never done this before, have you?"

His voice had that rumble to it again. The one that passed over her skin like silk, exciting every nerve.

She bit her lip. "Is it that obvious?"

"No," he whispered, palming her breasts again and tweaking the nipples until she moaned. "Just a lucky guess."

Her hips bucked of their own volition as he toyed with her. His erection lay against his stomach before her and she took matters into her own hands.

"Well," he said, his voice strained, "I was thinking the only reason you would still be a virgin was that you'd spent your whole life locked in a convent. But apparently that's not the case."

She leaned down and tongued the center of his chest, then the spot just above his navel. "Not as far off as you might think," she whispered through a curtain of hair.

He pulled his head back and gave her a quizzical look.

She gave him a light squeeze to distract him, then leaned down and nibbled on the shell of his ear before whispering, "Guardian angels don't get a lot of chances to consort with mortals."

Smiling, he wrapped his arms around her back and scooted down the bed until his shoulders were between her thighs. "Then we'd better make the most of what time we have."

At his first touch, her hips flexed of their own accord. At his second she was mindless. She devolved from a complex creature of intellect to something much more primitive. There was no thought, only sensation exploding white and hot within her body, and need. Desire so strong it stole her breath.

When Zane climbed back up to kiss her lips again, leaving a void of emptiness below, desire became greed and she swallowed him with her body. Enveloped him with her soul.

Time became meaningless. Yesterday irrelevant and tomorrow impossible to contemplate. She was awash in a hot molten river of *now*.

The fury rose. Heat and light boiled beneath her, around her, inside her until the desire detonated. It lifted her up, and away, scattering her until she settled slowly back to Earth like ash in the wind.

Chapter 10

ZANE could have lain in bed all night, watching Rosemary sleep in the dim light that slivered in around the edges of the curtains. She lay with her head on his shoulder, her breath tickling his chest, one arm draped over his waist and a smooth leg laced between his. If perfection existed, this was it.

Or almost it. Lying still gave his muscles a chance to stiffen, and his body was beginning to protest this afternoon's abuse. His head hurt and his shoulder ached. Much as he hated to let go of the moment, he needed to get up.

In the hallway he grabbed his jeans off the floor and slid them on, then grabbed the Tylenol from the medicine cabinet in the bathroom. He didn't bother to turn on any lights as he headed toward the kitchen to get a glass of water. He didn't need them, and he didn't want to risk waking Rosemary.

As he leaned over the tap, filling his glass, he felt something warm drip onto the back of his hand. Well, damn. He was bleeding again. Damned broken nose.

Not thinking much of it, he grabbed a paper towel to wipe up the mess, then walked over to the table to sit and tip his head back. The legs of the chair scraped over the tile as he pulled it out, and a wave of dizziness hit him. He fell more than sat down, blinking hard to clear the white spots in his vision.

When he could focus again, a dark puddle the size of a dinner plate stained the floor between his feet.

Double damn. Probably not just the broken nose, then.

His heart kicked into high gear. *Now?* God, why now? Why tonight?

Why him?

Pounding his fist against the kitchen table, he tried to stand, but his legs had turned to gelatin. The glass still in his hand shattered on the ceramic tile and he found himself lying on the floor staring up at the light fixture.

He could feel the blood flowing even more freely now, out his nose and his ears. Around the back of his neck.

Zane had never been a particularly religious man. He'd long ago forgotten how to pray and he'd never been a churchgoer. He'd sworn when the time came he would accept his death the same way he lived his life—taking responsibility for himself. But still, now that the time had come, he found himself asking for a little help from a higher power. For himself, and for Rosemary.

He wished it hadn't gone down this way. That she wouldn't be the one to find him, and have to live with that image forever. He would liked to have given her that much, at least, but it wasn't to be, because, as if his thoughts had summoned her, she stood in the kitchen entryway now wearing only his T-shirt, her hair tousled and her green eyes huge and frightened.

He had to give her credit. Her shock lasted only a moment, and then she was in motion, grabbing a cushion from a chair and propping it under his head, a dish towel from the refrigerator door to hold under his nose. Then she was up and running.

"Nine-one-one. I've got to call nine-one-one." She looked around, then at him. "Where's the phone?"

His voice came out thick, choked. "No. No call."

"Damm it, Zane, don't give me that! You need an ambulance. Where is the phone?"

He shook his head slowly. It was easier than talking. "No hospital. Don't want to die like that."

"You're not going to die."

Even as she said it, he could see in her eyes that she knew it wasn't true.

"Have a . . . DNR order on file anyway. Do Not Resuscitate. Nothing they can do."

She squatted by his side, fists clenched on her knees and tears in her eyes. "Don't ask me to do this. Don't ask me to sit here and watch you die."

"Okay." He struggled to a sitting position, his hands braced on the floor behind him. His head was still pounding, but he felt stronger. "Don't sit. Doctor said I might have a few hours once it started. Don't want to waste them. Let's go somewhere."

She laughed sardonically. "Go where? Out to dinner and a movie? You're bleeding."

He thought fast, but speaking was more of an effort. His tongue weighed almost too much to lift. "Out in the desert. My truck. Beautiful out there at night."

"You really are insane."

He looked up at her and knew his eyes were pleading, even if his words never would. "Every second," he said. "Full throttle."

She struggled with herself visibly, but in the end she did as he bade, as he'd known she would. The flow of blood had subsided to a slow trickle for now, so she wrapped him up in a blanket, handed him towels in case the hemorrhaging started again, and helped him into his truck.

He gave her a queer look when she hesitated before putting the key in the ignition. "Do you know how to drive?"

She searched her mind. The information would be there, given to her by the Father when she took human form, as was all information she would need to complete her task. "Yes."

They rode in silence until they reached a two-lane county road, where Zane pressed the button to roll down the passenger window and leaned his head against the door frame, looking up, enjoying the clear night sky and brilliant stars.

"Don't worry," he said when he caught Rosemary throwing him worried glances. "I'm still with you. Just enjoying the view."

The paved road led into the desert and eventually gave way to dirt. Zane pointed off to the right. "Turn here."

He smiled when she complied. "Now, go faster."

The truck bumped over the uneven surface. She gripped the steering wheel with white knuckles. "I don't think that'd be good for—"

He wanted to straighten up, to show her he could take it, but in truth he didn't have the strength. Instead he beseeched her with his eyes. "I want to feel the wind in my face. Just one more time."

Her lip trembled and he knew she wanted to refuse, but she stepped on the accelerator anyway. It wasn't the kind of speed he was used to, but the breeze at least ruffled his hair. He breathed the clean air in deep. It felt good. It felt right.

They drove for almost two hours, speeding up whenever the terrain wasn't quite so rough. He could tell she was beginning to enjoy the speed. Before long she'd be an adrenaline junkie like him. She'd changed, his girl.

She pointed out a cacti shaped like a bunny rabbit, laughing even while her eyes glimmered with unshed tears. He caught the yellow-eyed glimpses of nocturnal critters getting in a nighttime foray.

Finally his strength waned. She seemed to sense it and pulled near the edge of a plateau facing east, and cut the engine. Scooting across the bench seat, she pulled the blanket from his shoulders and wrapped it around both of them. He shifted his weight away from the window, into her, and rested his head on her shoulder.

"Too bad s'ill drk," he said drowsily. "Bet s'nrise'll be pr'ty."

She sniffed. "I bet it will."

"Wish coul see't."

"You will. It'll just be a few more hours."

But he knew he wouldn't. One last ragged breath was all the time he had. At 11:59 p.m. according to the clock on the dash, he drew it, and let go of life.

———

Rosemary had no idea how long she sat rocking Zane's still body in the cab of the pickup, but when she looked up, a blazing pink and yellow morning sky silhouetted the figure of Saint Peter floating beyond the front bumper. His white bartender's T-shirt had been replaced by cream-colored linen slacks and a loose shirt. The eagle tattoo on his bicep was gone.

Her breath hitched as she looked up at him. "He's gone."

"He's been gone for some time." His voice surrounded her. Filled her. There was reproach in it, but it was gentle. "Why haven't you taken his soul yet?"

"He—he—" A tear streamed down her face. The feeling shocked her. So this was what it was like to cry. Painful, and yet oddly comforting. "He wanted to see the sunrise," she explained, the tears falling in earnest now. "One more time. I—I couldn't deny him that."

"Then you have learned your lesson well." Peter smiled patiently as his image faded to dust and only his voice remained. "Let him see it."

She stared questioningly at the empty space where he had been.

His last words seemed to reach her from far away. "The power is in you."

Eyes wide, she slowly gathered Zane close and laid her palm flat on his cool chest. Almost instantly his eyes opened and found her gaze. His face was relaxed, pain-free as he looked out the windshield at the morning sky.

She felt the angelic glow envelop her, the weight of wings folded on her back.

Finally Zane turned to her, and she could see in his eyes that her true self had been revealed to him. "So," he said, his voice calm as if they'd been discussing flower arrangements. "Not my guardian angel, then."

"No. I am the angel of death. I've come to save you. Your soul, that is."

"Thanks for waiting. For letting me see this." He nodded at the windshield.

Her chin trembled. "You can see as many sunrises as you want where I'm taking you. You can *be* the sunrise. You can have anything you want. . . ."

"All I want is you." He brushed his knuckles across her cheek. "I love you, Rosemary."

She held him tighter, choking back a sob. "I love you, too."

With her head tipped down, she looked up at him through wet lashes and linked one hand with his. "Follow me?"

He lifted her chin and his index finger uintil their gazes met. "Anywhere."

___

"Every angel has to have a purpose, Zane," Saint Peter said. "Everlasting existence would get pretty boring without one."

Zane propped his booted feet up on the gatekeeper's desk, earning himself a raised eyebrow. "And you think I should be the inspiration man."

"You've inspired people with your courage for years. You're a natural."

"And while I'm busy inspiring people, I can take human form?"

"From time to time, if it's necessary."

"And while I'm in human form I can do anything I used to? Fly an airplane? Jump out of an airplane?"

Peter smiled smugly. Should saints be smug?

"You won't even need a parachute. Of course if there's something else you'd rather do, you can. You can have whatever you want."

"I want Rosemary."

Saint Peter sighed. "We've been over this. You can have any-*thing* you want. Not any*body*."

"What's the difference?"

"You can't have another angel. End of story."

"But I need a partner. What do I know about this angel cra— I mean business."

"You'll do fine."

"I'd do better with Rosemary."

"She's the angel of death. How is that going to inspire people?"

"Maybe it's time she changed departments."

Peter drew a deep breath and let it out slowly. "Angels do not change departments."

"Why not? Why'd you let her hook up with me anyway? She could have just taken me when I crashed into the lake."

"She had a lesson to learn."

He cocked his head. "What's that?"

"She had taken many souls. She'd led so many away from pain and suffering to a better place that she'd forgotten how important life is. How precious. She'd lost her empathy for the souls she brought home."

"So you reminded her how precious life is only to yank it out of her hands once she's held it?" He dropped his feet off the desk and leaned forward. "Seems kind of harsh."

Peter leaned back, considering. If Zane hadn't known better, he'd have said the man was flustered by the color that suddenly spotted his cheeks. "You may have a point."

"So you'll give it a try? Letting Rosemary work with me?"

Peter paused then sighed heavily. "On a conditional basis."

"Woo-hoo!" Zane lurched out of his chair and was out the door before the boss could change his mind. In the hall, he found Rose-mary anxiously awaiting the decision and scooped her into his arms. "He said 'yes'!"

Her smile was pure heaven.

He lifted her off her feet, crushed her to his chest and kissed her.

"I love you, Rosie," he said.

Against his neck, he felt and heard her heartfelt, "I love you, too."

From the door of his office, Saint Peter watched Zane and Rosemary practically skip down the hall, hand in hand. They were going to be trouble, those two. If a pair of angels could make a saint's life hell, they were bound to do it.

And still he smiled.